"This is a compelling tale with characters who imprint themselves on the streets of Glasgow." SCARLETT McGWIRE, *The Tribune*

"A very good read, which explores feminism and socialism with subtlety and intelligence." *Gutter Magazine*

"This is a thoughtful, neat and plucky book, much like its heroine. J. David Simons is brilliant at capturing the little oddities and foibles of his characters. The book is a riotous celebration of female empowerment." LISA GLASS, *Vulpes Libris*

"Simons' ability to capture the essence of his protagonist will really strike a chord; Celia's pain and challenges are sensitively rendered, her passion and stoicism enchanting. A quietly brilliant book." REBECCA ISHERWOOD, *The Skinny*

"Emotive, this is a thought-provoking piece of fictionalised social history." ALASTAIR MABBOTT, *The Herald*

"It is always a joy to find a novel which is such an entertaining and compelling read, is faithful to the history of the times and which also explores so many stimulating political themes." ALAN LLOYD, *Morning Star*

"Simons has brought off an unusual coup in getting under the skins of girls liberated by the conditions of WWI... He illustrates an intriguing strand of social history in a lively and gripping way." JUDITH MIRZOEFF, *Jewish Renaissance*

"This novel marries a vivid sense of place with characters who endear themselves to the reader, while tackling head-on the issues of socialism and the liberation – individual and gender – of the title." CAROL McKAY, *Northword*

"This informative, entertaining and ̇ ̇ ̇ ̇ ̇ ̇ ̇ ̇ book left a favourable impression long after I'd finished JANET WILLIAMSON, *Historical Nov*

G000255962

Novels by J David Simons

THE LIBERATION OF CELIA KAHN

J David Simons

Saraband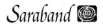

Published by Saraband
Suite 202, 98 Woodlands Road
Glasgow, G3 6HB
Scotland
www.saraband.net

ISBN: 9781908643841
ebook: 9781908643841

Printed in the EU on sustainably sourced paper.

First published by Five Leaves Publications in 2011.
This 2014 edition has been edited and revised by the author.

1 3 5 7 9 10 8 6 4 2

Glasgow
1915

One

CELIA HAD NEVER BEEN SURE how she felt about Sundays. She liked that the schools, the pubs and the shops were shut, that the locals scrubbed up and spruced up in their best clothes, that the streets were emptier and the parks busier. She even liked the sound of the church bells, their plodding patient summons to worship. She admired this distinction made between an ordinary and a holy day. But not the distinction between herself and the rest of the population. Between Christian and Jew. For despite her fondness for the Sunday peace, it also reminded her that this was not her Sabbath. This was the Sabbath that counted the Old Testament's seventh day of rest from a Monday rather than a Sunday. This confusion in starting point ending with her as an outsider. An alien. So when the doorbell rang and she stood to answer it, she knew that on this holy day, it would not be a Christian calling. But she was wrong. Not that she possessed some inner litmus test that could differentiate between Jew and Gentile. Although red hair was certainly almost positive proof. It was just that the blatant cockiness emanating from these two young men standing in the doorway could not possibly belong to a member of the Jewish race living in a land that God had not promised them.

"Moses Cohen?" one of them asked. This was the taller one with a hat shoved down to shade his eyes, a pus-coloured scar across his cheek. His companion was much younger, perhaps about eighteen. Skinnier too, with a nervy twitchiness about him. He was the one with the red hair. Both boasted skin pale enough to raise an initial presumption of illness or at least of days spent in places devoid of natural light. "Where is he?"

"I don't know who you mean," she answered curtly.

"Of course, you do." It was the red-haired lad who spoke this time, his voice nasal and mean as if the sound started from some nastiness inside his head rather than from his throat.

"Oh, you mean Uncle Mendel."

"We're not interested in his relationship to you," the taller man said. "We just want to know where he is. And what's this?" He was tapping at the decorative case of the *mezuzah* nailed near the top of the door jamb. "Is this a Jew thing?"

"Yes. It contains parchment of holy prayers."

"What happens if I pick it open?"

"You'll be cursed for life," she said, not knowing if this was actually true. But guessing she could not be too far off the mark given that God's punishments ranged from a plague of locusts to the death of the first-born male.

The man's fingers leapt from the casing. "Fuck," he said.

She was shocked. It wasn't as if she had never heard the curse word before. Just not in her home where the air had only been filled with the vocabulary of civilised conversation. Even the most minor profanity was forbidden, except for Yiddish put-downs that sounded far worse than they actually were. This man's Anglo-Saxon 'fuck' word hovered in the doorway where he stood. She wondered if the *mezuzah* might protect the hallway from its unholy invasion.

"Stop fucking around with that thing," his colleague said now that the sluice gates of cursing were open. And then to her. "We just want to know where your fucking Uncle Mendel is."

She realised she had remained rather calm despite this verbal onslaught. Not to mention the actual physical threat from these two men. "What do you want from him?"

But there was no time for an answer for behind her she heard the most awful wail and then:

"They've come," her mother screamed. "They've come again. I'm not going this time. No more. I've had enough. I've had enough of camps. Listen to me. Hear this." And she started humming the

4

opening bars of "It's a Long Way to Tipperary". Even the men in the doorway were dumbstruck as Madame Kahn walked up and down the hallway swathed in her dressing gown. Singing. "It's a long way to Tip…"

"It's not you they want, mother," Celia shouted. "It's Uncle Mendel."

Madame Kahn pulled in her gown, continued her promenade. "Mendel or me. What difference does it make? We are kin. But we are not your enemy. Look, look at these hands. I work my fingers into bones for making your uniforms. Into bones."

"Shut up," the taller man screamed. "Just fucking shut up."

Madame Kahn halted, brought the palms of both hands to her open mouth. Celia thought her mother might faint. Instead, she just seemed to deflate before her eyes into a cowering figure. Celia stepped back, put an arm around her. The poor woman was trembling in her grasp.

"What do you want from my Uncle Mendel?" Celia asked.

"He owes us," the nasal lad said.

"Owes you what?"

"Fucking big time." He reached into his inside jacket pocket. She thought for an instant he might be reaching for a knife. Instead he brought out a wad of papers, waved them at her. "Fucking debts," he said. "Gambling debts. All unpaid."

Madame Kahn looked up. Celia noticed she had calmed considerably now that her personal freedom was no longer at stake. "How much?" her mother asked. "How much this time?"

The taller man related a substantial sum in guineas.

"Moses Cohen is not here," Madame Kahn said. "He works in the Highlands. I don't know how long he will be gone. That is the truth. Half I can give you now."

The debt collectors looked at each other. "A month," said the nasal lad with an intimidating lean towards her. "That'll buy you another month. We'll come back for the rest then."

"You know about this, mother?" Celia asked.

Madame Kahn grunted. "It is not new. All my life I have to pay off my brother's gambling debts," she said. "Now stay here all of you. And I will bring the *gelt*."

The small bedroom was hot and dim, the curtains closed even on such a bright day. Her nose crinkled at the stink of boys. Of Nathan and Avram. Of their sweat and soiled linen. She managed to find a space for the tray on the bedside table before drawing open the drapes, dragging the window up a crack. But Nathan, propped up sickly on the pillows, winced at the light and she had to pull in one of the curtains until he was back in shade again. She sat down by the bed, laid a bib around his scrawny neck, felt the almost fleshless bones around his collar as she fussed over him. He stared back at her with yellowish eyes sunk into their sad, dark sockets as she used the bib to wipe the crust from the corners of his mouth.

"I'm sorry I'm late," she said. She spooned up some *borsht*, let it hover for an instant before his mouth until the dry lips unstuck and she was able to tilt the liquid into the gap. "But you don't really care, do you, little brother? I could starve you to death and you wouldn't say one word. Not one word to your sister. When was the last time you said anything to me? Anything at all. I can't even remember the sound of your voice." She gently poured another spoonful of *borsht* into his mouth, the gulping of the soup the only sign her brother was alive and conscious. Rabbi Lieberman had once suggested Nathan's condition might be associated with the legend of the *lamed vav* –the thirty-six righteous men who existed in the world solely to relieve the burden of suffering from the rest of humankind. Otherwise life would be too much to bear for the ordinary person. When she looked at Nathan, she could believe such a myth was true. Her brother's condition had certainly deteriorated since the beginning of this dreadful war, since the reports of the hundreds and thousands of casualties had begun to mount up.

"Two debt collectors came to see Uncle Mendel," she told him. "One of them swore at Mama. You should have heard it."

A voice from behind her. "Who? Who swore at Madame Kahn?"

She turned round. Avram stood in the doorway, a pair of muddied football boots slung around his neck. Next to him, his friend Solly, shining like the sun in a yellow goalkeeper's jersey.

"Tell me who," Avram insisted.

"I'd rather hear what the man said," Solly added. "Come on, Celia. Tell me."

"It's not important. Where have you been?"

"Flag day," Avram muttered.

"Selling pins for the Scottish Women's First Aid Corps," Solly said. "Avram got rid of them all. It must be his miserable face that wins over the wifies."

"You need football boots to sell flags?"

Avram grinned at his friend. "We finished early."

"Well, there's coal to be brought in. And carpets to beat. You should have come home right after you finished. You should have been here."

"All right, all right. I will do it now."

Solly stayed back in his guarding stance at the doorway. Like the goalkeeper he was. "What's put you in such a bad mood?"

"Get back to playing your silly games, Solly Green."

"Are we not old enough to know your womanly ways?"

"Just get away with you."

"We used to be friends."

"When we were at school, Solly. Things have changed since then."

"Like what?"

"Well, there's a war on, in case you haven't heard."

"I'm too young to sign up. But at least I work for a living."

"Taking illegal bets for your father? Standing in the lane looking out for the constable? That's not much of a living."

"You're right, Celia." Solly shifted on his feet. "You've changed."

He left her sitting there on the side of the bed, still with an empty spoon in her hand. She heard Nathan groan as his head shifted on the pillow.

"Oh, look at me," she said. "You must still be hungry." She dipped the spoon back into the bowl, but as she brought it up to her brother's lips, she noticed her hand was shaking.

With the heat gone out of the day, the night had come in quite cold. Celia sat alone in the kitchen, rocking in her mother's chair, listening to the flat as it creaked and settled. Everyone was asleep. She liked it that way, time to let her own thoughts calm to the clicking rhythm of her needles as she knitted some kind of a garment she could hardly remember what. A comforter? A balaclava for an unknown soldier? A pair of socks for her father? A winter scarf that stretched forever? It didn't really matter. Just good to be sitting there, sometimes a voice in the back-court, the light from the furnaces at Dixon's Blazes dancing across the dim kitchen, feeling more like a mother than a daughter. She thought about her Uncle Mendel. Of course, he had a partiality for a little too much *schnapps* – even she who was not very worldly in the ways of alcohol consumption could see that. But apart from a fondness for a game of *kalookie*, she never imagined her uncle was a gambling man. Rather he was a person with strong socialist views who cooked fish wrapped in damp newspaper over his fire until it peeled succulently off the bone. He told her Old Testament stories, read her the doctrines of Karl Marx, explained to her the secret meaning of the playing cards. How diamonds represented money and springtime, clubs stood for work and summer, spades health and winter, and hearts autumn and love. "Never be low in hearts," he would tell her as she sorted through her hand. "Especially in the autumn." "Why in the autumn?" "Because then the winter will be very cold." If the Jews had an equivalent of Santa Claus, she imagined her uncle would be first in line for the part, albeit with a tendency for too much Christmas sherry. But someone who could be the object of attention of those two gangster-types who had visited her home, this she found hard to believe.

She heard one of the bedroom doors open, her father's cough, footsteps across the cold hallway.

"You are still up," Papa Kahn said.

"And you shouldn't be. The doctor told you to stay in bed."

"I shall not be made a prisoner in my own house. By my own daughter. Anyway, I am hungry."

"The soup is still warm," she said, jumping up to attend the pot on the stove. "And there is some bread. I managed to get some rye this morning."

"Yes, yes. Some soup and bread I will have. But first a *schnapps*. A patient must have his *schnapps*. A sick heart needs a good kick."

He took the bottle of sweet brandy off the mantelpiece, poured himself a large glass, knocked it back quickly. He then filled the glass again, sat down at the table in front of his soup bowl. She watched his tired face as he blew noisily on his spoonful, quickly slurped down the hot liquid.

"You know I am taking Avram out of school? To work as a credit draper with Uncle Mendel."

"Yes, I know."

"He is a bright boy. But more important he brings money into this family. When Passover is finished, I will make the arrangements."

She picked up her knitting. Her father refused to look at her, staring sideways instead to the mantelpiece where the family photographs stood, sepia and stern. His cheeks were flushed now. The *schnapps* had done its work. She waited to hear the old complaints.

"I worry about your mother," he said.

"She says she was treated well."

"Physically, yes. But in her heart I know she suffered. Twenty-five years in this country. And then to be locked away. For what? For being a German. It is the humiliation. One moment she makes uniforms for the British army, the next she is locked up like a common thief. What did they think she was going to do? Poison their children? Pass on secrets? Secrets of what? How to fix a button? To stitch a hem? It is the humiliation. It eats and eats away at you."

He picked up his glass, drank back the contents, brought it down so hard on the table she was sure it would break.

"And now I have to make some declaration," he continued.

She broke off mid-stitch. So this was the cause of his irritation. "What kind of a declaration?"

"Some kind of statement about my nationality. All the Jews have to do this."

"A declaration you are Russian?"

"Yes, yes. That I was born in Russia. This means I am not German. That I am a friendly alien and not an enemy alien. But still an alien."

She rocked back and forth on her chair, watching her father contemplate his empty shot-glass. "Is it so bad to declare such a thing?" she asked.

"You don't understand, Celia. All my young life, I tried to escape from this Russia. From its persecution and pogroms. Now I have to declare myself a Russian."

"But it means you will never have to go to a camp. Like Mama."

"This is true. It also means when I am well again I can continue being a tailor making uniforms."

"What is so bad about that?"

"I help the British who help the Russians. This war. It plays with my loyalties. It makes me *meshugge*. Like a madman. What kind of a world is this?"

"It is not so bad here. At least there are no pogroms."

"Yes, yes, yes. To be a Jew here is no bad thing. But to be a German Jew like your mother is not so good. Ha! Better to be a Russian Jew. To declare loyalty to a country that hates you."

"Papa, you are tired. Please go to bed."

There was a time when she would have gone to stand beside him, let him stroke her hair until he settled. "My love," he would have said. "My little love." But instead, she rose wearily from her chair, pulled back the curtains to her cot in the kitchen, slipped into bed. She turned towards the wall as she heard the shot-glass being re-filled.

Two

MADAME KAHN WAS KNITTING like there was no tomorrow. It was something she had become expert at since her stay in the camps. After all, it had been the only distraction available to her. To manufacture mounds of useless garments while complaining in German to the rhythm of her task. *Eins, zwei, drei. Klick, klick, klick.* Celia watched her mother now as the needles flashed with such alacrity she wouldn't have been surprised to see them glow white with friction and the wool burst into flames. 'Like no tomorrow.' That phrase was something else her mother had learned in the camp. Everything was 'like no tomorrow' now. She cooked like there was no tomorrow, she ate like there was no tomorrow, she knitted like there was no tomorrow, she prayed like there was no tomorrow. Compared to her mother, Celia knitted like there were whole lifetimes of tomorrows. Which was what she was doing now in front of the kitchen fireplace, her mother sitting in the rocker while she crouched on a stool, with just the clicking of the needles for company, the occasional thought voiced as conversation.

"Soon it will be time to search the house," her mother said. "I have put out the pieces of bread for you to find."

"Yes, Mama. I will do it."

"I remember when you were children. When your father was in good health. How he hid the bread for you and Nathan in all the different corners of the rooms. And you two *kinder* went looking with a candle. It was like a treasure hunt."

"My favourite part of Passover."

"Ach, how times change." *Eins, zwei, drei. Klick, klick, klick.* "And that floral dress I made at the shop for that customer who did not pay. That should fit you."

"Yes, I suppose it would. It will be nice for when the summer comes."

"And you need to find yourself some friends. Also for when the summer comes."

"I have friends."

"Boys of your own age?"

"I know boys of my own age."

"Who do you know?"

"I know Solly Green."

"Solly is Avram's friend. Anyway he is a bookmaker's son."

"What is wrong with that?"

Madame Kahn shrugged. *Klick, klick, klick.*

"What is wrong with being a bookmaker's son, mother?"

"Nothing is wrong. I just think it may soon be time."

"Time for what?"

"To speak to Mrs Solomon."

"Mrs Solomon? The matchmaker?"

"Yes. The *shadchen*."

"Mother, I am only sixteen."

"You are nearly seventeen. And time passes quickly. You are very beautiful, my child. A good catch for some rich man. Not some bookmaker. But we must act quickly. Beauty fades. Like there is no tomorrow."

"I don't want a rich man." Celia noticed her mother's knitting speed had increased to a frantic blur.

"Want is not what we talk about here. Need is what we talk about. Your father is still not better. Nathan is… I don't know what has happened to that boy. Avram will send us a little *gelt* from the Highlands. Me, I work my fingers into bones here and at the shop. But it is not enough. Times are hard for us. We are poor."

"Have you been to the backlands, Mama? Have you seen the children living under sacks in the coalsheds? Whole families squashed into one room and kitchen? Dead bodies rotting in beds because there is no money to pay for a funeral. We are not poor. You do not know what it means to be poor."

"I know what it means to be locked up," Madame Kahn said, rocking more calmly in her chair. "Anyway. Better you find a husband than talking all this *Kommunist* nonsense."

"I am going to look for the bread."

"First you should go see your father. What kind of daughter never puts her head round a door?"

"He doesn't ask for me."

"Listen to me, Celia. Life is hard for your father. He has lost his faith in many things. In God, in this country, in his health. About all these things, he is angry. And perhaps he takes this anger out on someone he loves. A relationship between father and daughter can be very complicated."

"Is that what happened to you, Mama?"

"Just go see him."

Uncle Mendel came home for Passover. "Where is my favourite niece?" he asked, bursting into the kitchen, red-faced, open-armed.

Celia rushed into his grasp, felt the roughness of his beard against her cheeks, his body hot as always, like a perpetual furnace feeding off its fuel of chicken fat, black bread and *schnapps*. His large hands, fingers as thick as German *vursht*, patted her shoulders while she inhaled the smell of grass or hay or some other rustic aroma from his dusty jacket. She knew he would be looking over her head at her mother, busy creating the apple, walnut and cinnamon paste for the *Seder* plate.

"Ah, Martha," Uncle Mendel sighed. "Your famous *charoses*. The most bitter herbs it makes taste sweet."

"Don't try to sweeten me with your *schmaltz*," Madame Kahn said, without looking up from her task.

"Come, Martha. Your brother a welcome you can give. Then all about this terrible camp you can tell me." He almost danced over to her, held her by the shoulders. "And so slim you look. Like a young bride."

Madame Kahn wiped her hands on her apron, adjusted her headscarf, allowed her brother to kiss her on both cheeks. "You

13

stink," she proclaimed. "You cannot sit down at the *Seder* like this. Away upstairs and have a bath. *Gey, gey, gey.* Celia will heat some water for you."

A couple of hours later, Uncle Mendel sat down beside her at the *Seder* gathering, groomed, sweating and gleaming in his bright white shirt. Her father slouched on cushions at the head of the table while her mother manned her customary position at the opposite end with easy access to the range. On the other side of the table sat Avram and the one invited guest – Mrs Carnovsky – the wizened, chain-smoking, tea-leaf reading, old widow from across the close. Nathan remained in bed, oblivious to this re-enactment of his forefathers' bondage and escape from Egypt taking place around the kitchen table.

Against her mother's wishes, Papa Kahn insisted on leading the service as was the custom for the man of the house. Male hands were washed, the ancient story re-told, questions asked, *matzoh* broken, eaten or hidden, plagues recounted, the four glasses of wine drunk. Meaning pervaded everything. This was what she had learned since she was old enough to remember. The bitter herbs served to evoke life under the Egyptian lash, the salt water brought back the tears, the *charoses* sweetened the blows, the shank bone of the lamb reminded everyone of the sacrifice. And the boiled egg?

"The boiled egg is a symbol of the harsh suffering," Papa Kahn explained.

"Yes, yes," said his compatriot Mrs Carnovsky. "In Russia, the boiled egg means to suffer."

"*Nein, nein, nein,*" Uncle Mendel countered with a Germanic finger raised to the heavens. "The importance is in the roundness of the egg. The circle of life it represents."

"Mendel is right," her mother added. "The egg is the circle of life."

"*Feh, feh, feh,* to such a thing," Mrs Carnovsky said, dry-spitting into some imaginary spittoon by her side. "What kind of *meshugge* idea is this?"

"Now, now," Papa Kahn said kindly to his guest. "We are just having a little fun here."

"Fun?" Mrs Carnovsky spoke as if the concept were totally alien to her. "How can we make fun of suffering?"

"Of suffering we do not make fun," said Uncle Mendel. "But in the face of the circle of life and death, we are laughing." He picked up the egg. "Ha, ha, ha."

"*Feh, feh, feh,*" was Mrs Carnovsky's reply.

And with the debate over the egg concluded, dinner was eaten in such large quantities as to confirm Madame Kahn's assertion that there was no tomorrow. Then more glasses of wine were drunk followed by the boisterous singing of the many time-worn melodies. Celia felt herself giddy from the sweet alcohol, regretted wearing one of these new-fangled girdles that was surely impeding the path of the chicken, potatoes, *kneidlech* and *matzoh* through her digestive tract. If she could only unfetter herself in the same way her uncle had done in the loosening of his collar and belt, the release of his belly.

"So, so, so, Mendel," Papa Kahn muttered. "Soon Avram will join you. Do you think he will make a good credit draper?"

"Just fine the lad will do," Uncle Mendel replied, patting his stomach as if it were an old friend. "A good head for figures you have, *boychik*?"

"I love numbers," Avram said. "I was nearly top for arithmetic."

"Then a good businessman you will make. And a bicycle you can ride?"

"I never had a bicycle."

"And how will you go from village to village, croft to croft with your samples? I will see what I can do. But tell me, brother-in-law, of Russia what news do you have?"

"The war goes badly for them," Papa Kahn said. "Armies in retreat. No weapons, no supplies."

"Ah, this will make the Tsar very nervous. With this stupid war, his people he wanted to unite. Now against him they will turn. A revolution there will be. Mark my words. A revolution."

"I agree," Mrs Carnovsky added in a rare moment of concordance with anyone. "That is what my brother writes from Saint Petersburg. Or Petrograd. Whatever they call it these days. Revolution. It is in the air, it is on the lips. He says all is one big mess. The peasants come to the city to work in the factories for the war effort. But there are no places for them to stay, no food. People line up for days just for a crumb of bread. And there are no weapons for the soldiers. They are sent to the Front without guns. And everyone blames the Tsar. For the war, for the famine, for the lack of weapons, for the weather that destroys the crops. They hate him. *Feh! Feh!*" And again she sought out her invisible spittoon.

Celia regarded Mrs Carnovsky's outburst with admiration. As did everyone else for an unusual quiet settled over the table. Until Uncle Mendel leaned across to her father and asked: "Tell me, my friend. If there is a socialist revolution, you will return to Russia?"

"Hah!" Papa Kahn exclaimed. "Hah! Return to Russia? You must be sick in the head, Mendel. A screw loose. You think a socialist revolution will be good for the Jews? You think a country can stop being anti-Semitic overnight?"

"I think it will be good for the Jewish socialists."

"Why do you say that, uncle?" Celia asked.

"See, my young niece has an interest in revolution." His eyes shone at her as he answered: "If you are a socialist first and a Jew second, a new Russia could be a good place."

"Stop it, Mendel." Papa Kahn banged his fist on the table. A knife fell to the floor. "Stop filling her head with such ideas."

"Papa," Madame Kahn said firmly. "Calm yourself. It is not good to shout like this. Not good for your heart."

He ignored the admonition. "I will tell you something, daughter. I will tell you about this talk of socialist revolution in Russia. Some people here say it is we Jews in Europe who fuel it, who fund the unrest. That it is part of some Jewish master plan to dominate the world. Keep your head down. You know what I always say. The Jews should always stay low. Especially when…?"

"…when the Cossacks ride into town."

"Exactly, daughter. Now stay away from this Russia and its revolutions. I forbid such talk in this household."

"Papa," Madame Kahn snapped. "Listen to what I say. *Genug.* Finish."

"Yes, yes, yes, my friends," he said weakly, his skin pale like parchment, neither the wine nor his anger succeeding in making bloody inroads into his cheeks. "I am sorry. Let us sing the evening's final verses."

So together they sang the song of how God killed the Angel of Death who slew the slaughterer who slit the throat of an ox that drank the water that put out the fire that burned the stick that beat the dog that bit the cat that ate the little goat that someone's father bought for two coins of silver. For two coins of silver. For two coins of silver.

Celia helped her mother clear the table, bundle up the many pots and dishes into an old tablecloth to avoid tempting the rats. It could all be washed in the morning. Then she laid down in her cot weary in her bones but her mind tipsy with the thoughts of plagues, Elijah's return, slaughtered goats, the rebuilding of the temple in Jerusalem. She felt happy. In a rare, wrapped-up warm under the blankets kind of way. The presence of her family, the rituals, the songs, the traditional food, the wine, all providing her with a few moments of structure and comfort in a world growing increasingly hostile and confusing to her. Out in the hall, Mrs Carnovsky sharing her gold-tipped cigarettes of Balkan tobacco with her mother and Uncle Mendel. It was the only time she ever knew her mother to smoke, on these rare occasions after a few glasses of sweet wine. She heard the front door open and close, the exchange of wishes for a 'Happy Festival', and Mrs Carnovsky would be back in her flat to dry-spit a few more curses at her enemies, perhaps to read the leaves on the cup of a late night beverage. That left her mother with Uncle Mendel still talking in the hallway, the lingering dark-chocolate aroma of the tobacco, their mumbled conversation soothing her into sleep through the half-open door. Until she heard her mother's raised voice:

"...don't understand you. Always with the betting. And always with the losing, losing, losing. And always with me paying off your debts."

"I won't let it happen again. This is the last time. I swear it."

"How many times have you made that promise? Well, it's too late to make promises. Because I don't have the *gelt*, Mendel. I don't have it. I don't have enough even to pay next month's rent."

"Don't worry. It will be fine."

"Fine? All I know is that these two thugs, these two *betsemer*, will be back here for their money. And we have nothing to give them. They will harm you, Mendel. They will harm you for this. You have gone too far this time."

"Go to bed now, sister. You are tired. I will take care of this. Don't worry. I will take care of this. Of these things, I always take care."

"I am frightened, Mendel. They will kill you. Like the slaughterer killed that poor little goat."

"It was the cat that killed the goat."

"Well, this time it will be those dogs."

Three

HER MOTHER LOVED SOOR PLOOMS. Those sticky, lime-coloured balls with their tangy, fruity flavour. Even when Madame Kahn was in the camp, Celia would send her a care package every week stocked with her favourite confectionery. Now that Passover was finished, Celia was back at Glickman's sweet shop in London Road to pick up her mother's supply. She pushed at the front door but it would not open. It was only when she looked through the glass did she realise that her entrance had been impeded by the bent-down rump of a rather large woman.

'I'm very sorry,' Celia said, once she had managed to squeeze into the shop. Despite her apology, she expected a rebuke from this, now straightened, stern-looking customer. But instead the woman declared:

"I just don't know what to have. I absolutely love them all. So many choices. Dolly Mixtures, Ginger Creams, Macaroon Cake, Lucky Tatties." The dour features on her square face dissolved into a smile that displayed her sugar-besieged dentistry. "What do you think? You look like a young lass of taste and integrity."

Celia wasn't used to this kind of directness. For Glasgow Jews didn't behave in such a manner. They were certainly amicable enough within their own tribe. But when it came to dealing with the Christian world around them, they suffered a lack of confidence, an aversion to standing out from the crowd. Yet she found herself flattered by the openness of this Gentile attention, gave the question serious deliberation.

"I prefer the boiled sweets," she said eventually. "The Soor Plooms."

"And why is that?"

"They last longer."

"Och, that's a very practical answer. But it's not practical I'm after. I was merely thinking of indulging my sweet tooth."

"I just like the feeling in my mouth as the sweet gets smaller and smaller," she found herself insisting, wondering which of this woman's rotten teeth was the sweet one. "And that tangy taste. Until it disappears altogether."

"So you are not only practical. But willing to offer your opinions too. An interesting combination. Well then, I'll add some Soor Plooms to today's mix." She held out her hand. "Miss Agnes Calder. You may call me Agnes."

The woman's grip was firm, squashing up all her fingers as she gave her own name.

"Well, Celia Kahn. How is it that we have never met before? I teach at that primary school across the road there. I am here almost every day. It's either these sweets or the tobacco that will get me in the end." But given the woman's hacking cough, Celia reckoned it would be a bit of both. "Now tell me, where are you from?"

"The Gorbals."

"Where exactly?"

"Thistle Street."

"I see. So you and your family are not affected by these awful rent increases."

"We don't live near the shipyards."

"I was not asking a question. Merely making a statement."

"I'm sorry."

"Well, you may not be directly affected. But these increases involve us all. Greedy landlords exploiting the demand for property around the shipyards by hiking up the rents. Trying to evict poor working-class families for non-payment while the husband is away fighting. It's up to the women to protest this… this tyranny. Is that not right, Celia?"

"I think so."

"You think so? Well, lass, if the women don't, who will?"

"I don't know."

"You may have an opinion on boiled sweets but I can see in other important areas you are sadly lacking." This lament continued the following week when again she bumped into Agnes at Glickman's. This time the war itself was the subject.

"Do you think this conflict is a just one?" Agnes asked.

"All I know is that thousands of our young men are dying every day."

"That is true. Very true. And what are they dying for?" This time thankfully Agnes did not wait for her answer. "So the war profiteers can make their fortunes, that's why. Blood money is what I call it." She picked a piece of macaroon from her paper bag, popped it into her mouth. "We should become more acquainted, you and I, Celia Kahn. How does this Saturday suit?"

"Pardon?"

"Don't stand there with your mouth open. This Saturday?"

"I'm sorry but I can't..."

"A young woman has a mind of her own, hasn't she?"

"It's just that..."

"No excuses. Three o'clock outside St. Enoch's subway station. Please be on time."

At two o'clock on the day of her appointment, she sat in her mother's rocker swaying to and fro to the rhythm of the clock thumping away in the hallway, this plodding time-keeping always seeming louder, more insistent, on the Sabbath than on any other day. She felt her limbs heavy, resistant, pinning her to her seat with sixteen years of religious upbringing, each swing of the chair marking out her indecision. "I will go, I won't go, I will go, I won't go." Avram was busy at the kitchen table, sorting out for the umpteenth time his collection of cigarette cards. She had no idea what he saw in those expressionless faces of football players distinguished only by the colour of their strip. She watched as he flicked up one set of cards, placed them elsewhere on the table according to some secret logic.

"Billy Reid is not here," he sniffed. "Billy Reid. Do you see him?"

"Have you looked on the floor?"

Avram bent under the table. On returning upright, he scratched his head vigorously as if this scalp-scraping might assist his memory. "For the set, I need Billy Reid. Twenty-one goals he scored for Rangers."

"I have a terrible headache," she said.

"This morning he was here. Before we went to *shul*. Billy Reid."

"My head is splitting in two."

He ran a sleeve across his nose. "Twenty-one goals," he said. "The best player. Billy Reid. Where is he?"

"I'm going for a walk," she said, hauling herself up from the rocker. If God had really wanted her to stay, surely He could have pushed her body back to the chair there and then? "If Mama or Papa wakes, tell them I've gone out for some fresh air."

Avram glanced up and for a dreaded moment she thought he was going to ask to join her. Instead he said: "Billy Reid? You stole him. Give him back to me."

"Don't be ridiculous," she said, relieved that it was Avram's accusation rather than the Lord's wrath she was escaping.

She loved walking across Glasgow Bridge, passing over the tea-stained slurry of a river that divided the city. It was as if the Clyde formed the boundary to some fantasy land. Those broad thoroughfares, the tall buildings with their fancy façades, the gaudy emporiums with their stretched-out awnings, all beckoning her to enter from the dark, soot-clad confines of the Gorbals on the opposite bank. "Come in, lass," the Second City of the great British Empire whispered to her. "Don't be afraid. Come in and see the wonders of the Commonwealth. Tobacco and coffee, exotic fruits, fine teas and fabrics. Taste our bananas from the Indies, see our frozen meat from the Americas. Come in and sample and buy. Even on your Sabbath." And there was Agnes waiting for her under the subway clock, tapping her umbrella against the pavement in time to some invisible beat of impatience. She suddenly felt concern about the afternoon ahead of her. Perhaps she should turn back, but Agnes had already raised her umbrella in welcoming salute.

"I'm glad to see you are punctual. Wasting another person's time is tantamount to theft."

"I decided to walk," she said, as if a hansom might be her normal conveyance of a weekend.

"Let us go for tea. Come."

The tea-room stood on Sauchiehall Street. A tall, white-stucco façade with elegant lines, a curved bay window on the first floor, clusters of small-paned portals on the levels above. A hanging sign declared the place to be: 'Miss Cranston's Willow Tea Rooms.' She wondered who this Miss Cranston might be and where she had found both the funds and the imagination to construct a building of such bright and light feminine charm, stuck as it was between the dark soot-stained buildings on either side like a bride attended by miners.

"I can't go in," she said.

"Why not?"

"I just can't."

"Of course, you can. What's the matter, lass?"

"I'm not dressed properly."

"Och. Don't be silly. There's nothing wrong with your clothes."

"My coat is shabby. And my shoes…"

"As long as you are clean and you don't smell you'll be fine enough for these grand ladies. It's not as though I'm dressed to the nines myself."

Celia had to agree as she considered Agnes' small, black, unadorned bonnet with its narrow brim, the plain dark coat. "But I'm just a poor tailor's daughter from the Gorbals. You're … you're a teacher."

Agnes leaned in close to her. She could smell the tobacco on her breath mixed in with the tangy scent of Soor Plooms. "Let me tell you something," the older woman whispered. "The people in there are no better than you. Just remember that. No better. Put your nose in the air. Stick out your bosom. And make as if you don't have a bloody care in the world." Agnes pushed open the door, held it wide. "Come on, lass. Pull in your corsets and enter."

"I don't think I can."

"Nonsense. Come on. Come on. Quick, quick, quick."

She felt as if something momentous awaited her. The child inside her wanted to twist and turn and run all the way back to the Gorbals while another part of her desperately wanted to rise to this challenge. For this was not the Jewish world that faced her, full of its *dybbuks*, dark mysteries and unfathomable rituals. But ahead lay the white light of Christianity blinding her on a busy Saturday afternoon. She straightened her back, sucked in the tearoom air, put out her foot, crossed the threshold. A prim miss was already addressing Agnes.

"Can I help you, madam?"

"A reservation for a quarter past three. Calder. Two persons. The Room de Luxe."

"I will show you to your table."

Agnes beckoned, and Celia followed her companion and the waitress through the downstairs salon, stepping lightly on the thick carpet between the high-backed chairs, past the ladies in their broad-brimmed hats sipping their tea. Then up the twisting stairway, across the mezzanine, through the double-doors with their leaded glass panels and into a light, so-white room with its curved bay window and silver-painted chairs. Or perhaps they actually were silver. Silver to match the lampshades, the tea-trays, the cake-stands, the napkin rings, the cutlery on the stiff linen in this room where all the furniture and the windows ranged so tall and slender. Like willows. A chair was drawn out for her, she sat down at this table by the window, let out the breath she believed she had been holding ever since she walked through the door.

"Would you like the afternoon tea set for two?" the waitress asked.

"No, no, no," Agnes replied. "No scones, shortbread and sand-wiches for us, thank you. Only cakes – delicious, sugary cakes. Tea and cakes will be fine."

"I'm afraid the cake selection is not to our usual standard. What with the war and everything."

"Munitions we are able to manufacture with ease," Agnes grumbled. "But chocolate éclairs appear to be far too complex for the industrial mind. So what is on offer?"

"Marmalade cake, madam."

"Is that all?"

"I'm afraid so."

"Then that is what we shall have."

With the waitress gone, Celia followed Agnes' lead in slipping her napkin from its holder, spreading it on her lap. She noticed the dark tips of her own fingernails against the starched cloth, not unclean for lack of washing but ingrained with dirt from too many floors scrubbed, coal fires made and grates swept. She tried to hide these offending digits in the clasp of each hand as she stared out of the window at the display of moving millinery below – the bunnets, the bonnets, the occasional dark blue Glengarry of the passing soldier.

"Listen to that noise," Agnes said.

"What noise?"

Agnes pointed to the ceiling. "Upstairs."

She listened carefully. The low murmur of male voices. Footsteps across a floor. The occasional clicking sound. Then a cheer. "What's going on?"

"Billiards, my lass. That's what you hear. Men playing billiards up above, smoking their cigars, talking their man-talk, their war-talk, their merchant-talk. Men on top of us. While we sit daintily below, chattering over our tea. About what?" Agnes angled her head towards the three ladies at the table next to them. "The sale at Pettigrew and Stephens."

Conversation ceased as the waitress arrived with their order, set down the teapot along with the cakes. Then Agnes started up again.

"Tell me what you know about socialism."

"I'm sorry?"

"You'll get no polite chit-chat from me, lass. Socialism. What do you know about it?"

Celia picked up a sugar cube with a pair of silver tongs, watched as the granules dissolved in the brown murkiness of her tea. "I know what it means."

"Oh, do you now? Continue."

"It is the political philosophy of putting people before profit. Rather than profit before people."

Agnes wriggled herself upright in her chair. "My, my, my. Who taught you that?"

"My uncle."

"And is this uncle of yours some kind of a Marxist?"

"No, he is a credit draper."

Agnes smiled. "I see. A credit draper."

"He works for one of the warehouses in the city. Selling goods in the Highlands."

"I see. Well, do you have your own opinion of how we can put the poverty of the masses before the profit of the few?"

She didn't know if she had opinions on such lofty subjects. After all, she had never been asked about them before. "I believe there is injustice in the world," she ventured. "I just don't understand why."

"Now that is what I would call a sensible answer. It is important to admit what we don't understand. That is the first step towards wisdom."

Celia was relieved her admission had elicited such a positive response. She was also relieved when Agnes went quiet as she directed the attention of her fork towards her slab of cake. A silence that did not last long.

"I thought you might be interested in our socialist Sunday schools."

"I've never been to a Sunday school. I am not... I am not religious."

Agnes leaned forward. "Sip your tea, lass, and for goodness sake, relax. You're as wound up as a clockwork doll. I'm not talking about religious Sunday schools. I realise you are not of the Christian faith. You boast a certain complexion that would grace the great warrior and prophetess Deborah herself. I know today is your Sabbath, Celia Kahn. And by coming here on this day shows me you might have an interest in what I tell you. For socialist Sunday schools are run in opposition to the influence of religion. We believe in love and fairness and that the good things on earth are produced by one's labour, not by one's prayer. And if it makes you feel any better, we have our very own ten commandments. Not one of which you are breaking by having tea here today with me." Agnes broke off to cough so loudly that all other noise in the tearoom stopped.

"Are you all right?"

"I'm fine," Agnes wheezed, patting herself several times on the chest. "Just fine. But I feel I'm rushing things too much with you. Forgive me. Let's enjoy this tea."

Celia nibbled on her cake, listened to the roar from the invisible men above as one of their number succeeded in doing whatever a billiard player was meant to do. She liked what Agnes was telling her. But there was this one certain matter really bothering her.

"Agnes?"

"Yes, lass."

"There's something I want to ask."

"It is a person's duty to be curious."

"You won't think I am being ungrateful or impolite?"

"It takes a lot to offend Agnes Calder."

"Well then, if you believe in socialism, what are we doing here in this luxury tearoom?"

Her companion laughed loudly at this, a laugh that inevitably turned into a coughing fit. When she had calmed down, she was still chuckling when she flipped open her box of Woodbines with her yellowed fingers, extracted a cigarette.

"Now, that's a very good question," she said, lighting up. "It shows you're thinking. And my answer to you is this. Come the revolution, Celia Kahn, come the revolution and we'll all be having tea at Miss Cranston's."

"Is that the revolution that is going to happen in Russia?"

"Perhaps." Agnes blew out a smoke ring. "Something is in the air. Something is definitely in the air. But in the meantime, I might just have a little job for you."

Four

It was one of those beautiful days for the wifies with a warming sun and a drying breeze that set all the back-courts a-flutter with the whites of whipping sheets. Celia was out there with the rest of them, a bundle of clothes-pegs stuffed in her pinny, a couple in her mouth, as she forked the washing onto the line. It was only when the wind lifted one of her father's shirts could she see the back window of her own kitchen, her mother standing there flapping her arms.

"Thank goodness, thank goodness," her mother wailed as soon as she walked through the back door. Madame Kahn was marching across the kitchen, rubbing her hands up and down her skirt and against the front of her thighs as if she were trying to prevent the very action her own legs were carrying out.

"What's wrong, mother?"

"They are here."

"Who is here? Where?"

"These men. These dogs. These *betsemer*. I hear them upstairs in Mendel's flat. A few moments ago. Thud, thud, thud. Listen. Thud, thud, thud."

"I don't hear anything. Did you see them?"

"No, I did not see them. But I hear them."

"I thought they were coming tomorrow."

"They said they come in a month. A month it will be tomorrow. But what is a month? Thirty days? Thirty-one days? Four weeks? How do I know such things? How do I know what a month is in the minds of these dogs."

"I still don't hear anything."

"They killed him, that's why. They killed your uncle. How could they do such a thing?"

"I didn't know Uncle Mendel was back."

"Yes, yes. He came home yesterday. And now he is dead. Murdered in his own home."

Then Celia did hear a noise. The fall of something heavy on the floor above, causing the central light fitting in the hallway to judder. And then voices. Male voices. She rushed back out the doorway, up the stairway of the close to the first floor landing. The door to Uncle Mendel's flat was slightly open, she pushed her way through into the dark vestibule, waited momentarily for her eyes to adjust. The voices came from the kitchen. There was a leak of light from under the doorway. She looked around for some kind of weapon, seized a stout walking stick from the umbrella stand. Then quickly, she opened the kitchen door, marched in, stick raised, ready to lash out at the tall one, the one with the pulled-down hat who had been trying to prise the cover off the *mezuzah*.

Uncle Mendel, still in his hat, sat lopsided on the floor, an arm draped over a chair which most likely he had just fallen from. Solly was bent over him, holding the other arm, trying to haul her uncle to his feet.

"What is going on here?" she screamed, although why she was shouting she did not know. She was only about a yard away from the two of them, the walking stick raised half-way to the ceiling.

Uncle Mendel managed a sort of sloppy, embarrassed smirk while Solly was the first to speak.

"Christ, Celia. You scared me to death."

"Well?" she said. "Well? Well? What did you think you did to me? And my poor mother? She thinks you're killing my uncle."

"Damn," Solly muttered. "Madame bloody Kahn."

Amidst all her anger, she found herself smiling. A reaction to a childhood memory, knowing how Solly and all the other neighbourhood kids had been so frightened of her mother. That stout German woman who scolded them for the least noise, the simplest misdemeanour. Snatching Solly by the ear for doing God knows what and dragging him across the street to his father, Lucky Mo the bookmaker, so they could harangue each other in Yiddish and German, Solly stuck in the middle, his ear held to ransom. Not having the heart now to tell Solly that her mother was shrunk to half her size, shrivelled up inside too. But the memory had calmed her so she could say evenly:

"Just tell me what is going on here."

"I pulled him out the pub," Solly said. "He was in The Rabbie Burns, drunk as a lord, mouthing off about his winnings."

"His winnings?"

"Yes, he won a packet today."

"You see," Uncle Mendel slurred from his position on the floor. "All fine I said it would be. All fine. Uncle Mendel you have to trust."

"Won on what?" Celia asked. "Horses?"

"Well, not exactly," Solly said. "There isn't a lot of horse-racing these days. What with all the trains being commandeered for the soldiers, it's hard to get the punters out to the racetracks. So we have to be more imaginative in the type of action we can provide for those who still fancy a bet."

"Oh, it doesn't matter," Celia said. "Let's get him on to a chair."

"That's what I was trying to do."

"Well, let's do it then."

She let Solly drape her uncle's arm around her neck while he knelt down on the floor to get underneath the other arm. As she waited, she could smell Uncle Mendel's sweat, the alcohol seeping from his every pore. She could also hear herself whimpering. "Oh no," she thought. "Oh no. This can't be you. This can't be you, uncle."

Solly heaved the body upwards and she felt her uncle's thick fingers tighten on her shoulder as he was pushed to his feet, she doing nothing but helping him to balance. Then looking up to see her mother standing in the doorway, a poker in her hand.

"*Mein Gott!*" Madame Kahn screamed. "They killed my brother."

"He's drunk, Mama. Not dead. But drunk."

"*Vas? Vas?*"

"Not dead, mother. Drunk. *Shikker.*"

"*Shikker? Gott sei danke.*" Then her mother wagged the poker at Solly. "It's you. It's you, Solly Green. It's all your fault. A good for nothing. Always were. Just like your father."

"But, but …" Solly stammered.

"Martha," Uncle Mendel exclaimed. "*Alles ist gut.* Everything is fine." Then he vomited down the front of his jacket.

Celia cleaned up her uncle as best she could, dry-retching in the stench as she washed down his clothes, dabbed the crud from off his lips and his beard. Then together with Solly she managed to half-drag, half-walk him into the bedroom where her mother took over, getting him out of the rest of his clothes, putting him to bed. Celia mopped up the mess on the kitchen floor while Solly told her how Uncle Mendel had raked in his money betting on the football, not just the senior games but junior ones and school matches too.

"You'd better take this," he said, handing over a biscuit tin with a picture of Queen Victoria on the lid. "For safe keeping."

"What is it?"

"Take a look."

She opened the lid a crack. The tin was full of sterling notes and silver coins.

"Take your mother downstairs," he said. "I'll stay with your uncle until I'm sure he's well asleep."

"Yes, yes," she said. "Thank you." She liked that about Solly, his kindness and consideration for others. He had always been like that, even at school, looking out for Avram when he had arrived from Russia without parents, without language, without friends. It was so easy to overlook, she thought, a person's capacity for kindness when so much else was grabbing for attention. She told Solly she would come back up in a few hours to check on her uncle.

She returned with a pot of chicken soup. She expected the flat to be dark and cold but instead she found her uncle sitting on a stool in the kitchen, building up a fire in the grate.

"My favourite niece," he declared, looking round at her. His face was scrubbed ruddy, his beard neatly combed. He was wearing a freshly-laundered shirt.

"Your only niece," she said. "Here. Mother sent you up some chicken soup. But I see you are better already."

31

"Fit as a violin I am." The coal crackled and spat as he prodded and twisted with his poker. "Fit as a violin."

"You weren't a few hours ago."

Her uncle put a finger to his lips. "Hushshhh. This other Uncle Mendel you do not know. He is an impostor. A devil. A *dybbuk*. You must forget about him. Away with this man. *Avek, avek, avek.*" He flapped his hands in the direction he wished this alter ego to disappear. "But this Uncle Mendel you see now," he said, poking hard with a finger to his chest. "This is the real Uncle Mendel. Not a sinner. But a good Jew." He reached down and picked up a package wrapped up in damp newspaper. "An extra piece of fish I have in the ice box. All the way from the Highland rivers it comes. You want?"

"Yes, I want."

"Well, take off your coat and sit," he said, gleefully rubbing his hands together. "On the range put the soup pot. The fish I prepare. And a meal for kings we have."

She loved the way her uncle baked fish on the fire, the flavours steaming away on a bed of butter and herbs inside the wet paper. Just the smell of it could take her back to a time in her childhood when her uncle was her hero.

"Your mother's chicken soup is the best in the world," Uncle Mendel said as he slurped from a bowl he had raised to his chest, just below his beard.

"You only say that because she is your sister."

"No, it is true. The same anyone will tell you. Ask any Jew from here. Ask them in Thistle Street or Adelphi Street or Bridgegate. The same they will tell you. The best chicken soup in the whole wide world. And do you know why?"

She smiled at the old routine. "Tell me, uncle. What is the secret?"

"With a hen she makes it. Not a chicken. Hen soup she must call it. Not this chicken nonsense. Aha!"

And as if Uncle Mendel possessed some special sense that could see through wet paper, he announced the fish was ready. With a poker he dragged the singed newspaper parcels from the fire. She had already spread out a dish-towel over her lap to receive her meal. She gingerly pulled the paper off from the fish, letting out the steam, revealing the succulent white flesh. She picked off some of the meat, the hot fat searing her fingers as she popped some of the fish into her mouth. It was delicious.

"What is going on, uncle?" she asked between mouthfuls. "What is going on with this betting on football matches?"

"This Solly talks too much."

"He cares about you. After all, he brought you home from the pub."

"That other Uncle Mendel he brings home. That gambler. That drinker." He stuffed a large piece of fish into his mouth, stared at her with his watery eyes as he chewed. "A beautiful young woman you are becoming," he said when he had finished. He wiped the juice from his lips with the back of his hand. "Why don't we talk about you?"

"No, I want to talk about you. The real Uncle Mendel."

"The real Uncle Mendel?" he said, nodding his head around the room as if to some imaginary audience. "The real Uncle Mendel who smokes a pipe?"

"Yes, that one."

"Aha!" Uncle Mendel rose from his stool, crossed over to the mantelpiece for his smoking kit. He teased out a plug of tobacco from a well-worn leather pouch, stuffed it into the pipe bowl, puffed on the saliva-stained stem until the flame took and the sweet aroma filled the room.

"I am ready."

She laid aside the parcel of newspapers, licked the salt and butter from her own lips, her poor fish nothing more now than a heap of stripped-off bone, a tail and a head with its one dead eye staring at her. "Are you a social activist?" she asked.

"Me? If my job was here in Glasgow, yes. Many social problems there are here. But from the Highlands, it is very difficult. Why do you ask?"

"Because someone wants me to get involved with the rent strikes."

"This someone is who?"

"A schoolteacher I met. Agnes Calder."

"Ah yes, Agnes Calder."

"You know her?"

"Personally, no. But a well-known social reformer she is. Women's Peace Movement, women's rights, women's housing associations, women's everything. What does she want with you?"

"I am a woman too."

"Of course you are. And a very pretty one. But for a Jewish woman, it is unusual to be involved with such things. Our own battles, it is hard enough to fight. But if you want my opinion, to spread your wings is good. Very unfair these rent increases are. Very unfair."

"Do you think I should become a socialist then?"

Uncle Mendel sucked on his pipe, drifted into some reverie as if the smell and taste of his inhalation had set off some sweet and distant memory. "A socialist is not something you become," he said eventually. "It is something you are. Here in your heart." He tapped the end of his pipe against his chest. "As it is written in the Ethics of the Fathers – if I am only for myself, what am I?"

"So what am I?"

"This only you can say. But if in your heart, socialism is what you find, don't tell your mother. A rich man she wants you to marry. A *Kapitalist*. A man who puts profit before people. A man who does not bring hunger, rickets or lice into the family. Now if you do not mind, I feel very tired."

"Yes, I must go too."

Uncle Mendel accompanied her to the door, kissed her on both cheeks.

"I am glad we talk like this," he said.

"Yes, I am too. I miss you when you are away."

"That pleases me to hear you say," he said. "But just one more thing. A biscuit tin did you see? With this Queen Victoria on the front?"

"Don't worry, uncle. It is safe with me."

Five

FROM OFF THE TRAM just past Govan Cross, Celia had difficulty keeping up with Agnes, who trotted ahead despite her heavy build. Her no-neck, no-nonsense head turning round, shouting:

"Come on, lass, come on. There's no much time."

Celia scampered after her, running awkward with the large fishmonger's bell carried in both hands, one of her fingers jamming the clapper, but she managed to reach the top of the rise almost in tandem. The two of them breathless now, Agnes sweating, unbuttoning her coat collar, gulping in air. She was just grateful to put down the bell.

"Govan," Agnes muttered respectfully as she surveyed the grim urban landscape. "Aye. Govan."

She followed Agnes's gaze. Off to the north beyond the rows of tenements stood the shipyard cranes, the docks, the foundries, the munitions factories, the smoking stacks of the Scottish Co-op works. Closer at hand, the sheet draped outside one of the tenement buildings, scrawled with the blood-red, hand-painted threat: "God Help The Sheriff Officer Who Enters Here." Yes, this was Govan all right. Grey and defiant. A stronghold of resistance. She liked that phrase. It was one of Agnes'. But then again, Agnes boasted a whole lexicon of socialist rallying cries. She had heard enough of them on the tram over.

A window dragged open on a first floor. A poster was tacked to one of the panes. 'Rent Strikes Against the Increase' it declared. 'We Are Not Removing'.

"Trouble, Aggie?" a woman shouted above the crying of her cradled child.

"Aye, Lizzie. It's Jean Dunlop. Number twenty-six."

"Oh, for Christ sake. It disnae stop."

Agnes snorted in agreement. "What hour you got?"

Lizzie leaned her head back out of sight, bowing her baby's head dangerously over the sill as she did so. The crying stopped immediately. Lizzie came back into view. "Barely half-past nine."

"Good. There's time to call a meeting. Out the back-court at Jean's."

"I'll be right down."

"Tell the other women on the way."

"Aye." And the window slammed shut.

"That's one good thing about these sheriff officers," Agnes told her as they headed off down the street. "They only work between ten and four. Bless them. Just like my bowels. Regular as clockwork."

At the entrance to close number twenty-six, Agnes said she'd go up the stairs to speak to Jean, tell the poor woman the bad news. "You go out back, ring the bell."

In the rear courtyard, Celia saw a couple of children hanging around. Barefoot girls, they must have been aged about eight or nine, faces smudged with ash from playing in the midden. She guessed they had been looking for luckies. She used to do the same at that age, scavenge about in the ashes searching for some lost treasure. She came up with an earring once. Made of paste. But a dead cat was the more likely discovery. She could see the girls scheming away as they observed her approach, but they held back when they saw the bell. She took up position dead-centre in the drying green, drew herself up straight, gripped the handle in both hands, started to ring towards each of the winds. One of the wee girls put her hands over her ears. A window shot up straight away. Then another. And another.

"Is the sherrie coming?" a voice asked.

"It's not ten yet," she called back.

"What the hell's going on then?"

"It's a meeting, madam. Agnes Calder is calling a meeting."

"Oh, listen to you. Madam this, madam that."

She blushed at the teasing and the voice softened. "I'll just put the bairn down."

By the time Agnes had joined her, there was quite a crowd of women gathered, either leaning against the walls of the courtyard in their pinnies or hanging out the windows. Jean Dunlop came down too, pale and shivering, a baby in her arms, two urchins whining and twirling in her skirts.

Agnes had left her coat up at Jean's. But she was still red-faced and all swollen bosom in her blouse as she addressed her audience. "My spies at the Sheriff Court tell me Jean here is on the list for today."

"Forty-eight hours to get out," Jean Dunlop cried. "Forty-eight hours. That's what that fat bastard of a judge said. And me with a soldier-husband away fighting."

"Shame, shame, shame," the women cried in a chorus well rehearsed from previous evictions.

"The sheriff officer will be here some time before four," Agnes continued, now with a hand on Jean's shoulder. "And we'd like to give him a right good Govan welcome. Isn't that right, sisters?"

"I've got my wee bags of peasemeal," a woman cackled from her upstairs window.

"Mine's got flour in it," another shouted.

"I've got a chantie full of piss needs emptying."

The women were laughing and laughing and Celia smiled with them. Until Agnes put up both her hands to quieten the crowd. "What about the factory girls?"

There was silence now. Celia stiffened, eager for the response. Not knowing the answer herself, thinking her mind too young and muddled on the subject to know what was right, wanting some older, wiser woman like Agnes to say what must be done. It was probably what the audience wanted too. To hear what should be expected from those women in the munitions factory just down the road, packing cartridges, filling grenades, most of them fretting about their husbands off in France. Was it treasonous to down tools, to leave their workplace and stand in solidarity with these poor women fighting off the rent increases and the evictions?

"I'll go down to the gate," said Lizzie from up the street. "I'll pass a note through. Tell them what's going on. Let them decide for themselves what to do."

"Aye, that's a good idea," said Agnes. "Just give them the information and they'll make up their own minds. They'll know what's right. And not to be criticised either for getting it wrong."

"Maybe we can get the sherrie to come during the dinner hour," another woman suggested, her lips clamping on a cigarette as she spoke. "That way the factory girls could join us on their own time. Can you do that for us, Aggie?"

All the women laughed until again Agnes calmed them. "Well, you ken what to do, sisters," she said. "Celia here will ring the bell. Then it's battle-stations all round."

"Where do you want me to go?" Celia asked once the women had gone back inside.

"Go back up the rise to where Lizzie lives," Agnes said. "You'll get a good look-out from there."

"But how will I know it's him?"

"Well, he won't have a kitbag on his shoulder. And he'll be the only man wearing a bowler round these parts."

She took up her observation post on a low wall outside Lizzie's tenement, the bell resting across her lap, her gaze on the road coming up from the tram-stop. A trail of fresh horse-dung lay stinking on the tarmac, no-one coming out to scrape it up for the rose-bushes, gardening not being a priority for the Govan housewife in these troubled times. She turned her nose away from the stench, so full of fear and excitement she was she could hardly keep herself still, her foot tapping nineteen-to-the-dozen against the brickwork, her fingers playing a quick flute against the brass casing of the bell. She had prayed to God in heaven that the man would come early, that he would look down his list for the day and think to himself – 'I'll just start with Govan then'. For she had sworn to her mother she'd be back by noon to look after Nathan, complete the rest of the household chores. But it was getting close to midday now. That's if her eyes were seeing right and she could make out proper the hands on the clock tower of the Co-op building down in the town. She felt a droplet of sweat tickle down her spine, not knowing if it was from her anxiety or the heat.

"You must be hungry, lass?" It was Lizzie back with her bairn at her upstairs window.

"I'm fine, thank you," she called back across the front garden – no more than a patch of flattened weeds that could have done with a good hoe and some of that horse dung.

"Dinnae be daft. You'll need a full stomach to go whirling that heavy bell on a warm day like this. I'll make you up a piece. Meantime, why don't you get yourself a bottle of milk out of the cool of the close. Elspeth won't mind. She's no back from her shift yet. I'll sort it out with her later."

She shouted back her thanks, entered the darkness of the close, saw the whites of the two bottles standing on the doorstep. She chose the one not so deep in shade, picked off the cardboard top, sipped at the liquid, creamy and warm. By the time she was out in the open again, Lizzie was calling to her.

"Are you ready, lass?"

She put down the bell and the bottle, gave a little yelp and a curtsy as she caught the tight-wrapped wax-paper bag Lizzie dropped down to her. She opened up the parcel. Thick slabs of bread smeared with gobs of raspberry jam.

She was munching away at her piece, thinking about the time racing away, mulling over her loyalties to her sick family on the one hand and the Glasgow Women's Housing Association on the other, when she saw the bowlers. Not one, but two. That's what put her off at first. And the sun she was staring into. But there was no doubting it now, these were the sheriff officers. These two men in their dark suits and hats standing out against the light like burnt-out matchsticks, striding up the dusty road full of determination and legal authority. She threw away the rest of her sandwich, wheeled round, ran down the hill, swinging the bell to and fro in front of her like some mad priest with his thurible.

"They're coming," she screamed. "They're coming. Two of them. In their bowlers." She couldn't remember ever feeling so excited by anything before. The sheer exhilaration as well as the responsibility of it all. Could this really be her? Sixteen-year old Celia Kahn, a simple

Jewish girl from the Gorbals. Celia Kahn running against the law. Celia Kahn fighting for women rights, protesting against landlord tyranny, playing her part in the stronghold of resistance. She couldn't believe she had the courage to do this. "There's two of them," she shouted. "Two bowlers. Not bunnets but bowlers."

She arrived up front at number twenty-six, caught at the shoulders by the grip of Agnes Calder.

"That's fine, lass. You've done your work."

The close was packed solid with women, many with grimy faces, the female workers in their overalls from the munitions factory down-ing tools in solidarity. There were biddies too at the open windows with their little bags of flour and peasemeal lined up along the sills. Jean Dunlop and her bairns stood alongside Agnes who pulled Celia to the other side of her. She immediately stood to attention, her heart beating a clatter as if it were Prime Minister Asquith himself coming to visit Govan. Agnes nudged something into her hand.

"Your very own grenade, sister."

She squeezed the paper bag in her palm. Full of flour by the feel of it.

Behind her, the mood was still blethery and restless. Not like the raggedy line of children stood along the front of the tenements, strangely still and quiet, sucking thumbs or gobstoppers in their anti-cipation that something was about to happen but not understanding what and why. On the other side of the street, a few women hung around too curious to stay away.

"Get back to work, you lazy besoms," one of them shouted. "I've got a soldier-man in good need of your grenades."

"Well, he'll be in need of a roof over his head too," came the response from an overhead window.

"If he ever comes home to you," said another voice that trailed away in regret at the remark. But everyone had gone quiet anyway.

For all their bravado, it was the sight of the two men coming over the rise that had stilled the crowd of females. That familiar tension, Celia thought, when she heard her father come home from a long day at work, trying to gauge his mood. For many of the other women, it would be the smell of whisky breath they would be waiting for, or the deep grumblings, the slamming of the doors, the meals to be made, the living to be eked out of a pittance, the duties to be done in the marital bed, the drunken assaults to be endured, the babies to be churned out, some dead, others barely alive.

Agnes must have felt the mood change too for she turned round to face her companions, her voice steady, her expression defiant.

"Come on. Come on now. There's only two of them against our band of sisters."

The women roared at this and the men in their descent must have heard the noise too. For they stopped in their tracks, bowed their heads together in conversation, before continuing on their errand. Within a minute, they were stood in front of the wall of women, like some comedy double act Celia had seen at the Lyceum Music Hall. One round and sweaty-faced underneath his bowler, the other wiry and nervous, staring at his feet, looking like he'd rather be anywhere on earth than facing this mob of women. The heavier man stepped forward.

"Will Mrs Michael Dunlop please identify herself."

This request was met by a barrage of insults but again Agnes held up her hand.

"Let the officer speak his part."

The sheriff officer wriggled his neck inside his starched collar, repeated the request.

"I am that woman," Jean Dunlop said, her voice wavering.

"Yes, this is Jean Dunlop," said Agnes. "Wife of one Michael Dunlop, currently called to the Colours on the battlefields of France. Michael Dunlop, holder of medals for courage shown during the Boer War. And who are you, sir? Evicting poor families from their homes while other men lay down their lives for King and country."

The sheriff officer ignored this remark, which Celia thought he had every right to do, considering she knew Agnes to be a pacifist through and through, and any notion that a working man should lay down his life for King and country and the war profiteers was anathema to her. The sheriff officer continued to address Jean. "Do you pay a monthly rent?"

"I do," Jean said.

"Do you owe arrears on this rent?"

"Only in so far as she has not paid these unfair increases," said Agnes.

"I am not addressing you, madam. I am asking you again, Mrs Dunlop. Are you…?"

It started with just one bag. Not on any given signal but out of pure frustration and a sense of justice that had been simmering in Govan ever since the rent hikes had begun. A bag of flour thrown from an upstairs window, hitting the skinnier of the two men on the shoulder, star-bursting its white powder all over the dark suit. The women were silent at first as the full significance of an actual missile striking a legal representative of the Glasgow Sheriff Court sunk in. A couple of the children started to giggle and that was a signal for a full onslaught. Bag after bag was lobbed at the two officers, knocking off their hats, splattering their suits with a mixture of ash, flour, soot and peasemeal. The thinner of the two ran off quick back in the direction he had come, Celia lobbing her own bag of flour at him as he scarpered, hitting him full in the back. But the senior, heavier, man stood his ground, fending off the attack as best he could. The women worked themselves into a frenzy of abuse and flung objects while a few set about the poor man like wolverines to a kill. Someone yanked his jacket half-off so it pinned down his arms. He was pushed to the ground by the mob then picked up like a sack of Ayrshire potatoes. His shoes were dragged from his feet. And then a pause while some kind of decision had to be made about what to do with their captive. One woman was screaming:

"Off with his trousers. Off with his trousers."

"To the midden," another shouted.

"Aye, to the midden." That became the battle-cry. "To the midden. To the midden."

Celia found herself holding the sheriff officer's damp and wriggling foot, hardly remembering how she had gotten herself into such a prime position within the stramash. She noticed a hole in the sock, a detail that evoked a sudden swell of compassion in her. But the man kicked out, hit her square in the chest, knocking the breath full out of her. So she tightened her grip around his bony ankle and along with

42

a crew of other women carried the twisting torso through the close and into the back green. With about four women holding each of his limbs, the officer was swung back and forth, each swing eliciting a countdown from the crowd, starting for no particular reason at the number five. Four. Three. Two. One. And the body was let go to land in the pile of ashes.

The man lay there for a few seconds before struggling to his feet. The mood changed quickly. A climax had been reached and there was nothing more to be done. There was almost a sense of embarrassment as the sheriff officer attempted the impossible task of trying to clean the dirt off his clothes. One shoe was thrown back at him. Then the other. The women began to disperse quickly, Agnes moving quietly among them, whispering: "Remember. You couldn't see who did it. Too many to identify. Remember that. Impossible to see." And also: "Don't forget the march on the Sheriff Court on Friday. We need all the women we can get. All the women we can get. Friday. See you then."

Celia ran off too. Back up the road to the tram-stop. It was only when she got to the top of the rise by Lizzie's tenement did she realise she had forgotten the bell. She sat down on the wall where she had eaten her piece, waited for her breathing to return to regular, smiling, sensing something in herself she had never felt before. She was no longer simply a good Jewish girl, her father's hard-working daughter, her mother's support, the uncomfortable object of schoolboy leers. None of these women here viewed her as 'just a girl'. But as a person. A full person in her own right.

Six

"I AM LEAVING," AVRAM SAID.

She looked up from her jigsaw puzzle laid out in various stages of completion on the board across her lap, tried to blink away the dull pain behind her eyes. The completed picture should show a village in the Alps. But there was too much snow, too much cloud, almost impossible to tell which of these assorted white pieces was which. "What did you say?"

"I am leaving."

"I know. The day after tomorrow."

Her vision cleared, she could see Avram properly, standing in the kitchen doorway, wearing the new jacket her mother had made for him. They were about the same age, but he looked so grown up now. It must have been four years since he had arrived on their doorstep, sent to them from Russia by his mother to escape conscription into the army, even at his young age. Avram's mother, Rachel Escovitz, a childhood friend of her father's, a woman she knew Madame Kahn had come to despise in her imagination. A hatred which spilt over on to Avram. Although this new jacket might be the sign of a truce. Either that or the celebration of his departure.

"I will sell aprons," he said.

"And girdles," she added. "They are all the fashion now."

He blushed at that. It was the kind of adolescent boy's blush she had become familiar with. Their cheeks might be red but there was some other force that drove them beyond their shyness. "I have samples," he said. "If you want to try."

She laughed at that, a laugh of embarrassment, but she knew it would be hurtful to him. His cheeks only shone redder, like polished apples. She asked more kindly: "You must be looking forward to your new life in the Highlands?"

He moved further into the room, kicked out at some imaginary ball on the floor. "In the Highlands, there is no football."

"There must be football. Everyone plays football in Scotland, don't they?"

"Shinty. They play shinty."

"What's that?"

"I think they play it with sticks. Bloody shinty." He sat down, took a squint at her puzzle. "Hmmph," he said, with a kind of arrogance that made her think he had spotted the proper location of at least five pieces. "Not finished yet?"

"I don't have much time."

He sniffed at this. "What about you? What will you do?"

She lifted the board off her lap, placed it on the table. "I am going to be a clippie."

He rolled his eyes at her. "Of course you are."

"Every woman has a right to her economic independence. I will have my Corporation green jacket, my tartan skirt, my ticket machine. Every woman has every right."

"Papa won't allow it."

"Makes no difference. I'm still going to do it."

"You are too young. You must be eighteen to work on the trams. To take money like that."

"I'll lie about my age. Men lie to be in the war."

"Who will look after Nathan then?"

"Nathan will be well soon. You will see. I am sure of it."

"When I am away, you need to speak to him. He is your brother."

"I do speak to him. Every day when I feed him."

"But not properly. You need to speak to him properly."

"What do you mean? I do speak to him properly."

"I listened to you once. You just talk about yourself."

"But he doesn't say anything. I don't even know if he hears what I say."

"Still you must talk properly. Ask him questions. He hears. I am sure of it."

She looked over at the puzzle. To her surprise, she immediately found the piece of cloud she had been searching for. "I have something for you," she said. She stood up, went over to the mantelpiece, tilted up the base of the clock. "Here," she said, handing over the card. "Billy Reid."

Avram scrutinised the picture, then squinted at her. "What…?"

"When it is time," she said. "I'll come with you to the station." She left the room. Smiling.

She brought the bell along to the park, had gone all the way back to Govan to fetch it, one of the women having found it in the back green, handed it in at Jean Dunlop's. Agnes tucked it safe under the bench as they watched the young men playing football in a grassy area below. She only really saw old men in the public spaces these days. Or the walking wounded. Or boys too young to enlist. These ones must have been essential factory workers or just waiting to be called up. Stripped to their vests some of them were, even in this weak sunshine. Thin-ribbed, white bodies dripping their sweat. Shouting as they kicked the ball about, shivering when they weren't.

"The bell was my father's," Agnes told her, scattering some breadcrumbs at a burbling horde of pigeons around her ankles. "He was a fishmonger on the West Coast. He'd cycle twenty miles down to the pier at Oban when the catch was in. Mostly herring it was in those days. Then cycle all the way back to our village, his face red-raw from the bite of the wind. He'd ring his bell then, rouse the wee wifies to his cart, let his family know there was a living still to be made."

It was the first time she'd heard Agnes give out any personal information, her talk always concentrated on the great social injustices of the world. Even if it was only a bag of sweets she was buying at Glickman's, there would always be some political commentary to go with the purchase.

"I just love this spot, Celia," she went on with the same waver in her voice. "One of my favourite places in the world."

Celia lifted her feet off the ground, curled her legs under her body.

She certainly agreed here was a more relaxed rendezvous than the Room de Luxe at Miss Cranston's Willow Tea Rooms. But she didn't share Agnes' fascination with these wretched birds that did nothing more than cover these precious benches of hers with their spray of white excrement.

"What makes it so special?"

"From here I can see a straight line to the park gates, then again straight down the tramlines of Victoria Road, across the River Clyde, right into the town. It's like I'm sitting at the end of one of the spokes that drives into the heart of the Second City of the British Empire. Not that I'm in favour of empire, mind you. More like the hub of manufacture and trade as created by the honest toil of the working classes."

What with the clear sky and this vantage point Celia had a different sense of the city. Not the usual feeling of how it enfolded her, hemmed her in, cast its dark shadows, choked her with its soot and fumes. But how it spread itself out, gorged itself on the life-blood of the river, threw up its shipyards, museums, munitions factories and merchant buildings. "I can see the university," she said. "And all these churches. I can't believe how many there are. Eight, nine, ten …"

"I'm in two minds about the churches," Agnes grunted. "I do have to admit there is something quite marvellous about these grand spires, architecturally speaking. It's just what they stand for that bothers me."

Celia braced herself for another lecture on religion, opium, socialism and the wonderful achievements of the late James Keir Hardie, founder of Agnes' beloved Independent Labour Party, but instead two bags of flour were placed on the bench beside her.

"What are those for?"

"I've got a wee job for you."

"I'm hopeless at baking."

"That's not what I'm asking. Are you coming to the march on Friday?"

"I've got an errand to do in the town. I'll try to get away after."

"Well, bring these bags with you. I can sneak us into the Sheriff Court. If that bastard Fothergill wins his case on behalf of the landlords, I'm lobbing this flour at the man. I'd like you to do the same."

"For goodness sake, Agnes. I can't do that. We'll get arrested."

"Don't worry. I've got our exit all planned."

"I still won't do it."

"I'm not asking you to kill the man. This is peaceful protest. And direct action. But I cannae trust my aim. I need some back-up. I saw the way you chucked one of these at the sheriff officers. Don't tell me it didn't make you feel good inside. A woman demanding justice be served."

Agnes put on that pleading face of hers, the same one she'd used when she'd asked her to do the bell-ringing, her mouth going all sloppy, making her think the woman would just crumple and die if she didn't do what was asked. Then the pigeons flew up in a wing-flapping eruption scaring the life out of her as a ball skittered by, shearing the dead-heads off a bed of flowers by the bench.

"Throw it back, darlin', will ye?" one of the boys yelled.

She stooped, picked up the ball, found herself getting all self-conscious with her under-arm delivery but managing to hoist it back all the same. An accomplishment that raised hoots from the players. She flushed to the teasing but was enjoying the attention until Agnes rustled a brown paper bag of ginger creams in front of her.

"Don't pay them no heed. Nothing better to do than kick a piece of leather about."

"You can't blame them," she replied, picking out a sweet, one eye still on the youths below. "It's such a fine day. It could be their last game before they go to war."

"That may be the case. But what do you say about what I asked? After all you may not need to do anything. I'd like to think the sheriff will refuse to give legal authority to Fothergill for these evictions. If he's got a sense of what is ethical and right in the world."

Celia rolled the ginger cream around in her mouth, felt the spicy tingle on her tongue and gums. "All right. I'll do it."

"And afterwards, my socialist Sunday school's having a picnic in the Botanic Gardens. I thought you might like to come to that."

"If I don't get arrested first."

Agnes searched around inside her coat pockets, brought out a piece of paper covered in crumbs. "I've written the instructions where to go. You never know, you might meet some boys your own age. If you've a mind for such things."

She took the note, picked up the bags of flour, stuffed them in her message bag, strode off, down past the young men busy with their game of football, not a head turned to mark her departure. She decided on the long way home round the outside of the park, past the Victoria Infirmary, that impressive grey-stone building sprawled across the whole side of a hill that left even her young lungs breathless. She looked up at the wide hospital balconies where some of the male patients sat in their wheelchairs, others leaned on crutches against a back wall, heads raised to the weak sunshine. Sad and pale they were, all wrapped up in an assortment of scarves, greatcoats and dressing gowns. A couple wore peaked caps. One man had a medal pinned to his pyjama jacket. Most of them smoked cigarettes or pipes.

"Bloody war," she said to herself. "Bloody, bloody war."

Seven

CELIA HUNG AROUND THE HITCHING POST at the bottom of Buchanan Street where the carthorses were gathered for the haul of their wagonloads a quarter-mile up the easy slope to the station. The beasts were restless, flicking their tails, flies buzzing around the gunge lining their eyes, bothering her too, having to keep the pesky insects off her face with a constant wave of her hand. A boy weaved through their flanks, sweeping up the manure, left her wondering how much a person was paid for doing a job like that. And even though Avram wasn't in the mood to be obliging, she'd managed to get him to ask one of the drivers to give them a ride. For the fun of it really, given that his baggage was light enough to carry up the street, just a knapsack of his clothes, some samples for Uncle Mendel.

The cart-driver was merely a lad, his sleeves rolled up over brawny arms. He looked at her too straight for her liking, let out a shrill whistle, said:

"I shouldnae really… och aye… hop on."

She waited with her hands clamped to her waist while Avram swung on his bag and parcels, heaved himself on to the rearside of the wagon. Then she grabbed his held-out hand, pulled herself on board, careful of her own satchel with the flour inside. Bits of straw littered the wooden slats, squashed vegetables, a couple of tea-chests up the driver's end, plenty of space to spread out if she were careful of the splinters.

"Mind yer dress from the wheels," the driver shouted over the chests. "Don't want to be getting yer skirts dirty. Yer young fancy man wouldn't be wanting that."

"He's not my fancy man."

"Right then." The driver gave his brace of Clydesdales a flick, the horses began their plodding ascent.

She knew she should be feeling sad about Avram's departure hanging as he was off the backboard with the face of a graveside mourner, but all this fine weather, the flock of people, only served to fire up her excitement. A Salvation Army band struck up with its brass and its Christian soldiers chorus as they passed by St. Vincent Place, she couldn't prevent her legs swinging in time. Then the wagon pulled up sharp for a group of women crossing their path, two stern-faced matrons at their head stretching a white sheet declaring the procession's purpose – Defending Our Homes Against Landlord Tyranny. The cloth brushed over the pricked-up ears of the horses but the beasts just snorted, wriggled their thick necks, jingling the buckles and straps of their halters.

The wagon-driver sprang half-way up from his bench. "I'm with you," he shouted, pumping a fist. "Bloody landlords and their factors." Then, as if he felt the need to give some explanation, he twisted his head back. "On their way to the courts. For the big demonstration."

"I know," she said. "Protesting against those eviction cases."

"I've never seen so many folks in the town. Not even for the footba." The young man cracked a broad smile then flicked his whip. The team started moving again.

"How do you know so much about this?" Avram asked her.

"I read the newspapers. You play your football." Then to prove her point, she called out to the driver. "Are you getting any increases where you're from?"

"Aye, I'm frae Partick," he shouted back over his shoulder.

"That's one of the worst areas affected."

"Aye, all those workers from outside floodin' into the steel and engineering works. Landlords are rubbin' their hands like they're kindlin' fire with sticks. They'll either force the increases or have us out on our arses with the newcomers ready to step in. Meanwhile my faither's off in France fighting for King and country. And I could be joining him any day now."

"The Government and the sheriff will pay attention. You'll see. These wifies will make them."

"That's a fine way of thinking ye've got for being a lassie."

"I've got a fine way of thinking, lassie or not," she said firmly. "Now can you stop to let me off, please."

"I've no offended ye, have I? We're almost at the station."

"Please stop."

The driver pulled up the horses.

"Where are you going?" Avram asked.

"I'm sorry," she said, easing herself down off the backboard. "But I need to go. You should keep on to the station."

"I'm coming too."

"Please don't." But he was already gathering his baggage together in a scramble, jumping off after her. "Wait," he shouted.

She stopped, spun back at him. "I have to meet someone."

He fumbled in his pocket, pulled out a small box. "Here. Take it." He clawed back the lid to reveal a silver thimble.

She stared at his outstretched hand. "What's this?"

"I want you to have it."

"But your mother gave it to you."

"Please."

"I can't."

"Please, Celia. Please take it."

"No, no. I can't."

"Why not?"

"It's all you have left of her. It's too precious."

"That is why I want to give it."

"Oh, Avram. Don't be silly."

She looked round after she'd moved away from him, tried to catch a glimpse, but he was already smothered by the crowds, a little eye of hurt concealed within the storm of the marchers. She was swept up herself, driven across a George Square that was usually a blank open space with more statues than pedestrians, funnelled into a side-street, heading for the Sheriff Court. There were women, women, women everywhere, raising more noise than a Clydeside shipyard on launch day, the drums, the horns, the ricketies, the speakers on their makeshift platforms blaring out their causes.

She felt their anger. And sense of determination. But most of all, this intoxicating drug of power. The power of a united force. Of women together. Women taking control. It was like pollen floating in the atmosphere. She no longer felt herself as an individual. No longer Celia Kahn of 32 Thistle Street, The Gorbals. But part of something greater. Was this the revolution Agnes talked about? Her skin tingled and prickled with the potency of it all. She was sure these other women felt the same. She could see it in the jut of their faces, the delirium in their eyes, the shininess of their skin.

Above her, office windows gaped open, figures bent over sills to watch and wave. The procession began to slow, tiny steps forward now, bodies bunching up as they approached a junction. Something was going on ahead but she didn't know what. She worried about the time, one of the clock-towers showing she'd five minutes in hand, her nerves already all over the place without adding Agnes' displeasure to the mix. A belly-deep rumble rose up from beyond the Central Post Office, then a wave of squealing coming at her from the women in front as if someone had pinched them, told them to pass it back. People stacking up against each other, straining their necks for answers. She was being pushed from behind, forced up against the foxtail collar of the woman in front, fearful her satchel would be squashed, making her flour more ready for the baking than the throwing. Everyone peering this way and that as each row crept forward out of the side-street into the broader avenue of Ingram Street. And then she saw the reason for the delay. Coming down the road in a broad swathe of chanting, blackened faces, an army of men. Hundreds of them. In their factory-soiled jackets and dungarees. Some holding colourful ward banners, others waving caps, spanners, striding in step, to the sound of the bagpipes.

"Christ, it's no just a rent strike," a woman in front shouted. "It's a bloody munitions strike as well. The men have downed tools."

Their ranks mingled, flowed into each other seamlessly as if in some massive choreographed movement, two rivers of protest joining in their surge towards the Sheriff Court. Her feet hardly touched the road within the press of bodies, crushed up as she was against a lad with an oil-smeared face, a pale stripe across his forehead where his cap had been.

"Which yard are you from?" she asked, her voice scratchy from the shouting.

"I'm from Dalmuir, miss. But there's men here from all over. From Clydebank, from Cathcart, from Parkhead Forge. The factories are empty. They're bloody empty."

The main body of the march primed itself for its protest in front of the Sheriff Court while she headed off smart along the east side of the building. She found the entrance painted in its Glasgow Corporation green, knocked gently, her heartbeat stuck half-way up her throat as she waited. The door opened a crack, swung wide to let her in.

"Get in," Agnes said. "Before anyone sees."

She stepped into a cramped, dim vestibule with a wooden stairway leading off. Standing beside Agnes, a bespectacled lass with lank red hair, her arms clasped around a bundle of red-ribboned files as if it were her very own bairn she was protecting.

"This is Elsie," Agnes said. "She feeds me the advance information about the eviction notices. Our secret agent at the heart of the Scottish legal system."

"A clerk in the warrant office," Elsie said with a little laugh.

Agnes frowned, then asked. "What's happening outside?"

"The men from the munitions factories have downed tools, joined in on the march."

"Oh for Christ sake. It should just be us. Why do they always have to interfere?"

"Oh come on, Aggie," Elsie said. "Can you no forget about your feminist crusades for just one minute? We need the men to join us on this. Having the munitions factories idle will put far more pressure on Sheriff Lennox than a few harridans scratching at the courthouse door. The poor man's on the telephone right now to the Munitions Minister, Lloyd George himself. All the way to London." She nodded to the stairway. "Now up you go, the two of you. The gallery's packed to the rafters with the press. I'll keep this door unlocked."

"And the constables?" Agnes asked.

"They're all round at the main entrance. I'll leave you to it. I've got my own work to do."

Elsie was right. The place was packed. Not just the gallery benches but also below in the main courtroom. Hot and airless too, the closed windows holding in the stink of sweat, hair cream and cigarette smoke, keeping out the noise of the crowds. Agnes stretched herself up straight in the aisle, stuck out her bosom, surveyed the scene, just like that day back in Govan commanding her troops. A few of the reporters looked up, dipped their chins, flicked a hat brim.

"Why if it isn't Jimmy Docherty?" Agnes wheezed, addressing a lanky, grey-haired man scrunched in at the end of the back row.

"I'd doff my hat if I were wearing one, Comrade Calder."

"Writing your poison for the *Evening Citizen*?"

"It pays the rent. More than I can say for that lot down there."

"What's your headline? Strikers commit treason while country's at war?"

Docherty shrugged, smiled back as if he'd been caught out, a gold filling catching the light. Celia thought he'd probably been a good-looking man in his time. Before the alcohol had veined his nose and cheeks, pouched up his eyes. "Something like that," he sighed. "What are you here for? Enlisting supporters for the Bolsheviks? Or is it the Women's Peace Movement?"

"Just one revolution at a time."

"Is she one of your brigade then?"

"Not yet."

Docherty turned to her. "Well, don't let Comrade Calder indoctrinate you, lass. Or she'll have you burning down all kinds of buildings in the name of the suffragettes."

"I've got my own mind, Mr Docherty."

"I'm sure you have."

She gave him a slight curtsy, swept her skirts forward, sat down on one of the aisle steps. She'd never been in a courtroom before. "Have we missed much?"

"Quite a lot I'd say." Docherty showed her his legal pad with a page full of notes. "The factor Fothergill has refused to drop his eviction cases against the tenants for the arrears. Sheriff Lennox then tried to explain to this mob here that despite the passions raised by this issue, he could only decide the case on its legal merits. Needless to say that particular speech didn't go down well with the great unwashed, forcing a delegation from the protestors to approach the bench. Now they've all gone off into a wee back room to discuss the matter. I believe Lloyd George himself is being consulted, fact to be confirmed in time for the evening edition." Docherty scraped the back of his shaved-red neck with the tip of his pencil. "Meanwhile, I've never seen so many women in court in my life. Outside of a trial with a hanging at the end of it."

"Who was in the delegation?" Agnes asked.

"No-one I recognise. For the sheriff to meet with them at all is an extraordinary break with procedure. And a bloody disgrace, if you ask me, the court kow-towing to a bunch of anarchists."

"What do you think will happen, Mr Docherty?" Celia asked.

"My money's on a postponement, lass. Until the Government sorts something out."

"You're wrong there, Jimmy," Agnes said. "This crowd won't settle for anything less than these cases being thrown out altogether. Otherwise, Lennox will have a riot on his hands."

"It's no up to the crowd, Agnes. Or Westminster. Remember this is a court of law."

To confirm his point there came a command of 'all rise'. Sheriff Lennox bustled in from a side-door, a good deal of irritation on his face. A dozen or so men and women of the delegation followed, easing themselves into a line along a side wall, eyes to the ground, hands in a fold in front of them. She saw two other men take up position at a table before the sheriff. Agnes hissed over at her, drew a finger across her upper lip, then pointed down at the two men. The one with the moustache was Fothergill.

Sheriff Lennox settled into his chair, took his time sorting out the folds of his robe.

"Be seated!" an usher cried.

A unanimous thumph. Then silence. She felt as if the whole courtroom had taken a deep breath. Even the noise of the crowd outside had quietened.

She gripped her step with both hands, felt the rough wood dig into her skin, tiny ripples of nerves spreading out from her abdomen. Docherty beside her on his gallery bench, hunched forward, chewing on his pencil. Agnes heavy breathing behind her, stubbing out a cigarette on the wooden floor, giving her a tap with her toe, time to get ready. Her fingers trembled as she fussed with the buckles on her satchel, wished she'd brought her other bag, the one with the simple clasp. She could taste the bile risen in her mouth, a violent clench in her stomach, thought she might throw up over Jimmy Docherty and that smart suit he was wearing, didn't take a tailor's daughter to notice that. She imagined this must be how those soldiers felt in the trenches, snapping off the pin of their real grenades, pushing out of their shelter for a throw, never knowing if they'd get their heads blown off in the process.

Lennox surveyed his courtroom over his glasses, leaned forward to speak, appeared to change his mind, drew back into his high-backed chair. She watched him carefully, trying to second-guess the verdict, thought he had a kindly face, the sort of person who might be favourable to bending points of law in favour of what was right and ethical. Otherwise, any second she was going to be up on her feet with a bag of flour in her hand trying to target that shiny-suited factor man Fothergill with his slither of a moustache.

The sheriff cleared his throat, placed his hands on his bench, the white cuffs of his shirt sharp contrasting the black of his gown. She released the straps on both buckles, slid a hand inside, felt one of the flour bags, something quite comforting in the way it moulded into her palm. The silence filled the room, then snapped taut, waiting to be broken. Sheriff Lennox leaned forward: "On the understanding Parliament itself is about to consider legislation that will make the matter before this court redundant, the pursuer, Mr Daniel Fothergill, representing the factors, has agreed to drop all claims for ejectment." He brought down his gavel. "Case dismissed." And as if by some magical connection to this sound of hardwood on hardwood, the whole courtroom rose to its feet and cried: "Yes!" Everyone except Docherty.

"That's the whole concept of the law thrown out the window," he grumbled. "Mob rule is what I call it. And the interference of Government in the judiciary. They couldn't stomach the munitions industry grinding to a halt over this."

"The rent increases were unfair, Jimmy," Agnes said. "You know that."

"What do you think, lass?" he asked. "Does the end justify the means?"

She looked over at him as she buckled up her satchel. There was a weary wisdom about the man that made her think he could be right, that everyone else was wrong. Then she glanced at Agnes who'd moved down to the front of the gallery, smiling and shouting down to her colleagues in the main court room.

"Oh, I think justice was done, Mr Docherty," Celia said. "Justice was done."

Eight

CELIA RUSHED HOME FROM THE SHERIFF COURT, prepared lunch for her father, fed Nathan, headed out again quick before Papa Kahn had a chance to ask where she was going. She'd worry later about her mother's reaction to her absence. At Gorbals Cross, she caught the tram to the West End, the only passenger to tackle the chill of the open deck, felt she might explode from her relief and the excitement of the morning in the cramp of the lower tier.

She got off just outside the Botanic Gardens, at the red-brick station boasting its twin clock towers topped with those strange bulbous-shaped ornamental domes. She remembered how Papa Kahn used to point them out to her as a child: "These onion designs are just like in Russia. I come all the way to Glasgow but the architecture does not change. How can this be?"

She looked up at these domes now, then along Great Western Road, that grand tree-lined avenue with its central line of ornate street lamps stretching forever. Or at least as far as Loch Lomond. A boulevard which inspired Madame Kahn to respond to her husband thus:

"These silly domes might remind you of Russia," she snorted. "But this great wide avenue has the air of a Berlin *strasse* about it."

It also had the air of wealth about it. Here was where the rich dwelt. The textile tycoons, the coal barons, the steel merchants, the coffee importers, the shipyard owners. Here there was space. Here there was light. Here there were no rent strikes, no backlands, no over-crowding, no two families to a room, no men sleeping on rooftops, no unwashed children with rickets. Here she could watch a well-dressed matron strolling by with her young daughter in tow, both of them wearing matching fur-trimmed capes and mufflers. Here there was a university, an art gallery and a botanical garden.

The Botanic Gardens. Not just ordinary gardens like her own local Queens Park with its run-of-the-mill plant life. But as the entrance sign declared, these were 'horticultural gardens hosting impressive glasshouses devoted to temperate flora seeded and nurtured for botanical study at the University of Glasgow. Home to the noble and the exotic. The orchids, the cacti, the Australasian ferns. Housed under glass to replicate their indigenous climes and to protect them from the fog and smoke emerging from the city's industrial stacks and domestic chimneys.'

She thought about buying a newspaper. Why not enter the picnic with some reading material under her arm, ready to give her opinion on conscription, the battle of Verdun, or Europe's desperate entreaties for America to enter the war? But the newspaper-seller was not at his usual pitch by the gates. Perhaps the presses were stuck on hold until they had recorded Jimmy Docherty's court report. Instead she considered using her coppers to purchase a penny-lick from the vendor standing there with his ice-cart. 'Mr Luigi And His Famous Italian Ices'. She used to love these ice-creams with their secret ingredients from Italy handed down from generation to generation. But wartime restrictions had blanded out the taste. Better then to arrive at the picnic with an air of serious commitment than with a mouthful of unsatisfying dessert.

It wasn't hard to spot the socialist Sunday school picnic, gathered as it was away from the main paths on a gentle slope close to the river, placards from the morning's march stacked like giant kindling against the tree trunks. She was surprised by the number in attendance, there must have been about sixty souls standing around in a loose circle, adults and children alike, holding themselves against the cold now the sun was dipping past the tops of the branches. Agnes caught sight of her approach, her face still flushed from the morning's successes, beckoned her to join. But she decided to hang back further up the rise, with a view over what was happening, not ready yet to fling herself into the company of strangers. Some kind of ceremony was in process, the focus of attention on a pink-cheeked young man with the devout air of a priest about him whose words were directed towards a young couple, a swaddled-up baby in the cradle of their arms.

"…and so this child is not only a happy addition to these young parents and their kinsfolk but also a symbol of hope, faith and forward-looking courage for all the human race." The functionary paused, gazed at the child on whom he had bestowed such a massive responsibility before continuing: "We therefore meet in this public forum in order to reaffirm our conviction that every child born to our race, of whatever nation or colour, should be honoured as a new addition to humanity. And so as spokesman for this community, I ask by what name you wish this child to be known."

"Keir Hardie MacDonald", she heard the young father announce, fiddling with the baby's blanket as he did so. He was wearing his army uniform, probably back on leave to celebrate his doings of nine months previous. Either that, or he was off to the Front after the ceremony, might never see his son again. That thought made her pay closer attention as did his wife who snuggled in nearer to her man as the officiant said: "On behalf of all this company present, and of society in general, I welcome this child – Keir Hardie MacDonald – into the membership of the human family, and express a heartfelt desire that his life may be blessed with health and joy, that he may render service in a humble sphere or in the public sphere, to the social commonwealth, its fellowship, its order and its progress."

A number of the men shouted "hear, hear", then to her surprise the congregation started to sing, just like that, out there in the open, under the trees, not far from the glasshouses with their exotic ferns, with not a care for any members of the public that might pass them by:

'We this day your name inscribe
And whatever may betide
Always let your faith abide
Child of love, our comrade.'

The audience broke up quickly after that, smothering the young Keir and his parents with congratulations, while she carefully edged her way down the greasy slope. Agnes was waiting, her lips all pursed up into a smug smile. Celia couldn't blame her for that really, it had been her day so far.

"You managed to come," Agnes said.

"I decided I couldn't miss it. What with all the excitement of the morning."

"A victory for the solidarity of women against the exploitation of the working classes."

"What about the munitions workers?"

"Aye, them too. Though I'm almost sorry I didn't get a chance to throw my flour bomb. That Fothergill had the kind of face you wanted to powder."

"Oh, I don't know. I was shaking so much, I'm sure I'd have hit the sheriff instead."

Agnes laughed, rubbed her hands against the cold. "How did you like our little ceremony?"

"Yes, it was good. At least, I understood the words."

"Just a simple naming of a new-born child. Not a baptism or circumcision or some other barbaric covenant with church or God uttered in Latin or Hebrew. A simple naming. The family thought it would be nice to use the occasion." Agnes snapped open her hand-bag, had a look inside. "Och, I thought I had some sweets. Come on, let's have something to eat. And I'll introduce you."

A few trestle tables had been set up on the damp grass, she hadn't seen so much food and drink in ages. Large containers of ginger beer, lemonade and cider, plates of hard-boiled eggs, apples and cheeses, sandwiches smeared with jams and honey, bread loaves, Paris buns, sugar biscuits, even a large slab of butter.

"We're well in with the farm workers," Agnes explained. "Help yourself."

She couldn't resist a Paris bun on a plate, took a glass of cider as well, hard to hold on to the two items what with all the people she was being invited to meet, the handshakes, the names and faces blurring by her, lots of talk about the march, about the Government set to pass legislation to freeze rents until the end of the war. Agnes disappearing somewhere, leaving her to go back to the trestle tables, filling herself up with more bread and cheeses than her ration-fed stomach was used to, needing to wash it all down with another glass of cider. She was already feeling herself a bit flushed, not used to the alcohol, suddenly remembering Avram standing there in George Square with his mother's silver thimble winking at her from its velvet cushion.

A young man came to stand next to her. He wore a long overcoat, leather boots laced up to his knees, reminded of her of one of those Cossack soldiers her father warned her against. He leaned across her to pick up a sugar biscuit, she could see the white skin of his neck, a mole where his coat collar pulled away.

"The food's the best part," he said, on returning upright. He swept his hair back off his forehead. *Spülwasser blond*, her mother called that light-dark mix of colour – dishwater blond. Tiny craters of pockmarks were scattered across his cheeks.

"I suppose it is," she replied, her voice coming out all strange, hard to recognise herself in it.

"I'm called Boydie."

"That's a strange name," she said in a rush, not meaning to have spoken the words at all, just a thought in her head pouring out through her cider-loosened lips. "I'm sorry. That was rude of me. I haven't heard that name before."

"It's Gaelic. Boyd. Means blond." He pointed to his hair. "What about you?"

"What about me?"

"Your name?"

"Yes, my name. Celia. I don't know what it means."

He took a bite of his biscuit, stood there looking at her as he chewed, he might as well have been a Cossack measuring the worth of his horse, the way he scrutinised her up and down. With those pale blue eyes like a mirror, hard to know what lay behind them. He had a strange way of standing too, holding himself back from her as if her breath stank or he was about to be slapped. He wiped the sugar off his lips with his sleeve, she sipped on her cider.

"First time here?" he asked.

"Yes."

"For me too."

He continued to stare at her, she looked at her shoes, the wet blades of grass stuck to them, like little green flags after a parade. "Your parents are here?" she asked.

"My father sent me. He's a hard-nosed socialist. A union leader down the shipyards. But I came with some friends." He tilted his head towards a group of smirking youths. Then he laughed. "They bet me I didn't have the courage to speak to you. But I don't mind talking to you. With or without money."

She blushed at that, didn't know whether to be flattered or offended by this arrogant young man. "That's not very polite of you," she managed.

"I thought it was a nice to thing to say. A compliment."

"How much did they bet you?" She noticed she was back speaking in that voice again, the kind of tone she imagined those actresses in the cinema used as they smoked their lipstick-stained cigarettes.

"A half-penny."

"Is that all?"

He shrugged. "They're poor. But a half-penny means I can make a wish."

"What do you mean?"

"There's a bridge close by. The Half-Penny Bridge. Throw a coin into the river, make a wish."

"I've never heard of it."

"Perhaps I can show you."

"Now?"

"If you like."

"I can't do that."

"Why not?"

She took another sip of her cider, steadied herself against the side of the trestle table, how much alcohol could there be in pressed apples? "I don't want to leave the picnic."

"You enjoy this kind of meeting then?"

"I don't know. As I said, this is my first time."

He looked down at the table, seemed to decide against another

64

biscuit. "I prefer my socialism to be more radical. Not simple fables and stupid ceremonies. More militant."

"You would have liked today's demonstration."

"Today was good. Direct action is good. The march of the proletariat. I like that a lot. What do you think?"

"Direct action is all right. I'm just against all this killing and wounding."

"You don't believe in fighting for what is right?"

"I don't believe in going to war for anything."

"Ah Celia, you are still young."

She laughed, a little more loudly than she would have liked. But she enjoyed the way he used her name. "Young? How old are you?"

"I am old enough to fight." He glanced back to his friends. "Come on, let me show you this bridge. I'd like to make this wish with you."

"Is it far?"

"Five minutes." He pointed to the path that sided the river. "Along there."

"I need to speak to Agnes first."

"Who's Agnes? Your mother?"

"A friend. She invited me here."

"You need a friend's permission?"

"I just want to tell her where I am going."

"Come on. It's really not far."

She stood up on her toes, looked around. "I can't see her. If you're sure it's not far. But what about your friends?"

He grinned. "I don't need their permission either."

The path followed the course of the river, dipping under overhanging branches, wooden fencing-slats missing here and there, probably young boys broken through to net for tadpoles, smoke their cigarettes on the rocks.

"Where's this bridge?" she asked.

"Not far. Why are you rushing ahead?"

"It's getting cold. I just want to get there."

He tugged on her arm, forcing her to slow. "I need to tell you something."

"What?"

"I received my call-up papers this morning."

She stopped, the two of them panting, her head clearing slightly from the walking, the chill air off the river. She could smell alcohol on his misty breath, how had she not noticed that before? And the background trill of birdsong. A thrush. Such a hopeful sound.

"When do you have to go?"

"I'm not."

"What do you mean? Everyone has to go."

"I'll be a conscientious objector."

"You said you were a militant socialist."

"I'm all for violent revolution to promote the socialist cause. But my conscience forbids me participating in a war that is merely for the benefit of the capitalist profiteers."

She shivered, pulled in her coat, stamped her feet against the hard earth. She'd had enough of this Boydie and his Half-Penny Bridge. "That sounds like your father talking. What do you want to do?"

"I'm not a coward, if that's what you're thinking. Or a peace-crank. I'll explain my case to a tribunal."

"These tribunals only listen to committed pacifists."

"If they don't accept my position, I'll happily go to jail." He looked behind him as if the local police might pounce, cart him off to his nearest depot. "You're lucky. Women don't do anything about this damn war."

"That's not true. Look at the women on today's march."

He laughed at that, his lips pulled back ugly against his teeth. Like a horse. "It was the men going on strike that did it." He staggered slightly on his feet, falling back against the fencing. "I drank a little too much, a little too much."

It had become much darker, the light draining quickly out of the day. At the picnic, they would be starting to pack up.

"I'm going back," she said.

He stepped around her, blocked off her path, fumbling in his pockets for something. "You haven't seen the bridge?"

"There is no bridge. You lied to me."

He held out his arms. "You're right. There isn't any fucking bridge. Do you have any tobacco?"

"I don't smoke."

"I'd like a cigarette. That's what I really want. To smoke a cigarette."

"Let's go back then. My friend Agnes has tobacco."

"Yes, your friend Agnes."

"Come on," she pleaded. "Let's go."

He stood facing her, patting his coat for imaginary tobacco, shifting on his feet, finding instead a bottle of some amber liquid in his inside pocket. "Perhaps I will go to jail. To some fucking tiny, rotting, stinking cell. Or they'll shoot me for being a deserter." He pulled out the bottle stop, took a deep swig. He reached out a hand but she stepped back. "I want to kiss you," he said. "A man going into the army deserves a kiss."

"Stay away from me."

He threw the bottle on to the grass verge, lurched forward, grabbed her by the shoulders, began to push her back into the bushes. Low branches raked against her stockings, her feet slithered in the mulch underfoot, his weight pressing against her, forcing her knees to bend until she fell onto her back against the slope, Boydie on top of her, his body pinning her to the ground, one hand tight around her wrist, another flat-palmed against her nose and mouth.

"So what do you say?" he snarled. "Give a soldier something to remember."

She tried to bite his hand but her action only made him press harder against her mouth. She thought her teeth might cave in from the force. His other hand had abandoned its grip on her wrist, she could feel him trying to drag up the hem of her coat, her skirts. She tried to arch her body to push him off but he was far too strong and heavy, his weight trapping her upper arms so she could do little more than beat a fist faintly against his side. She couldn't breathe. Saliva was building up in her throat, choking her. His face above her, crimson, sweating, eyes bulging, those pock-marks. She could hear her own stifled cries within her head. He must have seen the panic of suffocation in her eyes for he let his hand slip slightly so it only covered her mouth. She snorted in the air, smelt the dampness of the earth, the mud on his palm, the alcohol on his breath. She could hear his breathing, her own gasps for breath, the hammer of her heart, the sound of the thrush echoing through the park. His other hand wriggled inside her skirts between their two bodies, between her thighs, searching out the slit in her drawers.

Nine

SHE DIDN'T CRY OUT when he split her, when her whole universe had split. She didn't scream at all. Even though she had the opportunity when his hand had slipped from over her mouth as he became more engrossed in seeking out his satisfaction. Her arms had freed slightly too so that she could beat hard on his back but he didn't seem to care. It was as if her own violent onslaught only deepened his pleasure. But she didn't cry out. Just suffered in silence. As a thousand years of practice within her race had taught her to do.

She stumbled up the path to the clearing where the picnic had taken place. Thank God there were still some people there. She only hoped that Agnes was still among them. She brushed away as best she could the mud and leaves from her coat, straightened her stockings. Underneath, her drawers were torn and stained. There had been blood on her thighs and some other fluid she had wiped off with a handkerchief. She ached from the tear between her legs, from the lead of his weight against her breasts. She had left her hat somewhere, the black velvet one she only wore for best. She gulped in a breath, walked towards the gathering, trying to keep her body upright. She had slipped and fallen down the grassy slope, that is what had happened, caught her head on a stone, might have even knocked herself out, look you can even feel the bump, how long had she been away?

"Where are your shoes?" one of the children called out as she approached. "Look, mother. She has no shoes."

She kept walking into their midst, one hand pinning her collar to her throat, the other bunched around the soiled handkerchief in her pocket. "I fell," she said to no-one in particular. "I fell down the slope. I am so sorry. I should have been helping. But I fell."

Two firm hands against her shoulders stopped her. "For Christ sake, lass," said Agnes. "What happened to you?"

"I fell, Agnes. I fell down the slope."

Agnes pulled her into her grasp, patted her head, picked out the leaves and twigs from her tresses. "Of course you did, lass. Of course, you did."

It was only then she started to cry.

She had no recollection of walking barefoot with Agnes through the Botanic Gardens to the park gates. There had been a ride in a hansom, she remembered that. And it had started to rain. The smell was so sweet as she listened to it drum on the leather canopy. She stared out from under the cab, watched the downpour cleanse the dusty streets, saw Luigi the ice-cream man pushing his cart in the rain. A penny-lick. She would have liked that now, her mouth so dry. Or even a glass of cider. There had been a flight of stairs after that, children running down them as she was helped upwards. It was the first time she had seen Agnes' home, her flat in the West End. Later she would remember thinking it was not as austere as she had expected. There was an ample hallway with quite a few doors leading off. Tall windows and high ceilings. Fine rugs on the floor. Through the fog of her distress the thought arose that the place was quite grand really for a teacher's salary. Piles of pamphlets everywhere. Come the revolution and we'll all live in posh West End flats. She was led into a large kitchen.

"I'm getting you into a hot bath as fast as I can," Agnes said as she fired up the range. "You sit down there. I'll bring you a blanket."

She watched as Agnes boiled up the water, tipped it into a tin bath in the middle of the room. Then she was made to strip, sit in the water, even though it was hardly six inches deep, watched with fascination as she splashed the last of the blood from her thighs.

"I want you to douche," Agnes said. "I'm going to add vinegar to the water. As much as you can possibly bear. Then I want you to wash yourself out."

She did as she was told. The sensation mildly irritating but it pleased her too to feel the acidity flush out the ugliness from between her legs. She smelt like a fish and chip shop. Wrap me up in newspaper and take me away.

"I doubt if the vinegar will do much good," Agnes kept saying. "It's old wives' tales really. But I've got nothing else to offer you. Except for this." Agnes handed her a glass.

"What is it?"

"Whisky. Drink it down. You'll feel better. And I'll fill up the bath now so you can have a proper soak."

When she woke, the rain was still coming down against the dark window-panes. She had a headache, a pain between her legs, a tingling around the tops of her thighs from the vinegar. The water was still hot. Agnes must have been re-filling the bath while she slept. Her neck was sore too where she had leaned her head against the cold tin. Agnes sat in a rocking chair by the fire, knitting at a pace that would have impressed even her mother.

"How long have I been asleep?"

"Not long. About fifteen minutes."

"Oh, it felt like forever."

She lifted herself up from the water but fell back again, as if her body was refusing entry back into this hostile world. She tried again. Agnes brought her over a large towel which she stepped into, the fabric scrubbing rough against her hot skin.

"I must go," she said. "My mother will be wondering where I am."

"You're not going anywhere," Agnes said, pushing her gently down into a chair. "I sent a neighbour's child over to your parents with a note."

"You don't know where I live."

"I know there's a Gorbal's tailor shop with your family name on it."

"What did you tell them?"

"I just said you were with a friend, you had a little turn, probably from something you ate, nothing to worry about, said you'll be home later. I'll make you up some food meantime. You should get your strength up while your clothes dry."

She saw that her dress, bloomers and stockings hung in a line over the fire. She closed her eyes. All she could see was Boydie's face, close up against her own, his lank, dishwater blond hair brushing against her cheek, the pox holes in his skin, the tree branches above. A grey sky, clouds moving in, rain on its way. The rest of her body gone from this picture in her mind as if she had been cut off from the neck downwards. The song of the thrush. She wished she could re-produce that precious sound. A boy at her school used to do that. Make bird sounds. No-one paid his skill much notice. But how wonderful that must be. To be able to carry that birdsong around with you always. She sensed Agnes in front of her now, felt a napkin placed in her lap. She opened her eyes, took the plate of macaroni held out to her.

"Eat," Agnes said.

Which she did. Scooped down her food with a spoon, dribbling the melted cheese on her chin like a baby, couldn't remember the last time she had felt so hungry. Agnes just watched.

"Thank you," she said, handing back her empty plate, hoping there was more but there wasn't. She asked for some water.

"It was my fault," Agnes said as she brought her a glass.

"What was your fault?"

"I saw you go off with him. That lad."

"Do you know him?"

"No. He's never been before. I don't know anything about him. His address. His family. Nothing."

"That's good then."

"Why do you say that?"

"I don't want to know anything about that fucking boy." She'd never used that swear word in her life before, although she'd heard it often enough, usually cringed to hear it. It felt good to say it now though. "Fuck, fuck, fuck," she thought. "I could say this forever."

"I'll never forgive myself," Agnes continued, without a flinch to her language. "I saw you go off with him. I should have known."

"Don't worry, Agnes. I'm fine now."

"Aren't you the brave one? You've had a bath and a wee whisky, that's all. But you're still in shock. You won't feel so fine tomorrow. And there's nothing we can do about it. If the bastard had beaten you up, bruised you a bit, broken a few bones, then perhaps the police would take an interest. Rape? They won't listen to a woman. There's no proof. It's his word against yours. And I know whose they'll believe."

Celia leaned back in her chair, listened to the rain. She didn't want any police. She just wanted to go on with her life as if nothing had happened. Except for that one question she so much wanted to ask in her ignorance.

"Can I get pregnant? I don't mean to be stupid, Agnes ... but the first time it happens ... what with all the blood and everything, surely a baby can't come from all that ... Can a girl get pregnant the first time?"

Agnes came over, kissed the top of her head, pressed her to her lap.

"Oh, my little lass," she said. "Oh, my little lass."

She gently pushed Agnes away. "Well, can I?"

"Yes, you can."

"I wouldn't want it," she cried. "I wouldn't want a child by him."

"Then I'd put your trust in either your God or luck. Rather in any vinegar. But let's not worry about that now. It might never happen."

"I do want to worry about it now. Can you help me, Agnes? Could you do something if it happened. Please."

"Yes, I could arrange something. But it would be dangerous. Too dangerous."

"I don't care. I'll do anything."

"Then it might be safer to have the child," Agnes said softly. "And kill the poor thing afterwards."

Glasgow

1918

Ten

"It is over."

It wasn't the sudden interruption that had startled her. It was the actual voice itself. It had been years since she had heard it. An aural insect trapped in an amber of sound. She looked up from the drab, tan section of linoleum she had been scrubbing. Standing in the kitchen doorway, her young brother. Nathan. She felt her heart swell. It was a tangible sensation as if this joy was an actual, physical commodity being pumped into her veins. She stood up, quickly walked over to him, drying her hands on her apron as she approached. Her first instinct was to crouch down, to lower herself to his height. But he was taller than her now. So she remained standing, staring at him. His hair totally white, blanched of colour after years without light.

"We must get you a new pair of pyjamas," was all that she could say to him as she fussed with the lapels of his jacket. He might have grown taller but he was as scrawny as a war-time chicken. "These ones are too small on you. Look, the sleeves are so short."

"It is over," Nathan said.

"What do you mean?"

But he didn't answer, just gazed ahead, his eyes blinking in the light. She heard the front door open. Over Nathan's shoulder, she saw her father enter the hallway. What was going on? He was never home at this time. In one hand a bottle of *schnapps*, in the other a newspaper.

"Look," Papa Kahn shouted, waving the front page that was just one bold printed word: PEACE! "The war has ended. The armistice is signed." And then: "Nathan? You are up?"

"Yes, Papa. It is over."

76

"My God, my God, my God," her father cried, holding his hands and their contents up to heaven. "What a day this is. What a day. Oh thank you, my Lord. Thank you, thank you." He kissed the top of Nathan's head. "Your mother will soon be here. She is closing the shop. No-one works today. We must drink to celebrate. Your mother will be so happy."

"I would like a bath," Nathan announced flatly.

She told him she would heat up some water, she would do anything, anything he wanted.

"Thank you," he said, turning back towards his bedroom. "It is over. But so many died."

Before he had made it back across the hallway, the front door opened again. Her mother, hat askew, breathless. As soon as she saw Nathan, she dropped to the floor, wrapped her arms around his knees.

"My son, my son, my son," she sobbed. "My son has come back to me."

Nathan patted her hat. "It is over," he said. "Time to start again."

While Nathan bathed, Celia looked out some old clothes of her father's, perhaps even something Avram had left behind. For there was nothing for her brother to wear. He had not been bought new clothes for years. He had only worn pyjamas and even in that department, she had become forgetful. That was the first thing she would do tomorrow. A new pair of pyjamas. Something special she could hardly afford from Paisleys the Outfitters. After all, she had not bought him a birthday present since when? Since before the war. She found a shirt with a collar needing mending, she could stitch that quick. And a brand new suit still in its brown paper wrapping –tailor-made for poor Simon Silverman. A few years ahead of her in school, he was one of the first to enlist, a fact the rabbi had announced with pride from the pulpit. He never came back. Now all that was left was this uncollected suit smelling of mothballs. She gave the items to her mother who dressed Nathan like a doll, it had been so long since he had put on clothes by himself. With the bedroom curtains hauled opened, Celia watched him as he sat facing the window, his hands gripping the arm rests, his head tipped back to the weak sunlight, his hair wet and combed. She remembered how as a child she would observe in wonder this new-born baby brother come into her life. And that was what she did now.

But there was little time for reflection. Neighbours were coming in and out of the flat, grasping her by the shoulders, shaking her as if the news were not real, pinching her cheeks. "Can you believe it? The war is over, Celia. Finished. *Genug*. We can live again. No more ration books, thanks to God." There was Mrs Carnovsky with her Balkan cigarettes, old man Arkush the baker, Dishkin the kosher butcher, Solly with his father, Lucky Mo the bookmaker, stinking the place out with fat cigars. Solly grabbed her by the waist, took her hand, danced her a few steps around the kitchen, right on the spot she hadn't finished scrubbing.

"Come," he said, his eyes all bloodshot from the sweet brandy. "Let's go outside. The whole of Thistle Street is dancing."

She laughed. "I have no time for such things. We have guests."

"The war is over, Celia. It's time to rejoice. You need to stop being so serious."

She felt his lips wet on her cheek. Again she laughed as she held him off. "I think you are drunk, Solly Green."

"I think I love you, Celia Kahn."

"And I think you love everyone today."

"Yes, you are right," he slurred. "I love everyone today. Where is that Judith Finkelstein? She will give me a dance. What a day." He poured himself another glass of *schnapps*, danced with it out onto the street.

She made a pot of tea, took it into Nathan, sat with him for a while. Friends and neighbours had asked after him but better to keep him quiet like this, introduce him slowly back to the world. She pushed his hair back off his brow, felt his forehead clammy.

"You need a haircut," she said. "Tomorrow, new pyjamas and a haircut. That's an order."

His eyes stared beyond her, out of the window, to the backcourt. A group of children playing in the midden. "You are so unhappy," he whispered hoarsely.

"What did you say?"

"So unhappy. What happened, Celia?"

"Nothing happened. It's just the war. It affected everyone."

"It is not just the war."

"What do you know, my little brother? You have been asleep for most of it. What are you? Some kind of mystic? A little Joseph with his dreams."

Nathan smiled. "I would like some tea."

She poured him out a cup. "Sugar?" she asked. "You see I don't remember if you like sugar. Of course, you like sugar. You must like sugar. You do like sugar, don't you?"

"You are crying, sister."

"So I am."

Later when all the visitors had left, when her father had gone to lie down, she went into the kitchen to wash the dishes. As she stood by the sink, she looked at her arms, wrist-deep in suds. How thin they had become, almost as wasted away as Nathan's. She could still hear people outside celebrating in the street, the wartime songs with their blind cheeriness she had come to hate, someone playing a violin, a bottle breaking. It was hard to believe the war was over. All the holes it had left in people's lives where loved ones had been. There would be no more daily casualty lists. No more nameless gravestones. No more sailors' funds and flag days. No more balaclavas to be knitted. There might even be butter on the table. A good slice of brisket. And perhaps she wouldn't feel so run-down all the time.

"There you are," her mother said, stumbling into the kitchen. "My beautiful little Celia."

"Mother. I do believe you are drunk."

"Yes, I do believe I am. My head is spinning like a clock. Dancing I was. I must sit." Madame Kahn crashed against the kitchen table, grasped for a chair, managed to ease herself down.

"I've never seen you like this before, Mother."

"Don't worry, don't worry. I am not becoming a *shikker* like my brother. This is a once in my lifetime event. How many war endings can there be to celebrate in my life? And my son. God has given me back my son. What is the date today? What is it?"

"November the eleventh."

"Then this day I will remember forever. November the eleventh. A holy day. The anniversary of my happiness. Why are you washing the dishes on such a day?"

Celia shrugged. "It was something that needed done."

"Well, leave them alone." Her mother made to rise from her chair, but slumped back again. "Come, come. Sit down."

Celia dried her hands, sat down at the table, took out her tobacco tin and a box of matches from her apron pocket. There was a roll-up all ready inside. She lit up, sucked in hard, such a good feeling that crispy tobacco taste, then the harshness in her lungs steadying her nerves.

"Now what will you do?" her mother asked. "Now the war is over. Now you have nothing to protest against. No more meetings. And demonstrations. And pamphlets to write. Everywhere there are these pamphlets. We have a house full of pamphlets. What is it with these damn posters and pamphlets? You stop a war with being strong. With tanks and guns. Not with these pamphlets. Thank God no more pamphlets. No more war, no more pamphlets."

"You don't really understand, do you, Mother? The women's movement isn't just about being against the war. That's only part of it. It's about equal pay. It's about giving all women the right to vote. It's about family planning and birth control. It's not just about the war."

"Bah! You talk like your Uncle Mendel. I don't want any Bolsheviks in this house. I don't want to hear this talk of revolution here. Not in this household. We are only loyal British subjects here. Better to put your attention on these young men coming home from the war. These Jewish officers. These heroes."

"I am not looking for a Jewish hero, mother."

"Well, you better find someone quick. Someone to put a smile on that beautiful face… because beauty fades… like there is no tomorrow."

Her mother quietened after that, closing her eyes until all Celia could hear was a light snoring. She sucked in the last of her cigarette, tossed it into a dirty cup of cold tea, not something she would have normally done, but did it anyway to spite her mother. And as she sat there in the darkening kitchen with the dusk casting long shadows across the room, the damp clothes hanging on the pulley above her head, the dishes still unwashed, she realised that the ending of this war meant a great deal to her. But it did not give her nearly as much hope as that revolution in Russia.

The population of Duke Street seemed happy enough. At least, no less dour, no less rowdy, no less talkative as they went about their daily business than any other pedestrians in any other street in the city. Celia had always imagined the presence of the prison would have an effect on them. Those forbidding arched gates, that stretch of so high walls, higher than a tram car, impossible to peer in even from the top deck. All that locked up evil, guilt and shame that resided there, hovering above the walled perimeter like a poisonous cloud that would somehow seep into the souls of passers-by. She supposed the locals had just gotten used to it. But for her, the sight of Duke Street jail made her shudder. A schoolyard skipping song forming her first impressions long before she had ever set eyes on the place.

There is a happy land,
doon Duke Street Jail,
Where a' the prisoners stand,
tied tae a nail.
Ham an' eggs they never see,
dirty watter fur yer tea.
There they live in misery.
God save the King!

She was singing the song to herself as she waited by the visitors' gate until a hard look from a wee wifie in front of her made her shut up. So she just stood there silent close to the wall, feeling herself cold in her very bones from the winter chill and the greyness of the building she was waiting to enter. Then a grinding of a key in the massive lock, the hauling open of one of the thick arched doors. A guard came out, fob-watch in his palm, regarding the time until three o'clock exactly, not willing to concede one extra second to those

81

inmates with the pleasure of a visitor to see. She shuffled in with the rest of them, gave the officer at the cubicle the name of Agnes Calder and her prison number. The man whistled as he scanned his register with a dirty fingernail. "Aye, the fire-raiser," he said, without looking up. She was told to turn out her pockets, surrender any packages for inspection, then wait in a freezing stone corridor. A guard would come to collect her.

The visitors' room wasn't much warmer. There was a grudging fire in a grate that was too small to heat the entire room. Rows of wooden tables, some with screwed-in links for the handcuffs to be locked into. And there was the smell. Not just the carbolic sloshed over the harsh stone walls and floors. But the sense of something else in the air. Something that could not be mopped and scrubbed out no matter how hard those on cleaning duty tried. The smell of dead-end despair that would cling to her skin and clothes long after she had left these walls.

Agnes looked terrible. Her coarse blue-white prison garments hung loose from her body, hard to believe this oversized uniform hadn't been given to her as some kind of joke. Her skin was colourless like the stone around her, her eyes sunk deep in their sockets, the essence that was once her friend retreating with them. The guard locked her cuffs to the table. The poor woman was trembling.

"How are they treating you?" Celia asked when they were left alone.

"Well, it's not just that the food's awful. But there's so much of it." She gave a little smile, then scrubbed hard at the inside of her wrist with her knuckles. "These clothes scratch you like a punishment all by themselves. How about you? How's life now the war's over?"

"We're all busy with the workers' strike for a forty-hour week. There's to be a big rally in George Square in support."

"I wouldn't put too much effort into the strike. The men can look after themselves. It's things like the family allowance we should be pushing for. Keep your mind on the women's issues."

"We're doing that as well."

"Aye, I hope so. It's easy to get distracted, get your energies drawn here and there. The men'll do it you. The union leaders and those bloody politicians. Now they see us women as a force to be reckoned with. Christ, it's so cold in here. Are you cold? I'm bloody freezing."

"I've got a coat on."

"A coat would be a fine thing. Rain, snow or sunshine, it's all the same uniform in here. At least, they could give you a blanket. A blanket and some hot water to bathe in." She scratched away at her skin again, raised her voice. "Aye, a blanket. An animal gets treated better."

"Come on, Agnes. What's going on with you?"

Her eyes darted around at the guards, the other prisoners with their visitors. Then bent over close, spoke hushed and quick.

"There was a hanging today. It was an awful thing. You could tell it was going to happen for they put up screens on top of the outside walls so those in the tenements overlooking couldn't see in. The prisoners kept away from their windows too, like it was a curse to watch it happening." She broke off to hack out a series of coughs. Celia could hear the flimsy, tarred lungs straining to their task. It was an awful sound. Then she finally settled, continued:

"They do it at eight in the morning that's the custom. A black flag goes up when it's all over. Then there's the bell. They ring that too. Not like a merry church bell. But slow and solemn. The chimes go right through you, cold and shivering. I've never been so upset in my life. I've got to get out of here."

"You've still got another eighteen months."

"There's men in here done far worse than burn down a bloody recruitment office," she hissed. "And got off with far less punishment. It's the women that get the harsh sentences. These male judges and their counsellors, they can't stand us suffragettes." Again she looked up, quick glances around the room. "I've decided on a hunger strike. Starve myself until they release me under the Cat and Mouse Act."

"I didn't think it was still on the books."

"It's no been repealed as far as I know. A lot of the suffragettes down south have used it. No reason it shouldn't work here. As soon as I become ill, they have to discharge me."

"Then as soon as you get well, they'll put you back in again."

"I don't care. I just want out. Even if it's only for a wee bit."

Celia looked around at the guards. "I wouldn't trust them. They'll force-feed you with tubes down your nose. Who's to stop them?"

"I'll take my chances. Do you recall Jimmy Docherty? The reporter from the *Citizen*?"

"The one at the courthouse for the rent trials?"

"Aye, that's the man. Well, get in touch with him, tell him what I'm doing. Maybe he'll get his paper to take an interest. After all, the fact of Agnes Calder no stuffing her mouth with food has to be of national interest, don't you think?" She laughed at this, then inevitably broke into one of her coughing fits. "Did you bring some baccy?" she wheezed.

"I handed it in at the gate."

"How much?"

"Two ounces."

"Well, the guards will take their share. I'll be lucky to get half. That'll do me though."

"I thought you were going on a hunger strike."

"Doesn't mean I can't smoke. Look, I've put you down as next-of-kin. Name and address. That means when I start getting sick, they'll send for you to take me out of here." Agnes tried to reach out to her with a cuffed hand. "I've nobody else, dearie."

Eleven

THE WHITE, GOLD-TRIMMED CARD WINKED at her from the mantelpiece. She could hardly get on with her housework because of it. When she came in from beating the carpets or bringing back the laundry or after dumping the ash-can on the midden, there it would be. Taunting her. There were actually two of them. The one on the left was for her parents so that didn't bother her at all. It was that one on the right. The one with the words The Jewish Servicemen's League scored out, replaced with the name Solomon Green. An invitation to a dance at The Marlborough in honour of those Jewish men and women who had served their country.

Her mother had been delighted, of course. Almost burst out of her corsets such was her glee. "This is your chance," Madame Kahn had declared, wagging a finger at her. "Take it. Or end up a spinster."

"Mother, I'm only nineteen," she protested.

"Already too late. You will be left on the sideboard if you are not careful. All these young men returning. All these heroes. I will make you up a special gown. Only the best material. And the latest fashion design. You will be the beauty of the ballroom. I give so many thanks to Solly for this."

"You don't even like him."

"Solly is all right."

"You always told me a bookmaker's son wasn't good enough for me."

"You think I want you for this Solly? No, Solly is … how do you say? … Solly is your Horse of Troy. Once you are there, these young

Jewish heroes will want to dance with you. I will supervise, of course. And I can give you advice. This one is a good family, this one not so good. This one is rich, this one…"

"Mother, I'm very fond of Solly."

"Look, this Solly is not so bad. But he is not for you."

Her mother was right. Solly was not for her. Still, she had agreed to go to the ball. Not because she didn't want to hurt him. Or because her mother had been so insistent. It had just been so long since there had been music and dancing and dressing-up in her life.

"Ahead of us, what a weekend we have," Uncle Mendel said as they raced along the freezing streets. "First George Square. Then The Marlborough. Socialism… followed by socialising. Aha! I like that."

It was all right for him, she thought, rushing along like this, with his fitness gained from traipsing the countryside day after day. But her city legs had difficulty keeping up.

"Please slow down, uncle."

"What's wrong?" he complained. "You are thirty years younger." But he slowed anyway and they fell in with the rest of the demonstrators heading for the square.

She felt like an old campaigner. It was the Rent Strikes all over again. Except this time, it wasn't the landlords she was protesting against. It was the employers. On behalf of those returned soldiers. With their forced 'pack up your troubles in your old kitbag' smiles, their haunted looks and their twitchiness. As if the trench mud had sucked out their very souls and the noise of exploding shells had forever shattered their nerves. Those who had survived without injury, who were still able-bodied enough to be a fitter or a welder, a boiler-maker or a caulker, a pipefitter or a toolmaker, for them there were no longer any jobs. That was what this rally was about, the unions wanting the working week cut from fifty-four to forty hours to create jobs for these discharged soldiers. The idea had a common sense about it. But she knew there was more to it than that. It was political too. It was a working class struggle. Labour versus Capital. All set against the volatile background of that revolution in Russia. The shipyards were out on strike, the engineering works were out, so were the miners, the electrical supply workers. The city was restless and nervous. Twitching like those shell-shocked soldiers.

A colourless sky. Breath clouds and tobacco smoke. She stood on frozen tip-toes, tried to see above the bodies to all sides of her. She looked for her own comrades in the Women's Peace Crusade, impossible to spot them among this huge crowd. Men clung to lamposts. The Red Flag swayed here and there, bleeding colour into the grey surroundings. The trams around the square stood still, disabled, powerless, their poles and pantographs plucked from the overhead wires by the strikers. Policemen mingled, batons drawn. Other constables on horseback, the beasts' flanks steaming, tails flicking, moving with the swaying hordes. On the steps of the City Chambers, the speakers in full swing.

Uncle Mendel brought out a silver-plated hip flask, took a swig, passed it over.

"What is it?" she asked.

"Highland whisky."

"Good." Better than the sweet *schnapps* he usually drank. She felt the metal cold between her teeth, then the bite of the liquid in her mouth, the slow burn down her throat into her belly. All around her, the crowd started to clap. Manny Shinwell had just finished his speech.

"Not bad for a Jew, eh?" Uncle Mendel said, blowing into his gloves.

It was the first time she'd seen Shinwell in person. In his buttoned-up coat, pipe in hand, urbane yet passionate. This Jewish union leader who had little to do with the Jewish community, this Jew who stood up, refused to be hammered down. But now Shinwell had gone inside the Chambers with a delegation to negotiate with the Lord Provost. Leaving her in this company of men, hardly a woman in sight, a sea of cloth caps, the mood pleasant enough but restless too. She could feel an edge to everything. This wasn't like the march on the courts during the Rent Strike. This was a deeper, darker confrontation.

A rumour quickly spread. A sheriff had come out on the steps to read the Riot Act.

"What's that you say?" Uncle Mendel asked the man in front.

"The fucking Riot Act."

"What riot?" she asked.

"Dinnae worry, lass. Someone's snatched it from the bastard's hands. He's no got anything to read now."

She felt the crowd ebb and flow, a dark mass with a collective life of its own. She moved in closer to her uncle. A roar up front. A surge forward, then back.

"The fucking polis are attacking," someone shouted.

"Jesus Christ, it's a baton charge."

"Holy Mary, Mother of God, the polis are attacking."

"Someone's come out of the Chambers."

"Shinwell's down. The polis have hacked down Shinwell. Shinwell's down."

"It's no Shinwell. It's Davie Kirkwood who's been felled."

"They've chopped Kirkwood. They've chopped Kirkwood."

"Jesus Christ! The constables are charging."

"Fuck. We've got to get out of here."

"Run! Run! Run! To the Green. To the Green."

Uncle Mendel grabbed her. And she ran with him. Eyes on her feet, fearful of falling, to be trampled by this fleeing mob. In Hanover Street, a parked lorry, tarpaulin unfurled, to reveal its load of empty bottles. The strikers grabbing the contents, the missiles flying over her head into the chasing horde. The smash of glass. On the roads. Against the building walls. Breaking the window of an abandoned tram.

"Uncle Mendel," she screamed. "Uncle Mendel."

She saw his body snap back, his hat flying, his hands grabbing at the constable's grip around his throat. She was already a few yards past him, had to fling herself out of the flow of people, flatten herself against a wall. She could see her uncle on the opposite side of the street, crouched down in a doorway, hands over his head, the constable flailing at him with his baton.

She pushed herself off the wall, looked to find gaps in the crowd running across her, weaving here and there, being pushed, cursed at, almost knocked over, until she arrived behind the constable. She meant to make a lunge for him but then she saw the unbroken bottle in the gutter. She grabbed at it, raised it high, had a thought to smash it down on his helmet, but something made her shift her target to his shoulder, just by the collar of his coat. The bottle came down hard on the bone, and the constable fell. Uncle Mendel looked up from his cowering stance in the doorway, one eye blue and swelling, blood running down the side of his head, staining his beard.

"*Mein Gott*," he said.

She looked at the fallen constable, his helmet knocked askew, the strap pulling awkward at his chin, his large ears, his thick moustache. She felt the rushing bodies brush past her, felt the neck of the still unbroken bottle in her hand.

"Celia." Her uncle was shaking her. "We must go."

"I've killed him," she said.

"Celia. Come on. We must go away from here. *Avek, avek, avek.*"

"I've killed him."

"No, no, no. He is not dead. I hear him moaning. Come on."

"But I want to go to the Green with the rest of them."

"Celia," he said, grabbing her chin, forcing her to look at him. "A policeman you hit with a bottle. We must go home. Here is too dangerous. Come, come."

Her uncle limped off ahead, a bloody handkerchief held to his head. She followed, a huge tiredness in her legs slowing her down, a feverish ache through her whole body. She just wanted to lie down somewhere, curl up in a doorway. But she walked on, the fog coming in thicker, ribbons of it all around her, clinging to her skin. She saw a tramcar rising out of the mist like some unleashed dragon as it was driven deliberately into the strikers fleeing from the Square. She saw men ripping up park railings, wielding them like battle-axes, fending off the police charges. All these scenes silently passing her by – no protests, no screams, no cursing – all sound blocked out by the pounding in her head.

"Throw away the bottle."

"I can't hear you, uncle."

"The bottle. Throw it in the river."

She moved over to the parapet of Glasgow Bridge, could hardly see the dark waters beneath through the mist, let the bottle slip from her grasp. She turned to look at her uncle. His black eye, his bloodied beard.

"Are you all right, uncle?"

"I lost my hat," he said, forcing a smile. "My good hat too."

"But are you hurt?"

"I will live." He leaned against the parapet, dabbed the cut on his forehead.

"Here, let me." She took a handkerchief from her bag, spat on it, wiped the blood from his brow. "It's not as bad as it looks."

"It is you I worry about."

He took her back to his flat, sat her down, stirred up the fire, gave her a whisky to calm her nerves, bring the colour back to her cheeks. He then went off to clean up his own wounds while she sat there staring into the flames, the coals spurting and spitting out their sparks, one hitting her shin, she hardly noticed. She felt like a stranger to herself, this other woman capable of such a violent act. Or perhaps this was who she was all along.

Uncle Mendel returned, lit up his pipe, drew up a chair. The two of them sipping their Highland malts, discussing politics in the firelight, no mention made of her striking the policeman.

"It is not good, this police charge," he told her, his right eye closed up, swollen like a piece of liver. "The government must be behind it. They are frightened. They think Glasgow is the new Petrograd. And perhaps they are right. At the edge of revolution we are. Revolt is in the air. Like gunpowder, it is. You can almost smell it. One little flame and ... whoosh. Like Russia it could be." He sucked on his pipe, drawing out a line of spittle as he removed the whitened stem from his mouth. "But strong leaders we do not have. A Lenin we do not have. A Trotsky we do not have. Our leaders are locked up. Or sick. A week of forty hours is all the unions want. But with the right leaders, we could have everything."

The next day's papers wrote up the police baton charge as 'Bloody Friday'. She searched for mention of a serious injury to a constable but the news was all about the ten thousand English troops marching into the city, the government too frightened to deploy Scottish soldiers for fear they might defect to the strikers. She came face to face with one of these young conscripts from down south when he held her off as she and her uncle tried to get back into George Square. His uniform hung off him like he'd picked up the wrong one in a hurry, he was just a lad really, looking terrified even though he was the one carrying the gun.

"Ye can't come in, miss," he said. "The area's sealed off." She looked beyond his outstretched arm, saw the guards posted outside the City Chambers, a howitzer on the roof of the post office.

"I heard they're sending tanks," she said. "Is that true?"

He gave her an apologetic grin. "Yes, miss. Parking them in the cattle market. Wherever that is."

"*Ich glaube es nicht*," her uncle said. "I don't believe it. Against the people of Glasgow, you bring tanks. Be ashamed of yourself, boy. Be ashamed of yourself."

She tried to lead her uncle away.

"Fire one shot and … boom," he shouted back at the young soldier. "We have socialists against capitalists, unions against employers. Now the English army against the Scottish workers. One shot, Celia… and in smoke it all goes up."

Twelve

THE OFFICIAL REPORT SHE GAVE to her family on her uncle's injuries was as follows: "He tripped over the edge of the carpet and fell badly against the door handle. He apologises but he is in no condition to attend the ball at The Marlborough Hotel."

"*Shikker*," her mother muttered, still angered by her brother's absence. She sat beside her husband, downstairs at the front of the tram specially commissioned to take the southside Jews of the Gorbals to the hotel. There was a second tram coming from across the river bringing its load of Semites from the West End. "He travels all the way from the Highlands for this dance, drinks too much, then falls over. *Shikker*. A drunkard. I lose patience with my own kin."

Her mother was wrapped up in a mink coat she'd brought from Germany decades ago, her father wore a dinner suit even though 'black tie' was not the requested attire. "I wear a lounge suit every day," he told her. "Tonight I must wear something special."

She sat across the aisle from them, next to Solly. She had never seen him so scrubbed up and smart before. Such a striking-looking young gentleman, she thought. With his double-breasted suit, bow-tie, two-tone shoes, hair slicked back. Already becoming a little thick in the jowls just like his father, Lucky Mo, but this slight heaviness giving him a grown-up, prosperous look. His hair starting to thin the way of his father's too. She had noticed that when he had bowed to her in the doorway, full of confidence and swagger, presented her with a posy of flowers, took her arm as they walked out to the tram, a gentle touch to her elbow as she embarked. There must have been other young women, she thought.

All the talk on the tram was about Manny Shinwell. Not that anyone actually knew him. The fact the union leader shared the same fore-fathers in Abraham, Isaac and Jacob appeared enough of a connec-tion. Even if his claim to fame was being arrested for incitement to riot. She wanted to say that he was not the only one to be arrested. Two of the other leaders of the Clyde Workers' Committee, Davie Kirkwood and Willie Gallacher, were also in jail. But that someone who was Jewish should make the headlines was all that mattered.

"Politics don't interest me," Solly told her as he tapped the end of his cigarette on a silver case. "No interest at all."

"Oh, Solly. How can you avoid what is going on all around you? After what happened on Friday."

"It's all the same to me. Capitalism or socialism, people will still want a punt on a horse or a dog or a football match. Hope and greed are a matter of human nature. Not a matter of politics. And Solly Green will be there to cater for those needs." He blew two smoke rings into the air to emphasise his point.

"What about all the poverty in this city? The overcrowding, the poor sanitation, the lack of jobs. Don't you care about anything?"

"I told you, Celia. Rich or poor, people still want to bet. Now the war is over, we're back to horseracing. We're busier than ever. My father's just ordered another telephone. That's four we've got in the office now. Telephone betting is the way of the future. No more stand-ing in the lanes with the odds written on the back of a shovel."

"What about the constables?"

"They turn a blind eye. And they're not shy about having a flutter or two themselves. Anyway, they've got better things to do with their time. Like keeping you socialists in order."

"Oh I despair of you, Solly Green."

"I don't see why. Don't you think Karl Marx liked a wee bet on the horses? I can see him now, getting up from writing that famous book of his, going down a back alley, slipping a few coins into the hands of a bookie's runner. Sixpence please on Bolshevik, running in the three-thirty at Ayr. Then back home to sit on his boils and start writing again. Half a mind on Communist revolution, the other half on the result of a race that could put food on the table. What do you think?"

She laughed. "I think you have a good imagination."

"Not imagination, Celia. Reality."

She let Solly go on to charm her parents while the tram lurched and screeched through the dark of the winter evening. She half-listened to the chatter in a mixture of Yiddish, German, Russian and English, marvelling at this little oasis of Jews safe within the tram's walls. It was like a Zionist's dream. Or at least the dream of the Territorialists who believed in a Jewish homeland whether it was situated in Palestine, Ethiopia or in a Glasgow tramcar. A spark from the pantograph overhead lit up the window, flashing her reflection back at her. There she was, just twenty-fours after troops had marched into the city, dressed up to the nines, travelling to a ball like some Jewish Cinderella. The shot Uncle Mendel predicted would set off a revolution had not been fired.

She had only been to The Marlborough Hotel once before. As one of many bridesmaids at the wedding of a distant cousin who had come to Glasgow from Germany before the turn of the century. She could only have been about five or six, but she recalled this German cousin boasting the largest moustaches she'd ever seen. She could have tied a swing to them, wondered whether they tickled, giggled when he raised the veil, kissed his bride. She remembered broad staircases, crystal chandeliers, one cavernous room leading to another. Red carpets, gilded cornices, gold patterns on the wallpaper. And so much food. Tables for meat dishes, tables for milk dishes. Tables for adults, tables for children. This cousin was dead now. He'd gone off to fight the Germans to prove he wasn't one.

The chandeliers were still there, many of the bulbs blown and blackened, the carpets footworn and faded, the wallpaper scuffed and torn in places. She had no idea what had happened to this place during the war. Did it just close down? Or had it served some military purpose? A recruiting station? A billet for the recovering wounded? Off in another room, she could hear a band churning out the old wartime tunes. Guests moved around the corridors, humming the melodies, stiff and awkward, looking like they had forgotten what it was like to have a good time. As she and Solly moved towards the music, she saw couples take to the dance floor, unsure of the steps and of each other. For one woman, it was a matter of how to be led by a man with only one arm. She noticed her own parents step up to the parquet flooring, tentatively at first, then finally taking the plunge as Papa Kahn swept up her mother into his embrace and they waltzed across the room. She sat down at an empty table, watched them while Solly went for refreshments. Strange to see them holding each other, looking into each other's eyes, their posture still rigid and formal, a man and wife, not just her parents. They seemed to be dancing in a different era, a time before women went to work, men went to war. Then the band perked up with some recent melody, her parents and other older couples drifting from the floor. She opened up her purse, took out her tobacco tin, lit up one of the pastel-pink Balkan Sobranies Mrs Carnovsky had given her to add a little 'Russian sophistication' to her evening. They tasted of toasted chocolate. Sublime. What was it Agnes used to say? Come the revolution and... we'll all be smoking Balkan Sobranies. She smiled to herself, realised she actually felt quite happy.

She teased Solly when he came back with a glass of lemonade and a bottle of beer, gently pressing him to take the soft drink, knowing he would.

"I didn't know you were a drinking lass," he said.

She took a swig direct from the bottle, raising a 'tut tut, tut' from Judith Finkelstein's mother as she swanned by. "There's a lot you don't know about me. Why don't you ask me to dance?"

Solly executed a bow, held out his arm, escorted her to the parquet floor.

"How do you dance to this new-fangled stuff?" he said.

"Let's make it a slow waltz. That's what everyone else is doing."

She felt his one hand against the small of her back, with the other he gripped her fingers. Such big hands, noticing hers tiny in his clasp. He had played goalkeeper after all, she remembered him alongside Avram in his bright yellow jersey, as bright as the sun, watching, protecting, ready to defend. He tightened his hold on her, forcing her head slightly more towards his chest, she felt the heat from under his jacket, saw the drops of moisture on his upper lip, the smell of hair oil, all too close for her to be comfortable, pressed like this against him, stifling her, suffocating her.

"I'm sorry, Solly," she said, pushing away. "I have to stop."

"Are you all right?"

"Just a little dizzy. It must be the beer, the heat. I want to sit down."

She felt her legs heavy, leaned on Solly as he led her back to her seat.

"I'll fetch you a glass of water," he said.

She picked up a programme card from the table, fanned herself. Perhaps it was the beer rather than having a man close causing her head to spin. But she felt better now she was alone, searched for another cigarette in her purse. A lit match appeared in the cup of a male hand. She looked up. A shiny, handsome face grinned back at her.

"Thought I might save you the trouble."

She bent her head, sucked in the flame, noticed the dark hairs on the back of the steady hand. When she drew away, the man leapt around beside her, nimble as a cat, pulled up a chair, sat down closer than she would have liked. He rubbed his smooth chin with his thumb.

"You're the Kahn girl, aren't you?"

"Could be."

"Are you or aren't you?"

"I suppose I am."

"And your name is?"

"Celia."

"That's right. Celia. I remember your family from Thistle Street. There was that brother of yours too. The footballer."

"Avram."

"Yes, yes, Avram. Everyone thought he'd play for the great Glasgow Celtic, he was that brilliant."

She sucked on her cigarette, puffed out purses of smoke with what she hoped was an air of Russian sophistication. "He wasn't my real brother though," she said, not sure what to make of this young man, leaning into her so familiar. "He came to us as a refugee from Russia. We ended up adopting him."

96

"Did he go to war?"

"He was too young. He's a credit draper now with my uncle in the Highlands. Who are you?"

"Jonathan Levy. Jonny."

"I don't remember you."

"My family lives in the West End. But we've lots of relatives in the Gorbals. We visit often."

"To see how the poorer half live?"

"It isn't like that."

"I still don't remember you."

"You were probably in pigtails when I was off to the war."

"You're not that old."

"The war makes you old. I'm just twenty-four though."

He did look older than his years, she thought, something in the smudged blackness under his eyes. As if they had seen too much in too short a time.

"Here's your beau," he said slapping his knee. And there was Solly back with a glass of water, a brandy for himself this time, looking like he might have downed another one on the way.

"My, my, my," Solly slurred. "If it isn't Lieutenant Levy of the Cameron Highlanders. The hero back from the Front."

Jonny shrugged, gave her an embarrassed look, then shook Solly's outstretched hand. "Lance-Corporal actually. Still playing goalie?"

"Gave it up for more lucrative endeavours."

"Are you really a hero?" Celia asked.

"Don't be shy," Solly said, a hand on Jonny's shoulder. "This man got a VC for knocking out a gun position at Loos. Captured thirty Huns in the process."

Jonny coughed out a laugh. "You've got me mixed up with someone else. No VC for me. Just glad to be back alive. And all in one piece."

Solly threw back his brandy. "Now you wait here, Captain Levy. I insist on fetching a drink for this hero."

"Bring one for Celia too." Jonny glanced at her, grinned as if he were doing her a favour.

"Don't bother, Solly," she said.

"Oh, come on," Jonny insisted. "It's party time."

"Thank you. But no."

Solly looked back at them, confused.

"A gin for the lady," Jonny said, waving him away.

She cooled herself with her programme, flicked off the ash from her cigarette far more than was necessary. "You shouldn't have done that."

"I was just being a gentleman."

She noticed his foot tapping the floor, but not in time to the music. "I don't need a man to tell me my mind, that's all."

He made a mock salute. "Apologies offered, madam."

She smiled, blew smoke in his direction. "Accepted, soldier."

"Start again?"

"I think you need to."

He didn't seem to know what to say after that. She watched him fidget, look over his shoulder for Solly. "What will you do now you're back?" she asked.

"I'll take up my studies again. I was nearly finished a medical degree at Glasgow University when I was called up."

"A doctor? That'll make your parents proud."

"Up to a point."

"What do you mean?"

"I don't intend to practise. Not right away at least. I want to get my studies under my belt. But after that I want to go to Palestine."

"With the army?"

"No, no. There are all these Jewish socialists going out there. Pioneers stoked up by the revolution in Russia. They're starting these agriculture communities called 'kibbutzim'. I want to go out there to work on the land."

"You could work the land here if you're so stoked up. Milk cows in Ayrshire. Rear sheep in the Highlands. Or would you rather be a Zionist?"

"I'm an idealist, Miss Kahn. The idea of building an agricultural community around socialist principles excites me. Creating a homeland for Jews in Palestine... that's merely a secondary issue for me."

"So why not start a *kibbutz* in Scotland?"

Jonny laughed. "The Jews here are not idealists. Or revolutionaries. They are pragmatists. Look at them." He swept his hand across the dance floor. "They just want to get by in life the best they can."

"You can't blame them for that."

"I certainly can't." He sprang up from his chair, stood at attention. She thought he was going to salute her again. "Now, if you'll excuse me," he said, with the slightest of bows. "I shall leave before Solly returns."

"But he's fetching you a drink."

"I'm sure he won't mind."

Thirteen

It was late when she awoke. Even with her eyes closed, she could sense the morning light playing on her lids through the thin curtain of her cot. How could this be? Where was her mother? She should have been in the kitchen by now, stoking up the grate, boiling up water for tea, sorting out Papa's breakfast before he went off to work. Her mouth was dry, so dry. And she had a headache. It was as if her brain were a bag of wet flour lodged inside her skull. She opened her eyes. She was still in her undergarments. Oh my, she thought. What has become of you, Celia Kahn? She folded her arms across her chest. How had she returned home? By tram, of course. The specially commissioned conveyance for the celebrating Semites of the Gorbals. Even her mother had been slightly tipsy. Singing. *It's a long way to Tipperary.* She remembered Jonny Levy. Lance-Corporal Levy. He took the other tram back home with those uppity West End Jews. She stretched out her hand, pulled back the curtain slightly. Her gown in a heap on the floor. What has become of you, Celia Kahn?

The ring of the front door bell. Who could that be at this ungodly hour? The butcher with his brisket? But not on a Monday morning. Not the fishmonger either. A delivery for the shop, perhaps. Or the knife-sharpening man with his sun-darkened skin even in winter time. She laid back down, her head heavy on the pillow, waited to see if anyone would answer. She heard a door open, a certain beat of feet that could only belong to Nathan. She closed her eyes.

The shaking of the curtain waking her.

"What? What is it?"

Nathan's voice. "It's for you."

"What's for me?"

"A telegram."

"A telegram?" She drew open the curtain. "Are you sure?"

Nathan raised his eyes at her. "You are Celia Kahn?"

She took the pale yellow envelope. Her name in funny little printing on the front. She'd rarely received a letter before with her name on it, never mind a telegram. Her thoughts racing towards the worst. Yet all her family were here. Except Avram.

"Well, aren't you going to open it?"

"Yes, yes, of course." She pinched open a corner, ran her nail under the fold, pulled out the single enclosed sheet of paper.

COME IMMEDIATELY STOP GOVERNOR STOP H M PRISON
STOP DUKE STREET

She covered her mouth with her hand. "Oh Agnes," she breathed. "Oh, poor Agnes."

She bought a bag of Soor Plooms especially for the occasion. Although whether the first thing a person wanted coming out of a hunger strike was a sweet to suck she wasn't sure. But for a stomach not used to digesting solids, it didn't seem such a stupid idea. There was no direct tram, quicker to walk all the way, save her money for the hansom to take Agnes back home. She needed the fresh air anyway to clear her head, sucked on one of the Soor Plooms for her breakfast as she crossed over the South Portland Street Bridge into the east side of the city. She was glad Agnes was getting out. She'd felt guilty she hadn't been to see her, no time even to contact that reporter Docherty from the *Citizen*, she'd been that busy with the strikes. She'd make it up to her though, take care of her the same way Agnes had tended to her after she was raped in the park, the only light then amidst her darkness. Yes, that was what she would do. Nurse Agnes back to health with plenty of hot baths, Soor Plooms, pots of tea, packets of Woodbines.

She had to knock on the prison gate given it was outside proper visiting hours, one of the guards coming to a barred slot, taking a good look at her up and down, examining the telegram passed through, then finally letting her in. At the reception cubicle, the officer didn't need to run his yellow-stained finger down the ledger to know who Agnes Calder was, just said to her, "Wait over there. I'll get someone to attend to you."

She went and sat on the cold bench, wished she had brought something to read, maybe even a bit of knitting, rather than just sitting there staring at the dank walls. She hadn't really thought through how it was all going to happen with Agnes, just assumed she'd have to collect her friend from the prison hospital, hopefully she'd be strong enough to walk to a hansom then taken home. A prison officer arrived with a large brown paper parcel.

"Are you the one for Calder?"

She stood up quickly. "Yes, I am."

"Well, here are her belongings."

"I don't understand."

"In the parcel. Her clothes. A few personal items. You can check them off from a list if you want to make sure."

"But where's Agnes?"

The officer looked over to his colleague in the reception cubicle, shook his head. "She's dead, miss."

"What are you saying?"

Again the officer glanced over at his colleague. "Dead, miss. Dead and gone." And then more kindly. "I thought you knew."

She let herself sink back down onto the bench. She had a handkerchief somewhere, she knew that. But it wasn't in her coat pockets. She also knew she was crying, she could feel the warmth of her tears on their run down her cheeks, but otherwise she felt cold. Two different parts of her, this inner part mourning her friend while these hands searched and searched in this pocket and that pocket, then her bag, while the officer stood watching her, this brown paper parcel in his hands which he eventually laid gently on the bench beside her as if it were a baby in swaddling. He put a hand into his inside jacket pocket. Perhaps he had the handkerchief she was looking for.

"She left a letter for you."

She took the envelope. Two communications to her in just this one day. This time her name handwritten, not those single strips of letters on the front of the telegram.

"Thank you," she said. Then wondering why she was being grateful to this man who had brought her this news, she began to feel an anger take over. "What happened to her? What happened to my friend?"

The officer took off his cap, tucked it under his arm. He had small, expressionless eyes. He didn't look like a bad man, she thought. But he didn't look like a good man either. Just someone who did as he was told, followed the rules, didn't ask questions. He spoke with some kind of an English accent. She hadn't noticed that at first. It made what he had to say sound more official.

"She died from the hunger, miss. Or at least complications deriving therefrom. It was her lungs that did for her in the end though. The prison doctor would tell you proper what it was. You can request a report. That would be your right. Being the next of kin as directed by the deceased."

"When? When did this happen?"

"A few days ago. Thursday, I believe."

"Why did it take so long to inform me?"

"Normally, you would be notified immediately. You are probably not aware but recent events in the city have taken up a great deal of our time and manpower. With the riots, I mean. There have been many arrests. We are detaining several people here within our walls."

She felt her body stiffen. "I am perfectly aware of recent events, officer. Now, can you tell me, where I might see my friend? Her body?"

"I'm afraid she's dead and buried."

"Buried? Where?"

"Here, miss. In the prison grounds. A death within these walls means the body of the deceased belongs to the state. The property of His Majesty's Prison Authorities. We have the right to bury all prisoners."

"Well, can I see the grave then?"

The officer scratched his head, replaced his cap, clicked his tongue against the back of his teeth. "I suppose I can take you there. The plot is nearby. Just quick mind. I've other duties to attend to."

She followed the officer as he opened up barred doors with a selection of keys, along corridors as icy as death itself, stone and steel, steel and stone, the stink of carbolic, not a drop of colour to the place. Grey, grey and more grey, then out into a dark sky and drizzle, a plot of land with a scattering of burial mounds, not as many as she might have thought, all roughly marked with wooden crosses, just the one standing out with a proper headstone. My God, she thought, this was where Agnes was to rest. Amidst the hanged and the damned and those just too frail to outlast their punishment. This had to be the grimmest place on earth, a graveyard within prison walls. The officer pointed to the far plot covered with fresh earth. She went over, stood at one end, head bowed, she just didn't have the words, wishing she had a Jewish prayer book with her and its mourner's prayer for the dead. Not that Agnes would have cared, being the atheist that she was. An arctic wind ripped through her, throwing up the skeletons of dead leaves to brush at her feet as it swept through this boneyard. In the distance, foundry stacks adding their bleakness to the already miserable sky.

"Now this Jonathan Levy," her mother said as she strode the kitchen. "A good family he comes from. Papa knows the father from Russia. Solomon Levinsohn. The name is shortened. To Levy. Levi. To be a Levi is to be from a family of priests of the temple. You know that, of course. Here this Solomon has a garment factory making *shmattes*. But in Russia, he completed his studies. He was an educated man. And the mother? Well, the mother I don't know. She is from Lithuania. But by all accounts, she is much younger than … you are not listening, Celia. This is important. Why are you not listening?"

"I have a headache."

"You have a hangover. That is what you have. You think I don't see you drinking with this Jonathan Levy."

"Mother. He came over and spoke to me for five minutes."

"Exactly. He came over. All the way across the ballroom floor. To speak to you. A man does not do this by chance. On a whim. To walk these fifty paces from one end of a room to another. He has intention. Intention to meet you."

"I thought he was arrogant."

"Arrogant? What has arrogance got to do with anything?"

"Mother, I don't feel well."

"You feel well enough to go gallivanting all over the city. Where were you first thing this morning? I come here to give Papa his breakfast and you are gone. What is this ringing of the bell so early in the morning?"

"Someone had the wrong address."

"Hmm. Anyway, this boy Levy. His family is respectable. A West End Jew. They have money. And he was an officer."

"A lance-corporal."

"Exactly. And he studies for a degree. Soon he will be a doctor. Not a priest of the temple. But a doctor."

"I don't want to disappoint you. But he's going to be a farmer in Palestine. He wants to live on a *kibbutz*."

"Ach. A *kibbutz*. This *Kommunistisch* nonsense. Remember that Greenberg couple? They went out to a *kibbutz* a few years ago. The community even raised some money to help them go. And you know what? After one year they are back. One year. And do you think I get my money back? Now, this Doctor Levy. He will see sense soon enough. What is wrong with you? You look terrible."

"Mother. I am going back to bed."

"Well, I am going to the wash house," her mother said. "Someone has to work around here. I would like to see the door handles polished when I return. The ironing needs to be done. And when you have finished, please cover the kitchen with newspapers. The man is coming tomorrow to sweep the chimney."

With her mother gone, she sat down at the kitchen table, took out the note Agnes had left her. She let her fingertips drift over each line of the coarse paper as she went through the words over and over again.

My dearest Celia.

I am writing this before I commence my hunger strike. If you are reading this, it means I have not survived. Please do not mourn for me. I have left instructions for you with my solicitor, Mr Sneddon of Sneddon, Baxter and Co., 179 West Nile Street. You were not only my comrade, but also my dear friend.

With love. Agnes.

From under her cot, she pulled out the brown paper parcel the prison officer had given her, cut the rough string with a kitchen knife. Inside were the clothes Agnes had worn when she entered the jail. A thistle brooch. And one other item. A book.

Fourteen

SHE KNEW EXACTLY WHERE THE BUILDING WAS given that it was right in the centre of the city but she had never really paid it much attention before. Except for its large clock, perched at just the right height, three storeys high, perfect for the naked eye of a young lady without a pocket-watch. It was one of those buildings with impressive columns and fancy balustrades that was never meant to accommodate the likes of her, yet when she entered and spoke to the young woman at reception, she was told to go on up without so much as an appointment or an escort. The liftman swiftly drew back the iron gate, gave her a nod as she entered. She eyed her reflection in the mirror above the dark mahogany panels, wished she had put on some lipstick.

"Where to, miss?"

"Third floor." The same as the clock.

She emerged directly into a hot room full of noise, tobacco smoke and busy bodies. Desks set out in rows, men on the telephones, women at their typewriters, message boys running here and there, almost tripping over her as she walked down the central aisle. She felt the yoke of flush around her throat as she searched out the familiar face but all passed by in a blur such was her anxiety and inability to focus on anything or anybody.

"Can I help you, miss?" It was one of the errand boys.

"I'm looking for a Mr Docherty."

"Jimmy?"

"Yes, James Docherty."

"Keep on going to the end, miss. Last desk on the right. By the windae."

Docherty was dressed down to his shirt-sleeves, his long legs up on his desk, telephone receiver to his ear. He cupped his hand over the mouthpiece when he saw her.

"Me?"

She nodded.

He raised one finger in the air, then pointed to the telephone. "One minute," he whispered. "Take a seat."

She cleared some papers from a simple wooden chair, sat herself down, watched Docherty as he listened to whoever was on the other end of the receiver and scribbled notes on a pad. His tie undone, his shirt collar soiled, two holes in the sole of each shoe, a cigarette behind one ear, the back of his neck red and lined, more like a farmer's neck she thought, baked raw from the sun. But it was the middle of winter and Jimmy Docherty sitting languid with his feet up at the offices of the Evening Citizen was not exactly the epitome of an agriculture worker. In one slick movement, he swung his feet off the desk, hung up the receiver on the switch-hook, leaned towards her, blue eyes bearing down on her, eager and questioning.

"What can I do for you, miss?"

"Miss Kahn. Celia Kahn. I met you once before."

"Refresh my addled and senior mind."

"At the Sheriff Court on the day of the rent trials. I was with Agnes Calder."

"I can't rightly recall. As you can imagine, there were more serious and distracting matters clamouring for my attention that eventful day. No doubt, Comrade Calder has played her part in this most recent riot. Which I'm glad to say has fizzled away to nothing. How is she?"

"She's dead."

He plucked the cigarette from behind his ear, tapped one end against the top of the desk. "Och. I'm sorry to hear that. A good friend?"

She nodded.

Docherty struck a match, lit up. A strand of burning tobacco escaped into the air, landed on the desk where it glowed on a sheet of paper until he stubbed it out with his thumb. She could have done with a cigarette herself. Rude of her to ask, she thought. Rude of him not to offer.

"I was rather fond of Agnes," he said. "But I always thought the tobacco would get her in the end." He inspected his own cigarette as if noticing the harm that lay there for the first time. "She smoked liked a double lum. And had a cough like an accordion with a hole in it. Is that the truth of what happened, Miss Kahn? The lungs?"

"She died in Duke Street Jail. Like you, they said it was her lungs. But I don't know whether to believe them. She was on a hunger strike, trying for release under the Cat and Mouse Act."

Docherty crouched forward on his desk, a bit like a cat himself. "The jail, eh? What was she doing in there?"

"She tried to burn down a recruiting office about six months ago. We all thought it was a stupid idea. What with the war turning in our favour, close to an end. I thought you might have known. It was all over the front page of your paper."

"I don't read that rubbish myself," he said, smiling. "Now, what exactly is your accusation here?"

"I think perhaps they tried to force-feed her. Tubes down her nostrils, food and liquids getting into her lungs."

"There would be a doctor's report."

"Yes, they said I could have one."

"Well, that would be a good first step before you accuse His Majesty's prison service of murder."

"Yes, it probably would." She felt hot now. She should have taken off her coat. A gentleman would have suggested that. Or offered her a cigarette. A glass of water perhaps. Her fingers played with the clasp on her bag. "The truth is I should have told you earlier. Agnes asked me to, right before she stopped eating. Said you might be interested in the story. Keep her name in the news. Let the public know she was on a hunger strike. Let the jail know they were under press scrutiny."

"And?"

She shook her head. "I forgot. I was just so busy. What with the march for the forty-hour week. I just forgot."

"So that's what this is all about."

"What do you mean?"

"You feeling guilty."

"Of course I feel guilty. She was a good friend to me. And I let her down." She glanced up from her fidgeting with the clasp. Docherty looked at her kindly.

"I'll tell you what," he said. "I've got some contacts inside Duke Street. I'll have a nosey around, see if I can find out how Agnes was treated. If the lungs got her, then no amount of press coverage would have saved her."

"You would do that?"

"That is what you came here to ask, isn't it?"

"Yes, I suppose it was."

"You could let sleeping dogs lie, of course. The official verdict favours your conscience."

"I'd rather know the truth."

"I suppose you were one of her comrades."

She nodded.

"Well, just let me say one thing to you, lass. From the mouth of someone who's seen something of Glasgow in all his reporting years. It's not your capitalism or your socialism or your feminism that you need to worry about in this city. If you're looking for "isms", it's alcoholism you need to be concerned about. That's the source of all the ills in this city. Every single one of them. The poor health and the poor housing. The way a man treats a man, a man treats a woman. The way a Protestant treats a Catholic and vice versa. Take away the drink and you'll have all the humanity you need without any of your political haverings. I dinnae touch a drop myself, of course. Temperance. That's what you should be pushing from those platforms of yours. Temperance. It's the devil drink that rots the soul of this city."

She said nothing. There was a mass of truth to what he had said. But she also knew it would take more than the advance of temperance to root out man's inequality towards woman. Still she was glad of his help. So it was with a great deal of humility she thanked Jimmy Docherty for his advice and his cooperation.

Twice she made an appointment with Agnes' lawyer. And twice she had to cancel. She couldn't get away. The whole household was sick.

Nathan had just gone down with the German measles. Four months out of bed since the war had ended, and there he was back between the sheets again with another attack from the Germans. Her mother was just recovering from Spanish influenza. The first wave had killed hundreds of people in the city the previous year. And then it had come back again worse than ever. But the virus had not reckoned for the defiance of Madame Kahn. "The Huns didn't get me," she said. "The British with their camps didn't break me. And the Spanish won't kill me either." Her father, more meekly, had also taken to his bed. But he had nothing more than a heavy Scottish cold, leaving her with a whole swathe of international infections to contend with as she ferried food and water to her patients, emptied bedpans, wiped cold cloths over hot brows. Dr Drummond had visited the last three evenings with his supplies of powders, quinine pellets and embrocations. At least there was money to pay his bills. Papa Kahn's tailoring business was doing well. What with all the soldiers back from the Front, back to civilian life, back to clothes they hadn't worn for years. Leaner frames from years of trench food and rations meant old styles needing to be altered. Or those with money in their pockets, new styles ordered for new lives.

She opened the front door, crossed the corridor of the close, grasped the brass knocker, rapped hard. She saw the shadow of Mrs Carnovsky behind the stained glass panels swaying down the hallway in her approach. The door opened a crack. The smell of brass polish and boiled chicken floated out into the stairwell.

"Oh, it's you again," the old woman said. "Don't go bringing me any of your foreign diseases."

"I'm perfectly fine. Can I use your telephone?"

"What is wrong with that father of yours, *bubeleh*? Can he not put his hand in his wallet to order a telephone? He's a man of the tailoring trade, after all. A business needs to be able to communicate, needs to keep up with the times. If an old woman like me can embrace these new-fangled inventions, so can a man like your father."

"You certainly are the modern woman," Celia said, knowing it was actually Mrs Carnovsky's brother, worried about his sister's health, who had insisted on the telephone. "Can I come in?"

"Yes, yes. *Komm, komm*. You know where it is. Meanwhile, I shall make some tea."

She sat down by the table in the hallway, fumbled with the awkward contraption, called the exchange, fidgeted with the wire until she was put through by the operator.

"I'm afraid Mr Sneddon has the influenza," the legal secretary said. "He is not taking any appointments at this time."

"Is there someone else who can see me?"

"What was the file again?"

"The estate of the late Agnes Calder."

"Let me ask one of the other partners."

The line went quiet. She could hear Mrs Carnovsky's kettle whistling away in the kitchen. Then the legal secretary again:

"This is Mr Sneddon's private case. Only he can deal with you. I'm afraid you will have to wait until he is better. It could be some weeks. The winding up of an estate is a very slow process anyway. Why don't you call back in a month or so, Miss Kahn. Or better still, wait to hear from us." Click.

She sat still for a few moments until she had regained her composure, then went through to the kitchen to thank Mrs Carnovsky.

"I have poured you a cup of tea," her neighbour said. "Drink before it gets cold."

She felt Mrs Carnovsky's gaze on her as she drank. The tea was too hot for her liking, but she gulped it down fast anyway, just so she could leave as quickly as possible. But no sooner had she replaced her finished cup than Mrs Carnovsky snatched at it, swirled the tea leaves around three times anti-clockwise, flipped the cup upside down on its own saucer. The old widow then ground the cup around three more times until it rested with the handle facing menacingly towards her. She stared at it, then up towards Mrs Carnovsky's smoke-teared eyes.

"Well?" the old woman said. The word came out more as a threat than a question. "Do you want to know your future?"

She shook her head. "Your readings are never good for me."

"What was the last one? I don't remember."

"It was a cross."

"Ah yes, a cross. Suffering. Did you suffer?"

"We've just had a terrible war. Now there's another outbreak of influenza. Everyone is suffering."

Mrs Carnovsky tapped a yellowed finger on the base of the cup. "Do you want a reading or not, *bubeleh*?"

"All right. Tell me."

The old woman picked up the cup, held it this way and that in the rare winter sunlight. "My, my," she said. Then resumed her scrutiny of the brown leaves against the white porcelain. "Look, look. What do you see?"

She took the cup, peered at the markings. "I don't know," she shrugged. "It could be many things."

"Come on, *bubeleh*. It is important you try."

"A fish? Is it a fish?"

Mrs Carnovsky slapped her thigh. "Yes, yes. A fish it is. A fish is a fine thing for the leaves."

"It is?"

"It means good fortune."

Celia laughed. "From where am I going to get good fortune?"

She kept the book hidden in a private compartment she'd made for herself between her cot and the wall. Her diary went in there too. And Agnes' letter. She covered it with brown paper as if it were a school book, but didn't write a title on the outside, not even her name. It felt profane keeping the text in the house, like secretly eating a strip of bacon off the *kosher* plates, knowing how such a sin would drive her mother into a state of hysteria. She had heard of the book's publication whispered by women colleagues in the peace movement. The Catholic Church was outraged. It was banned in America. She daren't even read it at night when everyone had gone to bed.

She decided to go to Langside Library. The one in the Gorbals was far too close, she was bound to meet someone there she knew. A drunk accosted her outside the building, one of those skinny, mean types with his tight face and corrugated brow, clinging on to a bottle filled with urine-coloured liquid as if it were life itself he was holding. Thinking he was being friendly or funny, or whatever else was going in his addled mind, he held out a hand in a drunken hello. A hand she must shake for fear the outstretched limb might turn to a palm-slap or a punch. "Gie us a kiss, darling," he slurred with his stink-breath. "Gie us a kiss." She pushed him aside, continued on inside.

Thankfully, the library was close to empty, the radiators being turned down, the one in the Gorbals usually piping hot, bringing in the hordes with nowhere else to go. She found herself a table in a corner, opened up to the title page. How Agnes had managed to smuggle a copy into Duke Street jail, she could not imagine. And now here she was holding this thin, clandestine volume in her hands. *Wise Parenthood – A Treatise on Birth Control or Contraception*. By Marie C. Stopes. She read:

"If the course of 'nature' is allowed to run unguided, babies come in general too quickly for the resources of most, and particularly of city dwelling families, and the parents as well as the children consequently suffer. Wise parents therefore guide nature, and control the conception of the desired children so as to space them in the way best adjusted to what health, wealth, and happiness they have to give."

And further on:

"The desolating effects of abortion can only be exterminated by a sound knowledge of the control of conception."

She had always considered her own attitude towards birth control a simple one – she practised social purity. She avoided marriage. She avoided sexual intercourse. She no longer gave any thought to her body 'down there'. Women had to be independent from a society structured around the lower natures of men. Her politics were her contraceptive, making her ignorance of sexual matters irrelevant.

But this book spared no detail. She learned about the workings of her own sex organs, how to fit a rubber cap, how to kill off sperm with the use of a quinine compound mixed with cocoa butter, how to rate other birth control methods such as the sheath, douching and *coitus interruptus*. When an elderly gentleman came to sit nearby with his newspaper, she scowled at his presence, turned her back. She read on. In her head, she could almost hear Agnes' Glasgow guttural dictating the words rather than Stopes' Edinburgh burr. How women with a history of miscarriages and poor health were held to ransom by the unprotected tyranny of men's sexual desires. How overlarge families equalled poverty for the working classes. Every so often, she would stop in order to reflect on the text. It wasn't as if Stopes' ideas were new to her. It was just that they were set down with such clear and rational thought. It was all so affirming. It was all so bloody obvious.

Fifteen

"You look exhausted."

She slowly raised her head from the newspaper spread across the kitchen table. Nathan was smiling at her. Her not-so-little brother, with his white hair and sad eyes, back on his feet after his bout with German measles. His nimble fingers and sharp sense of style turning him into quite the young tailor with a flair for the cut and the cloth, customers asking for him by name now. Nathan teasing their father about this, suggesting he might start a business on his own. "Mr Nathan's", he would call it, bespoke cloth-meister of the Gorbals, discounts available to returned soldiers looking to get back into mufti.

"I've been very busy," she said.

"I know. I never see you. Where do you go at nights?"

"Meetings. You know that."

"I thought you women had the vote now."

"If we're over thirty and married to a man of property. Anyway, we've got a lot more to struggle for than the vote."

"Elbowing your way into the sales at Pettigrew and Stephens?"

She couldn't help herself smiling at the comment. Nathan clapped his hands together. "Well, I finally made Miss Serious crack her face."

Madame Kahn bustled into the kitchen, discarding her apron as she walked. "Now, now, *kinder*. Prepare the table. It is time to light the *Shabbos* candles. Your father is waiting. And where is that brother of mine?"

"Is Uncle Mendel back for the *Shabbos*?" Celia asked.

116

Her mother pointed to the ceiling. "Who do you think is making that racket upstairs? He could put on his slippers. But no. He has to stomp around in those boots of his. Like a big fat *golem*."

Celia quickly folded up the newspaper, laid out the linen table-cloth and the Dresden china. Her mother placed a pair of silver candlesticks at the centre, a legacy from her own mother that could be traced all the way back to a great-grandmother from a pover-ty-stricken *shtetl* who still somehow managed to indulge in the luxury of owning such silverware. "These candlesticks are worth a small fortune," Madame Kahn would tell her. "They are your inher-itance. Your dowry. Unless…" The implications of the word "unless" were understood, a direct threat against marrying out of the faith. A bribe. She wed a Jew, she got the candlesticks. That was the deal. Or step over her mother's dead body, if she didn't.

She heard cheerful male voices in the hallway. Uncle Mendel greet-ing her father, then the two of them entering the kitchen, chuckling.

"Airplane fabric?" Papa Kahn said. "Clothes from airplane fabric? The boy is serious?"

"Good *Shabbos*, my dear family," Uncle Mendel said, ignoring his brother-in-law's question, spreading out his arms wide in bestowal of his greeting. "Good *Shabbos*." He then clasped Nathan in a rough hug. "Look at you. Look at you. A young man you have become."

She went over to kiss her uncle lightly on the cheek. His beard, more grey than dark now, smelt of lavender soap. "Good *Shabbos*, uncle." He smiled at her with his watery eyes, then skirted past her, opened the back door, peered out and up to the sky in a ritual she could remember for as long as there had been an Uncle Mendel and a Sabbath in her life.

"Where is the first star to announce the arrival of the *Shabbos*, eh?" he asked. "Bah! In this city smog, nothing you can see. To my cottage in the country, you must come. And a sky with a million stars you will witness. A million stars."

"Until then, Mendel," Papa Kahn said wearily, "we will just have to make do with the Sabbath commencement times as published in the *Glasgow Jewish Evening Times*. Now, tell me about this airplane fabric."

"*Shah*," Madame Kahn scolded. "First, the candles, then the airplanes. *Komm*, my daughter."

Celia went to stand by her mother as she lit the candles using a long taper ignited from the fire in the grate. With their hands miming a gathering motion above the candles, together they beckoned the Sabbath into the home. Celia closed her eyes, mumbled the blessing while Madame Kahn swayed beside her in silence for a good few seconds longer. She wondered what her mother's secret thoughts were during these quiet moments. No doubt, she would be asking God to bless her little family with good health and prosperity. But there were also probably some added desires too. That her brother should cease with his gambling and his drinking, that her son should continue in good health, that her daughter should not humiliate her with an inappropriate marriage. Her mother opened her eyes, breathed out a sigh both as an indication that her requests would probably go unanswered and also that her husband should proceed with his duties. Papa Kahn slowly enunciated the blessing for the wine, everyone responded with "Amen", and drank down the sweet concoction. Her father then cut and distributed the Sabbath loaf, so fresh from Fogell's bakery that it was still warm in her hands.

"No politics," Madame Kahn warned. "For once there will be no talk of politics at the *Shabbos* table."

"What is this airplane fabric?" Nathan asked.

Uncle Mendel poured out a glass of *schnapps* for himself, one for Papa Kahn. "It is Avram's idea," he said. "Out of airplane fabric, waterproof clothing he wants to make. For the farmers and the shepherds, the hunters and the fishermen."

"A *meshugge* idea," Papa Kahn said, as he blew noisily on his chicken soup. "Madness."

"A crazy idea it is not," Uncle Mendel corrected. "Today with an aircraft manufacturer in Carmunnock I met. Now the war is finished, rolls and rolls of the material they have left over. Waterproof fabric from the wings and the … what is this word? … fuselage. At a very cheap price I bought. There is more if we want."

"Then you are mad too. You can make clothing from such a material?"

"It is possible."

"I can make a few samples," Nathan suggested. "What does Avram want?"

"He suggests a smock," Uncle Mendel said. "Some leggings maybe."

"Let me have some of the material, uncle. I can do the designs, get the girls at the shop to make them up."

"See," Uncle Mendel said, pointing at Papa Kahn. "There is a young man open to change."

"I just want to know when Avram will come back," Celia said. "He's been away too long."

Uncle Mendel shrugged. "Up there, he has his own life. The work he enjoys. A good business sense he has. And football with a local team he plays."

"Football," Papa Kahn moaned. "Always with the football. And now with the waterproof clothing. Why can't he just be a credit draper?"

The next morning they all walked to the Great Synagogue in South Portland Street. "We shall go like a family," her mother declared as she tried to co-ordinate the event by stopping Papa Kahn and Uncle Mendel from going too early, her children from going too late. Celia had always despised the journey. Jew Street. Gentile Street. Jew Street. Jew Street. Gentile Street. Jew Street. Those were the descriptions mapping out the walk in her head ever since she was a child. The Saturday might have been the day of rest for the Jews of the Gorbals, but for everyone else it was business as usual. The coal wagon still came, the ash cans were still emptied, milk and post were delivered. People went shopping, pushed prams, lit fires, cooked hot meals, visited the park bandstands and the local libraries, traded with notes and coins. No Gentile was dressed up to the nines, carrying *Tallis* bags emblazoned with the Star of David as a shining symbol of otherness, staring straight ahead as if the Cossacks on their horses awaited around the next corner.

Starting out on her own Thistle Street was easy enough. After all, it hosted the most number of Jewish families in the Gorbals. She could relax then, pretend she lived in a city of Jews, a country of Jews, where Saturday was the official day of rest. But when she turned into Cumberland Street busy with its Saturday traffic and shoppers, the giant smoke-stacks of the electricity power station belching in the distance, she began to tense up, felt the trickle of sweat down her ribcage. When she was young, this was the point in their journey when her father would take her hand, she would skip along at his side without any sense of inhibition. Now, he just pressed on in front of her, back hunched, head down, while her mother clutched her coat collar, quickened her pace. Only Uncle Mendel with his long beard and sidelocks seemed oblivious to his foreignness as he chatted loudly with Nathan about Avram's idea for waterproof clothing. The next street, Abbotsford Place, was fine, there was her old school, several Jewish shops with their Yiddish signs above the doorways, all closed down for the Sabbath. Then it was across Bedford Street, another Gentile thoroughfare. She remembered one time seeing a non-Jewish classmate standing there with her mother. The young girl had started to raise her hand to wave but her mother had whacked her across the top of her head, 'shooshed' her, as if a bunch of lepers were passing. Finally, the ordeal was over when their little party reached the impressive façade of the synagogue on South Portland Street.

"You ran up those steps like the most religious woman in the Gorbals," her mother noted as they entered the haven of the foyer.

"And so did you, mother."

From her pew in the upstairs gallery, she observed the men of the congregation as they smugly went about the performance of their rituals. She watched as they murmured the holy texts in baritone under the cover of their prayer shawls, as they opened the Ark to collect the sacred scrolls, read from the *Torah*, faced this way, then that way, stood up, sat down, prayed for the dead, made a business deal with the living, shook hands with their neighbours, glanced upwards at their audience, nodded confidently at their wives and daughters. While she did what? Sat quiet in her primness, doing nothing except follow the service in her prayer book. She felt her mother nudge her.

"See." Madame Kahn dipped her head to a section of the male congregation. Celia looked down to witness the late arrival of a certain medical student from Glasgow University. She started so much at the sight of him that she knocked her prayer book off its ledge onto her mother's lap. Madame Kahn picked it up, passed it back to her, her lips curled into a smirk under her veil.

Jonny was waiting for her at the bottom of the stairway, smiling confidently, while she held on to the banister, observed her feet negotiating the steps as if her black leather patents were the most fascinating items on earth. She actually could feel herself shaking under his unwavering gaze. She guessed that after dealing with the threat of imminent death for two years in the trenches, a young Jewess in her Sabbath finery would not present much of a challenge to his nerves. She noticed he was wearing the same double-breasted suit as on the night she had first met him at The Marlborough Hotel. Silver cufflinks, matching tie-pin, even a silver thread reflected in his white silk *yarmulke*, his arm outstretched to greet her mother. Then he turned to take her gloved hand in his own before she had reached the bottom of the stairway. Standing above him, she could see the firm line of his parting that split his creamed-down curls as he bowed slightly before her. His hair was as black as polished coal.

"Good *shabbos*, Miss Kahn."

"Good *shabbos*, Mr Levy," she said, her voice emerging more high-pitched than she would have liked. "And for what do we Jews of the Gorbals owe the honour of your West End presence?"

Jonny released his grasp, stepped back from her, set his feet slightly apart, hands behind his back. Some kind of 'at ease' stance, she thought. "I have been invited to *Shabbos* lunch with the Samuels family," he said, rocking from side to side. "They live in Thistle Street. I assume they must be neighbours of yours."

"There are so many Samuels in Thistle Street, Mr Levy. You will need to be more specific."

"Meyer and Fanny. They lost a son, Joseph. He served with me during the war. I thought I would use the opportunity to attend the service here. It is such a beautiful synagogue."

"Surely not as beautiful as the one in Garnethill?"

"They are easily comparable," he said, before turning to address her mother. "Madame Kahn," he stated with a certain formality. Celia noticed her mother straighten, touch her hat.

"Yes, Doctor Levy?"

"That's very kind of you. But I am still only a medical student."

"Pardon my error," Madame Kahn replied. "I am always running a little ahead of myself. You were saying."

"Some of us from the West End Zionist Youth Group are going fruit-picking in Blairgowrie. I wonder if it would be appropriate to ask your daughter to accompany us."

"What would be more appropriate, Mr Levy," Celia said quickly, "is if you made your request directly to me. We no longer live in Victorian times."

He seemed unaffected by the rebuke, smiled at her in that confident way of his, then at her mother, then back to her again. "Forgive me, Miss Kahn. But a poor soldier from the trenches has been unable to keep up with the world of modern etiquette. I will therefore ask you directly. Would you like to come on an outing to pick berries in the company of the West End Zionist Youth Group?"

"The West End Zionist Youth Group," Papa Kahn repeated as he and Uncle Mendel joined them. "I've never heard of such an organisation."

"We intend to build communes in Palestine, sir," Jonny said, snapping out of his 'at-ease' pose. "*Kibbutzim.*"

"Jewish socialist communes in Palestine, eh?" Papa Kahn chortled. "My, my, what a concept. What do you think, Mendel?"

"You know what I think of such things. A true socialist does not need a Palestine. Socialist principles are universal. Even for the Jews."

"Excuse my brother-in-law, Mr Levy. But he is a Territorialist. He will put the Jews wherever they are told to go. Land is land is land. Even if it is in some jungle in Africa. Or even on the moon. Anywhere but where God promised them. Now about you and these *kibbutzim*. When do you intend to set off on your adventure?"

"I'm not sure, sir. I need to finish my degree first. But I've already started to learn Hebrew."

Papa Kahn moved in closer. "I would keep that quiet if I were you. There are some people standing in this very foyer who believe Hebrew can only be the language of the Book. Not to be used for everyday speech. God forbid if Hebrew is used to order a meal in a restaurant or to buy a train ticket. Even if that restaurant or railway station is in Palestine..."

"...Enough of this Palestine," Madame Kahn snapped. "I believe Mr Levy was talking about fruit-picking in Blairgowrie. I personally am very fond of strawberries. *Erdbeeren*. So delicious. They remind me of my childhood. How do you answer Mr Levy, Celia?"

Sixteen

It was early morning at Queen Street Station when she had to meet Jonny and the West End Zionists. But it was raspberries they were off to be picking in Blairgowrie, not the *erdbeeren* her mother craved. Apparently it had been a poor year for strawberries, the farmers leaving their thin pickings to the hired help – the tinkers, the travellers and the local labourers – rather than Glasgow folk on a fun day out with their careless hands and distracting talk. She was late even though he had insisted she must be on time what with three different journeys to make – two by train, one by horse and cart. So she was running up Buchanan Street with her wicker basket containing a couple of apples, her sandwiches filled with white chicken, a few extra made in a gesture of socialist solidarity for any of those with large appetites among the Zionist Youth.

She might have been tardy but she was no fool. She had brought with her a copy of the *Glasgow Jewish Evening Times* for protection. For in the early hours when the city was deserted like this, before the stores opened up and the traffic really got started, the rooftops belonged to the starlings. Thousands of them, with their endless screeching, excitedly discussing the latest gossip in birdland while dumping their liquid excrement down the sides of the buildings and onto the heads of pedestrians below. These birds would eventually turn the city white, she thought. Like that ancient Italian city with its volcanic ash. But she had her newspaper over her head to defend herself. For even her fast pace couldn't stave off the enemy above. Plop, plop, plop. She felt the paper flick to the force of the aerial bombardment. But even if the bird droppings had found her, her clothes weren't too much to worry about. Jonny had told her to dress appropriately for a day among the earth, the berries, the nettles and the brambles. She wore an old smock, a sleeveless cardigan and a floppy hat which she hoped would pass muster with these Zionists preparing to build farming communes in Palestine with their bare hands.

She was glad to see Jonny kitted out in his own berry-picking attire – a battered hat, an old tweed jacket with saggy pockets, twill shorts and long woollen socks. He was leaning against a side pillar at the station entrance, smoking a pipe, two large canvas bags at his feet. He swept off his hat as soon as he saw her.

"Where are the rest of them?" she asked.

"You're late. We've only got three minutes."

"But where are your West End Zionists?"

He shook his head slowly from side to side, smiled weakly. "There are no West End Zionists," he said eventually.

"What do you mean?"

"I didn't think your dear Mama would let you come on your own. So I just made them up."

"What on earth made you think I'd want to come by myself?"

"I thought you were one of those modern misses who didn't need a chaperone."

"You lied to me. You lied to my mother."

"I'm sorry. But what else could I say in front of her." He picked up his bags. "Look, I've got the train tickets. And we've got two minutes. You can either come with me. Or turn around, never speak to me again. Which is it to be?"

If his face had shown just one little look of that cocky confidence of his, she would have walked away. But instead, his eyes were flickering this way and that, anywhere but to gaze at her straight. A bird dropping landed in the space between them, splattering white excrement onto his boots. Divine retribution, she thought.

"I'm furious with you," she said. "So don't expect me to be all nice and friendly and polite. But I didn't get dressed up in my glad rags for nothing. Which platform is it?"

She hardly spoke to him all the way to Perth. Just took the window seat, watched the countryside steam past without a care for his fidgeting and various attempts to introduce conversation. She was still angry with him, but his behaviour had also given her the upper hand, allowing her to sit there calmly and in control, knowing she could bring this little stand-off to an end whenever she wanted. She was enjoying the views too now that the sprawl of the city had petered out and the sun was beginning to burn off the early morning mist. Only breaking her silence to murmur a reluctant 'thank you' when he brought her a mug of tea from the dining car, too much sugar stirred into it for lack of her proper instruction. He stared out the window too, his face looking quite handsome in profile, skin shaven clean, he must have woken up bright and early to do that, the sharp metal scraped sleepily across his chin and cheeks just for her. He pointed out Stirling Castle, a piece of information she ignored even though it was the first time she had seen the grand fortress perched up there on the craggy hillside, plumb centre in the middle of the town. Then there was the Wallace Monument standing there like some giant raised fist of defiance to the sky. Her heart lifted to the smell of the pine forests and the wheat fields sucked into the carriage through the open windows. One of the other passengers opened parcels of food for her bairns, the stink of boiled eggs adding to the aroma of the carriage.

At Perth, there was another train to connect them to Coupar Angus and on to Blairgowrie where she eased off slightly with her aloofness now that she had to depend on him for where to go next. He led her to a farm-lad with his horse and cart ready to take them the couple of miles out to the picking fields. They sat in the back among the bundles of firewood and jute sacks, the driver thinking himself to be some kind of tour guide, pointing out local features of interest as they plodded along.

"Salmon," he said as they crossed the bridge over the River Ericht. Then over on the other side. "Flax mills." On passing a cottage by the riverbank: "Mrs Beveridge. Wash mangled for a penny." A while later: "Walnut tree." And even: "Cows."

With the morning sun full out, she ignored the lad's sparsely worded commentary, laid her head back to rest on the jute sacks. There was nothing in her line of vision blocking out the cloudless sky. She could have been anywhere at any time in history. Just herself and nature. Banished from her mind was the city soot, the shipyard cranes blighting the skyline, the overcrowded tenements, the children with no shoes, the women with their hunched backs and their worn-out wombs, the men haunted by war, crushed by poverty, awash in drink. Here the air was fresh and clean, the grass was lush, the trees healthy, there were potatoes and berries in the fields. Out here, she was a nobody. Neither a woman nor a Jewess. Just a carefree soul on the back of a wagon, her cheeks hot from the sun and the excitement running through her. She wanted to laugh out loud. Not from any amusement. But out of sheer joy.

"We're here," the farm boy said as the wagon pulled into a court-yard. The lad turned round to look at them. "Water." He jerked his head in the direction of a pump, took out a fob-watch from his waist-coat pocket. She reckoned the lad must have been about thirteen but he had all these adult mannerisms about him, the way he screwed up his mouth as he looked at the watch face, the slow pace of his speech. "Hmmm," the boy said. "Eleven-thirty. I'm off to the station at three-thirty if it's a ride back to Blairgowrie you're after." He pointed out a track leading away from the yard. "The berries are down there. Keep going until you get to the tinkers, then take the next row along. Gaffer's name's Soutar. You'll get to hear him soon enough scolding the tinks. He's the one to sort you out with the buckets and the weighing and the paying. And mind, mister, to keep an eye on your lass there."

"Why's that?" Jonny asked, looking up from tightening his bootlaces.

"We cannae vouch for the behaviour of any of those men working down there," the lad said, scratching his head as if in all his young years he had already discovered the wayward ways of the adults of his gender. He then gave a shout to the horse, a shake of the reins and he was off.

She walked over to the pump, let Jonny work the lever while she splashed water on her face, cupped some in her hands to drink. She then did the same for him so he could fill up a couple of bottles he'd brought out of his bags.

"Forgiven me?" he asked.

"I haven't decided."

He ran his wet hands through his hair, his mood suddenly all light and cheerful. "Come on," he said, fixing his hat back on. "Let's go berry picking."

She strolled with him side by side for a good quarter-mile before they came across the tinkers working the rows. She'd never seen men so dark-tanned before, stripped to their shirts and vests, hands flashing quick for their penny-a-pound of rasps, mouths silent, eyes set hard on the task. Then they came across the man who had to be the gaffer Soutar with his flat-cap and purple-stained dungarees, sitting on a barrel by a rusty upright weighing-machine.

"You can start there," Soutar said, handing them a couple of buckets, nodding to a row. "Done this before?"

She shook her head while Jonny said: "Not since before the war."

"Well, I'll tell you some tips to remind you." Soutar scratched the back of his neck then had a quick examine of his nails. Deep-ingrained purple they were. "Just pick the full ripe ones. It's no use to us if you take the ones that are no ready. And it's no use to you because they won't ripen once plucked. Place them, don't throw them, into your bucket. Don't stack them too high or you'll squash them. Bring them up here once you've got a level of around three to four inches and I'll weigh them." He scratched again at his neck. "What have you got to carry them home?"

"I brought some containers." Jonny opened up his canvas bags, took out some shallow pots with lids.

"Grand," Soutar said. "And don't just pick the easy ones either. Search a wee bit among the leaves for the shy ones."

Celia walked down to her row, bucket swinging, beside her Jonny humming some stupid war-time song, she thinking themselves a couple of scallywags in their shabby clothes, like in some Charlie Chaplin picture.

"I can eat as many as I want," she said. "Who's to know?"

Jonny laughed. "That's the temptation. Just don't give yourself tummy-ache. That's what I used to do as a boy. Stuff my face for an hour, then have my belly hurt all the way home."

"You've got greedy eyes, Jonny Levy. That's your problem."

"And what are you? Some strictly disciplined miss?"

"Yes, that's me, I'm afraid," she said laughing, although she feared it was true.

She took one side of the row. The bushes came up to just about shoulder-high, so she could see Jonny working away on the other side, still humming away at his stupid song. She didn't have to search hard for the berries either, there were so many of them, coming off easy and squishy between her thumb and forefinger. She was all heated up now from the sun, the sticky leaves clinging to her skin, her fingers red from where the too-ripe berries had burst, bees and flies as plump as the rasps flitting all around her. She could feel the band of her knickers under her dress, itchy with her sweat. She took off her hat, wiped a sleeve across her brow.

"I've got enough," he shouted over to her. "See you at the end of the row."

When she had about a three-inch layer in her bucket, she went down to join him. He gave her a bottle of water to swig, then they walked up to where Soutar did the weighing and the calculating, poured the rasps gently into Jonny's pots, then started the whole process again. It was easy work but in the fresh air and the sunshine, she tired quickly. After their fourth trip up to Soutar, she was glad Jonny announced their work was done.

"I'll pay the man. Then we'll go down to the river for lunch."

They put the filled pots into the canvas bags, left them in the shade under Soutar's protection, walked down to the Ericht, Jonny saying he knew a spot from when he came as a lad.

"We Levys used to hunt in packs," he told her. "Everything we did – day-trips, summer holidays, weddings and *bar mitzvahs* – the whole family went. And I don't mean just first cousins. Fifth cousins, tenth cousins. A whole Russian village of Jews we were in our own right. We needed a separate rail carriage just for the food." He laughed, then looked down sadly at his feet. "It's been a bit different since the war though."

"We didn't have much of a family to lose," she told him. "My father's alone here in Scotland. My mother's only got her brother, my Uncle Mendel. My own brother Nathan was too young to enlist, thank God.

The same with Avram. Although he's only my adopted brother."

"I heard he's playing football now. For one of those Highland teams. Argyll Thistle."

"I didn't know that."

"Thistle have just drawn Celtic in the Scottish Cup. Half the Jewish men in Glasgow are talking about Avram like he's some kind of hero. Like Judah Maccabee. And they haven't even played the game yet."

"We hardly ever hear a word from him," she said. "He's got his own life now."

"Well, if he scores a goal, he'll be the most famous Jew in Glasgow. Apart from Mannie Shinwell."

He took her to a dry grassy area in the shade high up on the bank above the Ericht. They sat down, she set her basket between them.

"I brought enough food to feed an army," she said. "That's all your fault. You and your West End Zionist Youth. I want you to eat everything. It's not right to waste food."

"You needn't worry. I only brought an apple."

She picked out a sandwich for herself, drew her legs up and under her body, sat watching the river as she ate. It was so peaceful and picturesque, not a soul around, she wondered why she didn't take herself out to the countryside more often.

"The river's not usually as low as this," he said. "After the rains, it runs all swollen and powerful. That's when you can see the salmon leaping."

"Salmon leaping? Don't be daft."

"I'm not being daft. It's true. The salmon leap out of the water as they head up river to spawn. I've seen them do it with my own eyes."

She munched down on her chicken, not knowing whether to believe him or not, feeling a bit stupid for being a city girl with more knowledge about the times of the trams than the habits of fish.

"I suppose you would have to see it to believe it though," he said. "The wonders of nature."

He sat quietly after that. He had a sad look about him, she wondered whether it was the war he was thinking about. Hard to believe it was possible to go through an experience like that, not have the memories drift into your mind during these quiet moments. A whole generation of men wandering around full of these awful stored-up nightmares in their heads, she wondered how they could go on living, a society go on functioning. She picked a dandelion from the grass, her own fingers stained raspberry red against the yellow petals she plucked from its head.

"Did you volunteer?" she asked.

"No. I was a conscript."

"I'm glad."

"Why?"

"I was part of the women's peace movement. We were not exactly in favour of everyone marching cheerfully into war."

"There's a lot I don't know about you." He lay back on the grass, stuck his pipe in his mouth, but didn't light it. She stared at the river, trying to imagine salmon leaping upstream, such a struggle against the flow of nature in order to give birth.

"I'll be finished my studies in another few months," he said, more to himself than to her. "It'll be off to Palestine after that."

She plucked the last of the petals off the dandelion, blew it from between her fingers into the air, watched it float away. "A new life in a new land."

"That's a good way to put it. What about you?"

"What about me?"

"What plans do you have? When you're not trying to stop wars."

"When I'm not scrubbing floors, beating carpets, hauling in the coal, cleaning the grate and whitewashing the walls?"

He chuckled. "Yes, that's what I mean."

"Well, there's the family allowance for married mothers to be fighting for. Broadening the conditions for women's suffrage. Supporting the Independent Labour Party on equal rights for women. That's enough to be getting on with, don't you think?"

"You'd be perfect for a *kibbutz*."

"Me? If I wanted to dirty my hands in the soil, I'd get myself an allotment in Queens Park."

"I just thought a *kibbutz* would suit your socialist principles. To each according to their need, from each according to their ability. You can't get more Marxist than that."

"I'd rather apply my principles to the people of Glasgow. Why get up and go somewhere else?"

He struck a match to his pipe-bowl, she watched him suck the tobacco alight, she liked that hiss and crackling sound as the dried leaves caught. "Glasgow's problems are just too entrenched," he said. "I'd rather start somewhere from scratch."

"That's a strange attitude for someone who wants to be a doctor. I imagined you'd have a limitless desire to heal the sick. And there's plenty here in Glasgow."

"Sadly, the extent of my compassion is limited. I'm prepared to care for my family, my friends, my neighbours and my community. But beyond that, I just let the world take care of itself. That's why I admire someone like you."

"You admire me?"

"For taking on all those causes, helping people you don't even know."

"Only the women," she said. "The men can look after themselves."

"You don't really like men, do you?"

"In my experience, they're either too weak. Or they're putting down women to feel strong."

"That's a pity."

"Why's that?"

"Because here's another."

The newcomer had to be one of the travellers, a short, stocky man, flat-capped, shirt-sleeves rolled up tight, trousers both belted and with braces. He stood about twenty yards off, beckoned them with a wave.

"What do you want?" Jonny shouted.

The man didn't reply. Instead he crouched slightly, legs set apart, body lowered, summoned them again with his fingers, the way a master might entice his dog.

Jonny called again. "What is it?"

The man remained silent but his gestures became more impatient.

"Let's go with him," she said.

"The farm-lad warned us off the gypsies."

"I've nothing against them."

Jonny held up his hand to indicate 'wait'. Quickly they packed away their picnic things, went after the man. He didn't let them catch up but walked ahead, turning around every now and then, beckoning them on.

They followed him to a barred gate left open, along a path through the trees, the sun poking through the leaves and branches where it could, speckling the dry carpet of needles and cones underfoot. She breathed in the freshness of the pine, the smell of far-off burning wood, hiked up her skirts so she could walk faster.

They came to a clearing. Unyoked caravans were parked in a rough circle, facing into each other, all with their stovepipes jutting out of the roofs, some painted plain, others boasting elaborate designs. A couple of fires smouldered away at the centre of the camp, pots heating away among the cinders, the rich aroma of a meat stew. A woman sat on the steps of one of the caravans, weaving a basket, thick black hair down to her waist, a scattering of silver-tin buckets at her feet. She looked up, narrowed her eyes, then retreated to her task.

"Where's he gone?" Jonny said.

"I can't see him through the smoke."

"He can't have disappeared."

"There he is," she said, spotting their guide beyond the far-side caravans. "He's still asking us to come over."

They didn't cross the campsite directly, but walked around the rear of the wagons. Piles of pots and churns lay around, clothes hung on lines, a roped-off paddock where a dozen or so horses grazed without an ear pricked at their passing. It was so quiet, she thought. If the men were away picking in the fields, where were the women? And where were the children? When they had walked about half-way round the wagons, they found their man standing in a clear space near to a thick pole dug firm into the ground. He smiled at them through broken teeth, swept off his cap to reveal a band of pale, sun-starved skin across his hairline, pointed with a stick to a large dark mound on the ground at the pole's base,

"What is it?" she asked Jonny, her eyes stinging from the smoke off the campfire.

Jonny took off his hat, ruffled the sweat-matted hair at the back of his head. "I don't believe it."

"What is it?"

"It's a bear. It's a bloody bear."

"Hey ho," the gypsy said, holding up his stick. "Have I got a show for you." He started to gently prod the body of the beast. The bear shifted its head from the cradle of its arms, opened its eyes, stared right at her. A pulse of fear, excitement and revulsion all wrapped into one ran through her whole body. The man poked again with the stick. The bear opened its huge jaws. She could see its pink maw, the fangs, its thick tongue. Then it uttered a painful yawning sound.

"Hey ho," the man said, whacking the bear lightly across its back with the stick. "Dance time."

The animal shook its head, it was only then she noticed the cuff around its neck, the chain attached. Slowly, the bear heaved itself up onto its front paws, raised its rear until it rested on all fours. This time, it let out a growl. Not a ferocious sound, more like a tired groan. She took a pace backwards, just managed to stop herself urinating in her knickers.

"I don't like this, I don't like this," she said. "We should go."

"Wait a moment," Jonny said. "Let's see what happens."

The man took his stick, held it above the bear's snout, began to slowly raise it higher. The animal stretched to follow the path of the stick until it heaved itself up on to its hind legs, straining against its chain. Standing full, paws raised, it was a massive beast. Yet she could sense its weary sadness, its spirit broken. The gypsy reached into his trouser pocket, brought out a mouth organ. He wiped the instrument against his shirt sleeve, started to play with one hand, the other jiggling the stick above the animal's snout. The bear stumbled from one rear leg to the other in a pathetic jig.

"Come on," she said, pulling on Jonny's arm. "This is cruel."

"Yes, yes, in a moment."

"Stay," the gypsy shouted. "Free show, free show. Don't go, my friends."

She could hear the mouth organ start up again behind her as she strode across the middle of the encampment, the smoke from the fires tearing her eyes, she couldn't be sure of the entrance point back into the woods.

"What are you running for?" Jonny asked on catching her up, grasping her arm. She shook him off.

"Why didn't you come when I said? You should have come…"

"…Hey, hey, *gaji*." It was the woman weaving baskets on her caravan steps "Hey, hey," she shouted again. "Come here."

"Ignore her," Jonny said.

The woman stood up. Broad-shouldered she was like a man, her long hair so black it surely had to be dyed in youthful contrast to the wrinkled face it framed. "You," the woman said, pointing at her with a fearsome finger. "You. The *gaji*. Come here."

"Let her be," Jonny said. "She'll just want to sell you her weaving."

But there was a commanding strength in this woman's voice that made disobeying almost unthinkable. "I want to see what she's after."

"Suit yourself. I'll wait for you here."

She walked over to where the gypsy stood on the steps. As soon as she was close enough, the woman grabbed her hand, tried to claw open her fingers. "Let me see, let me see," she kept saying. "Let me see your palm."

She managed to pull back her hand. "What do you want?"

The woman started touching her hair. "Such black, black hair, dearie." Then her fingers stroked her cheek. Hard leathery skin against her own. "Dark skin, dearie. Where you from?"

"Glasgow."

"Heh! Heh!" The woman half-laughed, half-cried, her mouth a cavern of blackened stumps. "Tell your Auntie Jessie where you're really from?"

"I told you. I'm from Glasgow."

"That's a place for red-haired bairns, skin the colour of milk. You've got the Roma blood in your veins. Jessie can tell."

"My father's from Russia."

"Ah. *Russka Roma*."

"No, no. We are Jews."

"Jews," she said, smiling so that her face cracked into a web of deep lines. "Jews too are wanderers on this earth." She wiped her hands

135

down the sides of her skirt as if to bring an end to the matter. "Now why don't you buy one of my tin buckets? To carry the berries I'm sure you been picking. Or why not a pot to pee in for one of the bairns you and that handsome Jock over there are bound to have?"

"I haven't got a penny on me."

"Why not ask yon Jock to give you twelve. For a shilling will buy you a brand new bucket of tin."

She was just about to call to him for the money when he came wandering over through the smoke. "She's not got you buying something?"

"A shilling for the best tin-craft in the land," Jessie hissed. "You'll pay double in that city of yours."

"Come on, Jonny," she pleaded. "I want to show these folk a kindness."

"Aye," Jessie grinned. "A kindness. We're all alike, you and I."

Madame Kahn stood at the kitchen table, inspecting the contents of the different pots that lay there. "I have never seen so many berries in my life," she said. "We have enough here to make raspberry jam until the Messiah comes. Those West End Zionists, they make you work hard. Did you enjoy yourself? The sun on your skin looks good."

"It was a good day, mother. But it is late. I am tired."

"And you must thank this Jonny for the bucket. Whatever you want to say about these gypsies, their tin-work is excellent. This bucket also will be here when the Messiah comes."

"I am glad to hear it."

"Now where are all my jars?"

"You are going to start making the jam now? It's nearly midnight."

"Don't worry about me. I enjoy making jam. It reminds me of my childhood. I like the soft feeling in my hands. But then we make with *erdbeeren*, not with these raspberries."

Celia was too tired to help. Instead, she just went to her cot, kicked off her shoes, lay down fully-clothed, listened to her mother sing as she worked away with her simmering pots, the smell reminding of her day in the fields, of farm lads with adult ways, of bears and berries and gypsies.

Seventeen

SHE HAD JUST COME BACK FROM THE STEAMIE, her hands full with a basket piled high with clean linen, still warm and smelling of bleach and soap. The basket she'd put down in the small entrance hall inside the storm-doors, she was struggling to find her keys to the flat when she heard a sound on the stairway. At first, she thought it was a dog whimpering and she preferred to just let it be, not having any affection for the upstairs' neighbour's mongrel that would bark her awake most nights. But the sound persisted, something plaintive and beseeching about it that made her curious. So she closed the storm-doors slightly against her basket what with thieving kids happy to run away with anything unguarded, slowly ascended the stairs. She kept her body in a lean in front of herself, twisting her head upwards, her legs ready to scarper in case she had to. As she approached the last few steps to the first floor landing, she noticed a mound of dark clothing in a pile outside Uncle Mendel's flat. Her first thought was that he had forgotten to take his washing in, her second one being a flash of memory of the gypsy bear tied up to the base of the pole. Then she realised the groaning was coming from this very pile of clothes. She raced up the last few steps, knelt down by the body that lay there.

"Uncle Mendel, Uncle Mendel," she cried, shaking his moaning body. "What happened?"

Her uncle was lying in a pool of yellowish liquid and she feared the worst embarrassment for him. But then she saw the uncorked, empty bottle of whisky at his side, smelled the stink of cheap liquor not that much dissimilar to the stench of disinfectant. Her uncle's face was buried into his folded arms on the cold stone floor, his hat still clinging to his head but off at an angle. She shook him again, he turned his face towards her, his lips slurring some incomprehensible words.

She moved in closer. "What? What did you say?"

"Keys."

"Yes. Your keys."

"My keys. I cannot find."

"Here, let me help you to your feet."

"Go away," he shouted. " *Avek. Avek. Gey avek.*"

"Uncle. It's Celia. I'm here to help you."

He buried his face back into his arms. Then his back heaved up and down. "Leave me alone," he sobbed. "Leave me alone."

She took off his hat, placed her hand on the back of his neck, felt the skin there, hot and sweaty. "Let me help you."

"You cannot help me," he sobbed. "Just leave me alone. Leave me to die."

She patted his jacket pockets, found the one that contained his keys, a huge bunch of them, she could be here for days deciding the one that fitted. She tried the few marked out from the rest with coloured tape, miraculously the third one successful in the opening. She knelt back down beside her uncle.

"I can't do this on my own," she whispered. "You're going to have to help me."

"Just go away. *Gey avek.* They will kill me."

"Who will kill you?"

"These thugs. These *betsemer.*"

"No-one is going to kill you. But I need to get you into your flat."

"First they beat me. My body is blue and black. Blue and black. Now they will kill me."

Gently, she lifted her uncle's head from its rest on his arms. Then she grabbed his wrists, tried to pull him up and across the threshold.

"Come on, uncle. Help me. Please help me."

He finally began to move, raising himself with much effort and groaning on to his knees. But that was as far as he was able or willing to go. So with her pulling his outstretched arms and the slow movement of his knees, she was able to get him to crawl into his own hallway before he collapsed in a heap again. She closed his front door, locked it, sat down on one of the hard-backed chairs, until she had regained her breath. The hallway was dark but she couldn't be bothered getting up to put on a light. Her uncle had fallen asleep anyway, she could hear his light snoring like a cat's gentle purr. She must have drifted off herself because she woke with a jolt to some loud banging on the front door.

Thud, thud, thud.

She almost jumped off her chair with each blow, grateful at least for the door having wooden panels rather than the stained-glass of the flats on the ground floor. Thankful also she'd locked the door, refrained from turning on the light.

"Moses Cohen, Moses Cohen," a voice teased. "Open up. We know you're in there."

It had been years since she had heard it but she recognised the whiny, weasely sound of the young, ginger-haired lad who'd come round the first time to collect her uncle's debts. Hard to forget a voice like that, so mean and menacing in its delivery.

"Moses Cohen," the lad continued. "Your piss is all over the hall-way. You been wetting yourself again?" Thud, thud, thud. Then the sound of the empty whisky bottle being kicked away.

"Open the fuck up!" Another voice this time, must have been the other man, the one with the cream slash across his cheek, the hat kept low on his brow.

Uncle Mendel stirred on the floor but the snoring continued. She wrapped her arms around herself to stop the shaking. The handle rattled on the door, the voices dipped to a murmur. A harder thud this time, one of them must have been taking a run then a shoulder to the wood, the whole door shuddering to the blow. She heard a few curse words after that and a sense the men had moved off but she couldn't be sure. Perhaps they had gone to fetch a sledge-ham-mer or an axe. She waited in the darkness, her body held stiff, her breathing slow, letting the clock in the hallway tick away fifteen minutes, twenty minutes. After half an hour, she got up, slinked into the kitchen, tip-toed across the room to the window, slid her head out slowly from behind a curtain from where she could see down to the entrance of the close. No-one there. She moved back into the hallway, knelt down in front of the doorway, checked the slither of light from the outside landing for the shadow of legs and feet. Uncle Mendel groaned and her heart lurched. Very slowly she turned the key in the lock, eased open the door. She half-expected it to be slammed back in her face. She peered out into the landing. No-one there. She raced down the stairway and out into the street.

She ran and ran, her pinny flapping, her legs all over the place. She headed for Florence Street. It wasn't far, just to the end of her own road, then along two blocks. A couple of men unloading coal from their wagon, whistled, called after her: "Whit's yer hurry, lass?" She kept on running, looking out for the tenement of her destination, not sure which one, only that the outside window on the second floor had been pointed out to her once before. But she had a good memory for these things, a picture in her mind, she could even remember the curtains, a yellow floral pattern. And there they were, the same flowery print, hadn't been changed in the few years since she'd been shown the place. And why should they have been? It wasn't the kind of flat that demanded a high standard of decoration. She found the close entrance, ran up to the second floor landing, her chest sore from the lack of breath, she just stood there outside the door with hardly the strength to lift the brass knocker. She saw also that there was a bell, a dirty white button which she pressed. The ring was clear though, like upper octave notes on the piano quickly trilled. She rang again. Her hand against the door jamb as she gulped in the air, hoping it wouldn't be Lucky Mo but his son who answered it. A slot in the door at about eye-level slid open. She hadn't noticed that before.

"Who is it?"

"It's me. Celia. Please let me in."

It seemed to take forever as locks were undone, chains removed. The door opened.

"Oh Solly, thank God it's you."

It was just a one room flat, thick with smoke. Bedroom and kitchen all rolled into one, the toilet communal between the landings. Solly took up position in a battered-leather swivel chair behind a large desk on which stood four shiny-black candlestick telephones, wires and cords all in a tangle, a couple of ashtrays stacked high with twisted butts, and a scatter of paper slips, some skewered on one of these thin wire contraptions meant to keep the office desk neat and tidy. The walls were pinned with newspapers displaying the day's race meetings. The window behind his head was so dirty there was hardly a need for curtains to be drawn to stop the light coming in. He was down to his shirtsleeves and braces, hands behind his head, sweatstains under his arms. He nodded for Celia to sit in a rickety wooden chair in front of his desk.

"Still seeing that Jonny Levy?" he said.

"What do you mean?"

"That night at The Marlborough. I brought you flowers, escorted you to the ball. And what did you do? You hardly talked to me all night. And I haven't heard from you since."

"I'm sorry, Solly. I had too much to drink that night. I don't remember much of what happened."

"I'll tell you what happened. You used me."

"Solly, I didn't come here to argue."

He went silent. What with the grey light coming at her from behind the window, it was hard to make out his face. She looked around the rest of the room. A rusty sink, a giant safe taking up one whole corner, a couple of mattresses on the floor.

"You sleep here as well?" she asked.

"No," he said, his voice calmer now. "We just take this place during the day. A family lives here at night. Keeps the polis off our tracks." He brought his fingertips together in a bridge. "So what brings you here for the first time in your life?"

"I…"

One of the phones rang. He leaned across, lifted the receiver a fraction, then replaced it. "Go on."

"It's Uncle Mendel. He's in trouble."

Solly gave a little swivel in his chair. "So I heard."

"You know about this? About these men trying to kill him?"

"I don't know if they will actually kill him. What would be the point? Maim him, perhaps. Break a few bones. He owes some bad people some serious money. You just can't do that, you know. Drink and gamble. One vice at a time is what I say. You've got to keep a clear head in this game."

"What can we do to help him?"

"We? It's not my problem. I helped him out the last time he was in trouble. As a favour to you. He's not my responsibility."

"Solly. What's got into you? This is Celia. I've known you all my life. Help me. Please."

Again Solly swivelled in his chair, side to side, giving a little creak each time. Another telephone rang, the *tring, tring, tring* tearing at her nerves. He raised the receiver, slammed it back down. Then he turned his chair sideways to her so he was staring at the wall, at the safe, his fingertips back touching again in a bridge. She noticed how clean and trim his nails were and she imagined this was a usual pose for him, the way he considered matters of business, rocking back and forth, gazing at dark corners. "Avram," he said, his voice coming out all scratchy. He cleared his throat. "Avram. Avram is the key."

"Avram? How can he help? He's a credit draper in the Highlands. He's got no money to pay Uncle Mendel's debts."

"That is true. But he's also playing for a non-League side in a cup-tie against Celtic. Mendel might be able to help me out there."

"What do you mean?"

Solly laughed. "What do you know about football?"

"Nothing."

"And the intricacies of betting on football matches?"

"Nothing."

"Then why should I waste my time explaining. Just let me say that Mendel's plight, Avram's footballing talent being unknown to the usual Glasgow punter, and the clever mind of one Solly Green might make all parties concerned very happy."

"You can do that?"

"On one condition."

"And what is that?"

He turned his chair to face her. "Come here." He beckoned her with a solitary finger. "And take off that stupid pinny."

She sat where she was. Some noises outside the window. It must have been the lamp-lighter for an orange glow started to spread across the filthy window pane, slowly turning to yellow. She wondered when the night-time occupants returned.

"They won't be here for another couple of hours," Solly said, reading her thoughts. "Plenty of time." He patted his thighs. "Now, come here."

"Don't do this, Solly. We're friends."

"Only when it suits you."

Again she didn't move.

"Come over here." His voice harsher now.

She rose from her chair, taking off her pinny as she moved round the desk.

"That's a good girl," he said.

She didn't recognise his voice anymore. She didn't recognise herself either. As if it were just her body here in this room while she was off somewhere else. Sitting by a river, watching the salmon leaping, feasting on chicken sandwiches, the white meat so delicious in her mouth. She reached the other side of the desk, turned her back on him, he pulled her down on his lap. She felt the chair give slightly, thought their weight might be too heavy. She could hear his breathing, the touch of his fingers as they brushed her ear, stroked her neck.

"You're cold," he said. And she wasn't sure if he meant her skin or she was cold as a person. She was trembling too.

He placed a hand on her belly, the two of them rocking back and forward on the chair, the street lamp casting a garish glow across his skin, reflecting off his watch. His other hand moved round to her breast, the palm cupping her, she could feel the heat of it through her blouse, her own skin icy cold, his breathing hoarser now. Then suddenly, he arched his body with the forward motion of the chair, and she was pushed off him onto the floor.

"I'm sorry, Celia. I'm sorry, I'm sorry." He kept wiping his hand across his brow as if to erase the memory. "I don't know what I was thinking. What was I thinking?"

She lifted herself up from the floor, picked up the pinny that was lying there, tied it back round her waist.

"I was so happy you were coming with me that night," he said, his voice not directed at her but towards the dirt-stained window. "I even bought a new suit. New shoes to dance you around the floor. And then you just ignored me. As if I were worthless."

She looked down at him. There were tears in his eyes. Two grown men sobbing in one day. What was the world coming too?

"Let's forget this ever happened," she said.

"Yes, yes, yes, Celia. Let's forget it. We shall wipe the slate clean. Start again, yes? I'll try to sort out this mess with Mendel. I can't promise anything but I'll do my best. This football match with Avram could be the solution." A phone rang. And this time he answered it.

Eighteen

THE SWEEPS WERE JUST FINISHING UP, father and son they were, the elder up on the roof with his brush and wooden ball attached, his son down below with his soot bag stretched out in the grate, the sacking sealed round about. These two shouted 'hey, hey' to each other up and down the flue in a signal, but Celia had heard some call 'oi, oi' or 'down below' and other slang of the trade. But whatever their call and however well she supervised them, laid out newspapers in preparation, got them to wash up afterwards, they always left a black film in their wake that inevitably ended up in her hair and on her skin. So these four times a year when the sweeps were in, she made it a point to have herself a bath in the evening, otherwise she wasn't far off looking as smudge-skinned as these very tradesmen themselves.

It was on this afternoon before her evening bathing that Jonny Levy decided to turn up. Just like that. She hadn't seen him for weeks, not since their trip to Blairgowrie and suddenly there he was, coming round completely unannounced with one of his army pals. It was just as well her mother had answered the bell, keeping the door on a chain until she had time to escape into the main bedroom before the unexpected guests were ushered into the kitchen. Madame Kahn then brought her in a basin and a towel to wash off the soot, along with a change of clothes.

"It is good he calls like this," her mother said as she dabbed at her cheek with a damp cloth. "It shows he feels comfortable with our family."

"I think it's very rude, if you ask me. Who is his friend?"

"Robert? Or perhaps it was Robin. Or Roger. You know how I am with names. When I am introduced, my head goes into a spin. Now I must go prepare some tea."

By the time Celia appeared in the kitchen, Jonny and his pal were seated around the table, sipping tea and eating digestive biscuits off her mother's best china brought over from Germany. Made in Dresden. Only used on the Sabbath. Or if the King and his counsellors were ever to drop by for a visit. Jonny rose at her entrance.

"I'm sorry to just pop in like this," he said.

"It is a surprise."

"A welcome one I hope." He indicated his companion with a stretch of his hand. "I'd like you to meet Robert. Robbie."

Robbie made a vague attempt to rise from his chair, then sat back down again. She noticed his suit too tight and short on him, his skinny arms poking out of his sleeves. "Pleased to meet," he said, then cracked his biscuit in half on her mother's best plate, popped a piece into his mouth, chomped away.

"It's just a flying visit," Jonny went on.

Flying visit? She'd never heard that expression before. Must have been something he'd picked up in the war. Like all those other phrases imported from the army. 'A-1', 'cushy', 'muck about', 'over the top'.

"We've just had the sweeps in," she said, not knowing why this should be of interest to anyone. "It always feels a bit dusty after they've left."

"You wouldn't notice," Jonny said. Robbie meantime ran his finger across the table-top just to check.

"Doctor Levy was telling me," her mother said. "It is Doctor Levy now, isn't it?"

"Yes, it is. I graduated last week."

Her mother smiled as if the Messiah Himself had just arrived in the kitchen. "Doctor Levy was just saying there is a concert at the bandstand this afternoon. Perhaps you would like to go."

"Will the West End Zionists be coming this time as well?" Celia asked.

"Just Robbie and I."

"Well, West End Zionists or not," Madame Kahn said, pouring herself another cup of tea. "I think you should go, Celia. It is such a lovely day. I can manage the ironing and the cleaning. And preparing the dinner. Off you go with these fine young men. You don't need an old woman like me for company."

Jonny made some flattering remark to her mother which made her tuck in her chins in a sort of girlish embarrassment. Then she shooed them all out into the street. Robbie, with never any intention to go listen to a bandstand concert hung back in a doorway to light up a cigarette while Jonny led her gently by the elbow down the street. It was Flora Harris' young daughter, she with the one eye from the careless use of a knitting needle some years back, who called after them: "Celia's got a boyfriend, Celia's got a boyfriend."

She walked with him in silence for a while without any firm direction although she knew they were generally heading for Queens Park where outdoor concerts were held. A pillar box narrowed their passage along the pavement, forcing him in closer to her. She felt something pressed into her hand, then his fingers in a wrap around her own. She looked down. She was holding an orange.

"Where did you get that?"

"It's from Seville. I've kept it in an ice-box for months."

She took the orange, smelt its skin, the faint tangy flavour, a souvenir of some distant sunshine, slipped it into her coat pocket, kept on walking. He went quiet on her after that, acting a bit twitchy, fidgeting away with his hands, putting her on edge too. She wouldn't have minded one of Robbie's cigarettes, something to calm her nerves.

"I've booked my passage," he said. "Now that I've graduated."

"You're going to Palestine," she said, the words coming out flat, not even inflected into a question, more as a statement to herself.

"Yes. Palestine."

"When are you leaving?"

"In about six weeks."

She walked on, thrust her hands in her pockets, felt the orange there, surprised the warm-coloured skin should feel so cold. "What's on the programme?"

"Programme? What programme?"

"The bandstand programme. Or isn't there any concert?"

He pulled her to a halt. "Come with me," he said.

"To the park?"

"No. To Palestine."

She laughed although she hadn't really meant to. This was a serious matter. "Why would I do that?"

"You know what I'm asking."

"That's the point, Jonny. I don't know what you're asking."

She realised they had come to a stop outside her father's tailoring shop. In the window, a mannequin in a dinner suit, the cloth bleached in places by sunlight, a dead rose in the lapel, the display had been there for as long as she could remember. Beyond the glass, she could see her father working at a jacket on his long work bench. She could see the glint of the pinheads from a wrap across his forearm. She turned to look at Jonny. She noticed the skin on his cheeks and chin blue-black shiny from the lack of a shave, his eyes wide and questioning.

"Why do men always disappoint me?" she thought. "Why do they always disappoint me?"

* * *

Celia had been in his office for over five minutes and he had not said a word. Instead, Mr Ronald Sneddon, senior partner of Sneddon, Baxter and Co., Solicitors and Notaries Public of West Nile Street, Glasgow merely perused the legal documents before him, occasionally glancing up at her over his glasses and muttering, "hmmhmm, hmmhmm." It was a dark office with any light that could have shone through the large window being blocked off by the closeness of an ugly blank wall opposite. Within this lack of sunlight, Mr Ronald Sneddon presented himself as a rotund silhouette, hunched over a desklamp that bore down exclusively on the text in front of him. She read off some of the titles on his bookshelf – *The Principles of Scots Law, Cases Decided by The Court of Session, The Scottish Law Review, Acts of Sederunt* – until the lack of light forced her to give up her task. She took off her gloves, folded them on her lap. Mr Ronald Sneddon emitted some more 'hmmhmms' before finally looking up.

"Do you know why you are here, Miss Kahn?" he asked. "Apart

from the fact that the late Mrs Ferguson left you a note to come to these offices."

"Mrs Ferguson? No – I'm here because of Miss Calder."

"Ah, yes. You could be forgiven for not knowing such a thing. For Miss Calder was only wed for a few weeks. She and her husband, Kenneth Ferguson, married just before the war. Then in a pique of patriotism I have never understood, he volunteered as soon as hostilities broke out. He was one of its first casualties. He was a captain. He was also a partner in this law firm. A dear friend." Mr Sneddon poked his glasses further up his nose. "I can see you are nonplussed by this information, Miss Kahn. Well, I am afraid I am going to surprise you some more. Perhaps you would like a glass of water before we continue? Or I can ask my secretary to bring us some tea?"

She did not want water or tea. She only wanted to know why her late friend would conceal such an important detail from her. And yet she had to prepare for more news to come. She shivered herself further upright on her chair, altered the position of the gloves on her lap so that the bottom one was now at the top. "That is very kind of you, Mr Sneddon. But please continue."

"I will therefore ask you again. Have you any idea why the late Mrs Ferguson asked you to attend these offices?"

"I can only assume it is to help with organising the disposal of any furniture or personal items. She rented a flat in the West End. I visited there many times."

"The rented flat to which you refer was actually owned by my late partner who, on his death, left it to his widow. Mrs Ferguson was a woman of property. And coupled with the fact that she would have been over the age of thirty years had she continued living, she would have had the right to vote under the restrictions of the Representation of the People Act 1918. A fact which I am sure would have pleased her suffragette sensibilities. Hmmm." Mr Sneddon glanced down at his papers, ran a fat forefinger from one line of text to another, then continued. "All this brings me to the point of this visit. Which is that Mrs Ferguson has willed you a liferent in this property to which we are referring."

"A liferent, Mr Sneddon?"

"Yes, a liferent. The name is an apt description of its purpose. You have the right to live in Mrs Ferguson's property for as long as your natural life. Should you choose to give up this right at any time, then be so kind as to inform me accordingly. I will then arrange for the disposal of the asset and the proceeds will be distributed to various charities as instructed."

She touched her breastbone as she had been taught in deportment class. Inhale. Then a long exhale. Inhale. Then a long exhale. Calm the nerves and the female disposition. Act like a young lady. Back straight. "Do I understand correctly that I am to receive a free tenancy of Agnes' … Mrs Ferguson's flat?"

"Under certain conditions."

"But Mr Sneddon. Even if I wanted to, I cannot afford to live in a flat on my own. I have no income. I cannot pay bills or rates or insurance."

"Your concern is perfectly understandable. But let me assure you that all bills for your necessary use of the property shall be paid for by this firm on behalf of Mrs Ferguson's estate. For a period of five years. After that time, while your actual occupation shall remain rent-free, you will have to assume responsibility for these other costs. At such time, you may decide to give up your liferent and I will dispose of the property as previously described." Sneddon sat back in his chair, causing his buttoned-up waistcoat to expand dangerously over his large belly. He fanned himself with the pages of Agnes' will. "Mrs Ferguson also stipulated in her final testament that the property … and here I shall read … 'should be used partly for the continued hosting of committee meetings for socialists and feminists alike as well as to provide a focal point for the distribution of information related to … hhhmmm … birth control.' These are the only conditions." Sneddon rose from his seat, walked his bulky frame to the door, switched on an electric light as if this somehow would help illuminate her thoughts. She could hear his breathlessness as he waddled by her on his return to his chair.

"I understand that this may be a bit of a shock to you," he continued, his complexion now reddened from his brief excursion. "A pleasant one I hope. As you know, it is a rather attractive property in a tree-lined West End street. But, if you will allow me, I also believe that I can help clarify Mrs Ferguson's intentions towards you. She did say to me when I asked the reason for her rather unusual bequest that she would like to offer you an opportunity. 'So that Miss Kahn will have a chance to be herself,' she said to me. 'To be herself.' Those were her words. Only you, of course, know what that means. Would you like some time to think about all of this?"

"Yes… yes, I would. I cannot respond to this now. All this information is rather overwhelming."

"I am sure it is. Why don't you take the keys from reception, Miss Kahn? Take yourself over there for a visit. Perhaps after that, you can tell me what you decide. For five years at least, the property will be totally paid for, maintained, and administered by myself. On production of the relevant receipts, of course. You have been allocated some public duties. But beyond that, all you have to do is enjoy the accommodation as you please."

She had never visited the vacant home of a deceased person before. As soon as she had crossed the threshold, it felt that all of Agnes' furniture and personal possessions in this flat were dead too. As if Agnes by virtue of her ownership had infused these items with a certain essence that had now disappeared with her passing. The armchair sagged, the upright piano silenced, the desk-ink dried to a crust, the fire-irons redundant, the silver-handled hairbrush rendered obsolete, the uncollected post unread and irrelevant. Surfaces were layered with dust. The wall clock in the hall had stopped. She stood on a chair, took down the rather heavy timepiece, wound up the mechanism, put it back. She listened as the renewed ticking began to restore some of the lifeblood back into the empty flat. She opened windows, cleaned surfaces, beat carpets, polished brasses, sorted out piles of clothes, stacked out-of-date pamphlets, so many pamphlets, it was a wonder the place had not gone up in smoke. A solitary spark from the fire onto one of these piles and Agnes could have been burned alive by her own pamphlets of protest. A suffragette sacrifice. A witch at the stake. She bundled up the piles of papers, took them out to the midden.

Back in the flat, she collapsed into an armchair, sat splay-legged like a man, like Agnes, lit up a cigarette, watched the smoke curl around this space she had the right to live in for the rest of her natural life. She had a liferent in that fireplace over there, that dresser, that Ottoman, that coat-stand, that piano, those samplers. Come the revolution, Agnes, and we'll all have liferents to fancy flats in the West End. She smiled to herself at that notion. But what was she thinking of? She couldn't live here by herself. What would she tell her parents? Young women didn't live alone unless they were elderly spinsters with deceased parents, war widows with young children, or prostitutes. Yes, that was what her mother would call her if she told her the truth. A prostitute. Or more likely in Yiddish – *kurveh*. She rose from the armchair, moved into the bedroom, dusting surfaces as she went. She had a liferent in this bed, this mirror, these ornaments, this tallboy. "Why not just leave me a few pieces of your silverware and be done with it, Agnes? Those I could have sold to pay off my uncle's debts." She opened up a drawer in one of the bedside cabinets. Inside, a bag of Soor Plooms, stuck together, covered in fuzz.

She sat down at the dressing table with its smell of stale make-up powder, picked up the silver-handled hairbrush, faced the mirror. It was divided into three hinged sections, so she played with the wings until she could see the profiles of all these Celias stretching back forever and into infinity. What did the millionth image of her reflection look like? Or the billionth? Would she be older or younger in time? She scraped the brush through her hair, feeling the bristles harsh against her scalp. She stroked harder, watched the tears wash over her eyes, dampen her lashes.

"I should have been there for you, Agnes," she said to her reflection. "I should have been there for you." She leaned into the mirror, nipped some colour into her face. "But if that Jimmy Docherty finds it was your own smoke-stained lungs that got you…" She twisted open one of Agnes' compacts, patted some powder on to her cheeks. "…I might just take you up on your bequest."

Glasgow
1923

Nineteen

"Celia, Celia," her mother called. "Come and see this. *Komm, komm, komm.*"

"A minute." She finished pinning the brooch to her collar, glanced quickly at her reflection in the mirror above the kitchen mantelpiece, went out into the hallway. The electric lights, full on even though it was still afternoon, illuminating the shiny black device that sat on the hall table. Her father, mother and Nathan standing there beaming smiles at her as if Moses himself had arrived on their doorstep with the Ten Commandments.

"Well?" Nathan asked. "What do you think?"

"What can I say? The Kahn family have finally entered the modern era."

"About time too," Nathan added. "Every home should have a telephone. I can't believe you waited this long, Papa."

"Just because it is new, does not mean it is good," Papa Kahn said. "Before if you wanted something done, you would go and ask. If you wanted to see a friend, you would go and visit. There would be real, human contact. You shook a hand, you kissed a cheek, you saw the look in their eyes. Now you get lazy. You stay at home. You only hear a voice."

"It's not such a bad thing," her mother said. "With my varicose veins, I shouldn't have to *schlep* up and down this building shaking hands and kissing cheeks with my neighbours."

"It pushes human relationships further apart," Papa Kahn warned with a wave of a bony finger to no-one in particular.

"And it brings those further apart closer together," Nathan countered.

"Who is so far apart?" Papa Kahn grumbled. "Everyone I know lives in the Gorbals."

"What about Avram?"

"Avram?"

"Yes. Why don't you call him? I have the telephone number of his clothing shop in Oban."

"I can do that? I can telephone all the way to Oban? This is a miracle."

"Yes, Papa," Celia said. "Call Avram. Tell him it is time to come home. Staying away from us all these years, it is ridiculous." She put on her beret, ran her fingers over the telephone as she passed. Quite beautiful it was, like a glossy black daffodil. "Now, I must go."

"Where to this time?" her mother asked.

"A meeting in the West End."

"Another meeting? We are like a bed and breakfast for you. Kahn's B&B. At Celia's convenience. When will it be time for you to come home?"

"I don't know. I will probably stay overnight at Charlotte's. It is safer than travelling across the city in the dark."

"I see. And this Charlotte? Do her parents own a telephone too? In case we need to speak to our only daughter."

There were five of them. Five women. They made up the core. Apart from herself, there was Charlotte, Maggie, Big Bessie and Christine. The Suffragette Five. She had known them for several years now, up through the ranks of the socialist Sunday schools, then the Women's Peace Crusade, sitting together on various other committees on the way. Intimidating they had been to her at first, before she settled down to being one of the pack. A pack of she-wolves. Or bitches. Ready to scratch and bite if threatened. Not only by men, but also by each other.

Big Bessie was large and in charge with a wrinkled face that could collect raindrops in its folds, plump upper arms that wobbled when she laughed. Charlotte was the wealthy, stylish one, the one with the men's suits, the crimson slash of lipstick, the long cigarettes. Then there was Maggie, the former munitions worker with real muscles from handling all those shell-casings during the war, still wearing her boiler-suit even though it had been years since she'd seen the inside of a factory. And finally, Christine, a tiny bird of a church-going woman who barely spoke a word, making Celia feel heavy and loquacious by comparison.

Charlotte was her favourite. She got on well enough with the rest, but they tended to come together as comrades and part as comrades once the work was done, without a real friendship struck in between. These flexible relationships reminding her that feminism and social-ism could unite them yet the day-to-day demands of religion and class could still divide. But here they all were now, sitting around a table in the kitchen of her liferent flat, passing round a bottle of cream sherry to share, four candles at the centre lit in memory of the years since Agnes' death, Maggie with a reminiscence to tell.

"I recall one time Agnes was out on one of these big union marches," she said, her mouth turned down grim even though the anecdote was a fond one. "You know what she was like, looking around for some kind of raised spot from which to better berate the masses. She ended up getting four hefty miners to fetch a wooden hoarding, hoist her up on it onto their shoulders so she had herself a platform. Half-way through her speech about higher wages for the workers, one of the miners below her shouted: 'I can see up your skirts.' To which she replied quick as a wink: 'Well, that's the only rise ye'll be getting if ye dinnae let me get on with ma speech.'"

Celia laughed along with the rest of them despite having heard the story many times before. Still it was good to think about Agnes again. She just hoped she could properly honour her memory this night. After all she had been preparing for it for years. Big Bessie picked up a small brass bell, gave it a delicate shake. The meeting came to order.

"Comrades, comrades," Big Bessie said. "It is four years since our dear friend passed. If she were alive today she would probably be turning in her grave at the sight of what's been going on in this great city of ours…"

"Ye cannae say that," Maggie hissed.

"What can't I say?"

"If she were alive today, she'd be turning in her grave. That's a mixed metaphor or something."

"Jesus Christ, Maggie, I was only making a point."

"And the point is…?"

"That poverty has bitten so hard in this city, it breaks my heart to witness. The dole queues are longer, the women can't eke out a living from the parish relief, more and more bairns are dying of the tuberculosis, free milk in school is being restricted. Half the children in my wee lassie's gym class cannae exercise because their limbs are twisted with rickets. People are sick and starving. They used to talk about Glasgow being Moscow on the Clyde. But any socialist fight's been beaten out of the working class by the twin fists of unemployment and despair. It's a disgrace and an embarrassment. Families are better off in Munich and Vienna. And they're the ones who lost the war. We've done our best to support the political struggle with a few successes. We've now got ten Labour MPs pleading our cause in Parliament. But what are we women to do? We need to change our tactics to tackle the wretched nature of things. And given that this day is the anniversary of our comrade Agnes' death, I believe Celia has something to propose regarding our old friend's legacy."

Celia stood up, looked around at the four faces staring back at her through a fug of tobacco smoke, strange to be feeling so nervous given she'd spoken out to these women so many times in the past. She picked at the brooch at her collar, Agnes' brooch, the one that had come to her in that plain brown package from the jail. "As you know, when Agnes died she left me a liferent in this flat…"

"Why you?" It was Maggie again, folding her thick arms as she stared straight at her. "Aye, why you? I always wondered that."

"Oh, Agnes always had a wee fancy for our Celia," Charlotte interrupted with a couple of puffs of her cigarette into the air. "Didn't you know that, Maggie? She preferred those dark, svelte young things to you big beefy types." Charlotte's bright red lips broke into a smirk. "Isn't that right, Celia?"

She said nothing, knew it was better to leave Charlotte's little innuendos alone, otherwise she would just come back at her with another.

"Don't play coy with me," Charlotte continued to poke. "I've never known you to mention any male love interest in your life. We just assumed you and Agnes were… how shall I put it? … sapphically entwined."

"Well, you assumed incorrectly," Celia said, left with no choice but to defend the blush to her face. "In fact, with your gents' tailoring, I always thought it was you who were…"

"… I've no heard ma Archie complain about my beefy proportions," Maggie piped into the conversation.

"That's because he's a butcher," Charlotte responded. "He likes a nice juicy slab of meat." More laughter. Big Bessie rang the bell again.

"For goodness sake, comrades. A few glasses of sherry and you're at each other's throats. Now please let Celia continue." Big Bessie peered over her nose at the company then back to Celia. "Well?"

"As I was saying, when Agnes died she left me a liferent in this flat so we could continue to hold our meetings here. But there was another condition too. I've held back talking about it because it's a touchy subject and we've had other matters on our plate. But I feel now the time is right to pursue Agnes' wishes. Because so many of the problems that Bessie has just mentioned could be solved by doing so. And that is to further the cause of birth control in this city." She held up Stopes' book. *Wise Parenthood*. "Has anyone read this?"

Silence. A few intakes of tobacco, ash flicked into saucers, chairs scraping on the lino.

"Where did you get it?" Charlotte asked.

"It was among Agnes' possessions from the jail."

"What's your point?" Maggie asked.

Celia took a breath, steadied herself. "If we really want to lift families out of poverty," she said. "If we really want to rescue women from the tyranny of their husbands' sexual appetites, this book clearly tells us the road to follow."

"And what road is that?" Maggie again. "Victoria Road? Argyle Street?"

"Giving women proper knowledge about birth control."

Again silence. To her surprise, it was the normally quiet Christine who spoke first.

"It's not right."

"What's not right?"

"You asking us to discuss this."

"Why not?"

"All this sex talk. It's men's business. Down at the pub with their smutty tongues."

"That's the whole point," Celia countered. "It is about women talking. About women taking responsibility for their own bodies. It's about lifting women out of their ignorance."

"It's loose women's talk," Christine went on, wringing the silver wedding band on her finger as she spoke, her neck flushed from the yoke of her Fair Isle sweater right up to the hairs on her chin. "Whores' talk."

"You're a married woman, Christine," Celia said, trying to keep her composure. "Where did you get your information on sex?"

"I told you. I don't want to talk about this."

"What about you, Bessie?"

Big Bessie's loud laughter broke through the tension. "I'll tell you what my dear dead mother told me." And here Bessie put on a voice of a prim matron. "The bairn comes out the same way as it got in."

"That was it?"

"Aye, that was it. The entire words of wisdom imparted before I was wafted away to the marital bed. She might as well have been talking about a wee lad scampering up a chimney."

"One black hole's same as any other," Charlotte said.

Big Bessie scowled. "Enough of your cheek."

"Well, I'm still not having anything to do with a contraception crusade," Christine insisted.

"Why are you so against it?" Celia asked.

"Because I'm a Catholic, that's why."

"How many children have you got?"

Christine wrapped her arms around her thin body. "Six."

"And how many have you lost on the way?"

"Another three."

"Have you not done your insides enough damage?"

"My man will have nothing to do with any contraception. And

neither will the priest. I don't know what you Jews do in the bedroom. But no-one's telling me to go against the word of the Pope."

"I'm not in favour of birth control either," Maggie said. "And I'm no a Catholic. I just think you've got to let human nature take its course."

"Let man's nature take it's course you mean," Big Bessie sniffed.

"Doesn't matter whose nature," Maggie replied. "I dinnae want to walk around with any rubber appliance inserted up my secret passage."

"What about you, Charlotte?" Celia asked.

Charlotte was flicking through the pages of Stopes' book. "I'd like to read this. Anyone else after me?"

"I'll have a go," Big Bessie said. "But I'll tell you what worries me. It's all very well giving women information about birth control. But where are they going to get the money to pay for it? I cannae see your average working class wifie asking for extra money out of her man's pay packet. 'Excuse me, Tommy. Can I have a few extra pennies to buy a Dutch cap?' He'll probably thinks it's a new bonnet from Holland I'm after."

Charlotte cornered her afterwards in the hallway. She had a habit of talking up close like some kind of spy. Perhaps it was a habit she had picked up during the war. 'Careless talk costs lives' the posters used to say. She had always thought Charlotte was a bit of the Mata Hari type anyway, her voice coming out hoarse and breathless on a gust of tobacco.

"I apologise for teasing you back then," Charlotte whispered.

"I didn't mind really."

"Well, I just thought… you know… never knowing you with a man in your life. There isn't anybody, is there?"

She shook her head.

"I'm sorry. I've embarrassed you."

Celia stood there as Charlotte fingered the collar of her blouse then patted it down flat. It was a strange action yet something her father would have done, Papa Kahn checking on the texture of the cloth before making sure it sat just right. "It would be a pity if you didn't have someone though," Charlotte continued. "Given that you've got yourself a nice little love nest here."

"I'm a social purist, Charlotte. No sexual intercourse. No marriage."

Charlotte smiled. "Well, that's the best form of birth control, isn't it? So what's made you get on your high horse about Stopes then?"

"It's something Agnes believed in. And I happen to agree with her. And now that one of the Labour councillors in Govan has started agitating for a family planning centre, I thought it was a good time to get involved."

"Bessie's right about the cost though. It's all right for the middle-classes like Stopes to be wittering on about contraception. It's the working-class women who need it most. Yet have the least means to pay for it."

"I agree. If you've just got feminism without any of the socialism attached, you just end up with a whole lot of privileged women sitting around being aggressive. We need to get the message and the means of contraception out to the poor. I was hoping we could get some kind of funding. Maybe from the Labour Party. Buy in come caps from France, distribute them for free."

"I see you've got all this figured out." Charlotte looked around, then moved in even closer. "I could contribute a little something myself."

"What do you mean?"

"My father, as you probably know, is very wealthy. It would be no great hardship to deprive him of some loose change to further the feminist cause. After all, he could do with a little birth control himself given the way he goes around distributing his seed." Charlotte flicked a quick smile at her.

"That would be very helpful."

Charlotte returned her attention to fingering her collar again. "I was also wondering whether you might consider renting out a room."

"I thought you were an heiress living in a grand mansion?"

"Well, I happen to have a gentleman in my life at the moment. And having access to a pleasant room in the West End would be extremely convenient. Utmost discretion guaranteed from all parties. And the best practice of birth control firmly in place."

She laughed to herself. Charlotte had trapped her nicely. An offer of money on the one hand, a friendly favour on the other. But then again, she'd never told Charlotte she used her as a cover story whenever she decided to bed down in Agnes' flat for the night. "Why don't you read the Stopes book," she suggested. "Then we can talk again."

Twenty

To be late was to steal someone else's time. That was what Agnes used to tell her. If that were the case, she certainly was a thief now. For the clock at Gorbal's Cross told her she was late for dinner. And not just any dinner. But the meal before the *Kol Nidre* service, the mountains of food necessary to sustain her during the fast of *Yom Kippur*. The Day of Atonement. When she had to repent for all her sins of the last year so that once again her name could be written in the Book of Life. She stepped up her pace. Jew Street. Gentile Street. Gentile Street. Jew Street. Her own Thistle Street almost empty, no doubt all the sinners busy indoors getting dressed up for synagogue or already at table stuffing their faces. As if twenty-four hours or so without eating or drinking was the greatest hardship that could befall them. She knew poor families elsewhere in the city for whom a mere one day of starvation would be a blessing.

The flat was surprisingly quiet. Dark too, all the doors off the hallway sealed against her, the telephone already unplugged for fear it might ring during this holiest of days. For a dreadful moment, she thought she might have missed dinner altogether, that her family were already repenting in the synagogue. She opened the door to the living room. A figure rose from one of the chairs to greet her.

"My God," she exclaimed. "Look at you."

Avram. He had left a boy, returned a man. What had happened to that little Russian immigrant? Tall and straight he had become, cheeks chafed from the country air, a fine suit on his back. A credit draper turned successful purveyor of waterproof clothing in Oban

163

High Street. Smocks, coats, hats and leggings all made from airplane fabric, designed by her brother Nathan, manufactured by the staff at Kahn & Son Tailoring. Avram. Her own personal hero those few years back when Solly had concocted some football betting scheme to release Uncle Mendel from his gambling debts. "Don't ask," Solly had told her at the time. "Just don't ask. But everything is fine. Avram saved the day. Your Uncle Mendel is safe."

She dumped her bag full of notebooks and pamphlets down on a chair. "Don't you have a hug for me?" she said.

He came towards her, clasped her around her waist, swung her around, making her feel like a bride. Once he had dropped her back onto her feet, she held him at arm's length, then moved in to kiss him on both cheeks.

"Is that a kiss for a comrade?" he asked.

"That's a kiss for someone I've missed very much." She looked him up and down. "My, my. You've grown up."

"So have you. You look beautiful."

"Thank you. Beautiful but with bags under my eyes." She danced around him as if he were a model on display. "A brotherly compliment, I assume."

"I'm not your brother."

"Might as well be." She let herself drop down into an armchair, took out a packet of cigarettes from a coat pocket.

"They let you?" he asked.

"They can't stop me." She picked up the chunky solid-silver lighter usually reserved for guests. She flicked at the lever several times but without success. "Damn," she said, rummaging again in her coat pockets until she found a box of matches. "Why are you staring?"

"You've changed."

"You mean I smoke and swear."

"Perhaps."

"Perhaps you are wondering what happened to darling little Celia?" She blew a couple of purses of smoke into the air. Just like Charlotte, she thought. She realised she was starting to do that quite a lot recently. Copying her friend's mannerisms.

"You were always different."

"Not 'always' surely?"

"Yes, always. I remember you wanted to be a clippie. You could only have been sixteen then. The last time I saw you, you were off to a demonstration in George Square."

"You tried to give me that silver thimble. And I refused to take it. Oh, Avram, you must forgive me. I was so heartless."

"I forgave you a long time ago."

"Good. That's one less sin I need to repent for later."

He laughed at that, they both did. "Go on, sit down," she said. "You're making me nervous."

He hiked up his trousers at the knees, sat down opposite, crossed his legs. His shoes were polished up so fine she fancied she could see the ceiling reflected in them. In fact, everything about him was just right. The handkerchief straight-lined in his top pocket, the starched-white collar and cuffs, the knot of the tie, the crease in his trousers cut sharp, the socks gartered up tight, she realised he would want to impress. This immigrant child who had once turned up on their doorstep with nothing. He tapped his fingers on the arm of the chair.

"You must have other men chasing you now?"

"I'm a Jewish spinster through and through. Twenty-three years old, left on the shelf. Even dear Mama has given up on me."

"I find that hard to believe. What about that chap Jonny Levy?"

"How do you know about him?"

"Uncle Mendel mentioned a while back he'd been courting you."

"Courting me? He took me berry-picking once in Blairgowrie."

"I remember him. He used to play football with us on the streets. A bit older though. What happened to him?"

"He went off to Palestine to build a *kibbutz* with his own bare hands."

"Socialism in the sunshine. That would be right up your street."

"Sometimes I threaten Mama and Papa that I will go there too. If you don't let me do this, I'll just go off to Palestine to see Jonny Levy. They hate it."

"I thought they would like you going off with a Jewish boy. You'd get to keep the candlesticks."

"They don't want me going to Palestine. They're in favour of

Zionism for all the other Jews. But they believe they have a perfectly good Jewish homeland right here in the Gorbals. Jerusalem on the Clyde, they call it. Anyway, what about you? Have you found yourself a pretty country lass?"

"I think I have."

She felt the slightest twinge of remorse. It was the way he had lifted her up this now, spun her around. No-one had ever done that to her before. Easy as you like. "And who is she? This country lass who has stolen your heart. I can't imagine there are many Jewish girls residing north of Loch Lomond."

"Her name is Megan," he said. "And she's not Jewish."

"Mama and Papa will not approve. Have you told them yet?"

"I don't need their approval. I'm not their real son. I'm also a young man of independent means living far away from this Gorbals *shtetl.*"

"Tell me about her."

He rubbed his palm back and forward across his chin, suddenly all thoughtful. "It's a difficult situation."

"What do you mean?"

"She's pregnant."

"My goodness. You're going to be a father."

"It's more complicated than that. It's not my child."

"I don't understand. If it's not your child then…"

"She doesn't want it. She's come down here for…" His voice trailed away, he sat staring at his hands.

"For what?" she asked.

"To… to get rid of it."

"You mean an abortion."

He reddened at the word, looked furtively around the room as if a constable might jump out at him for just saying it. "Yes, an abortion," he whispered. "I'm paying for it. And I've come down with her to make sure she'll be all right. She said there was a good chance it would be fine. If it was done early."

"That's just her being brave. It's a bad business. You've got to be lucky to survive, early or not. If she doesn't bleed to death, the infection can kill her."

"How do you know so much about it?"

"It's my business to know these things. Are you sure this child isn't yours?"

"I told you already."

"Well, you're going to an awful lot of bother for someone not carrying your own."

"I suppose I am."

"So where is she, this Megan?"

"I've put her up in an hotel in the city."

"When is the appointment?"

"Seven-thirty this evening."

"Right in the middle of the *Kol Nidre* service."

"She didn't want me around anyway. But I'll try to get away right after synagogue is finished. Just to make sure she's all right."

"And I'll come with you. This is woman's work, Avram. You wouldn't have a clue what to do."

Her mother stood at the doorway. "I see the wanderer has returned," she said, looking at each of them, dwelling smugly on the ambiguity of her statement. "Ah yes, returned for the High Holidays without telling anyone. Expecting dinner to be on the table. Just like that." Her mother tried to snap her fingers in emphasis but failed.

Twenty-one

YOM KIPPUR. The Day of Atonement. To confess, to ask for forgiveness, to start life afresh. Yet looking down on the congregation from her perch high up in the synagogue all she could think about was death. Death, death, death. The death of an unborn child – her own child. Was that not the sin that could never be forgiven? No matter how much she fasted, beat her heart with her fist, she still felt it as the murder of an innocent life. It had been years since she had consciously thought about her own abortion, somehow locking away the memory in some secret vault in her mind. But the poison from that event still seeped through to her life, staining her every mood, word, deed and dream. Agnes, God bless her, had arranged everything, ferrying her to and from some place in the East End in a hansom, made the necessary excuses to her parents for her absence. She had found the best woman she could to carry it out. Not some back-street abortionist working in a pool of infection but a retired mid-wife willing to take a risk with some proper sterile tools in exchange for the nice wad of guineas Agnes had put on the table. The danger had still remained great. But she'd caught the pregnancy early, her bleeding moderate, staunched quickly, the foetus discarded unseen and without fuss. And then she was back to scrubbing floors and white-washing walls as if nothing had happened. Except for the ache in her scraped-out womb. She refused to remember her rapist's name, yet she thought she saw him once. Walking along Buchanan Street in the city, hands in his pockets, watching his pock-marked reflection in the store windows, her reflection there too, witnessing his passing, his free and swaggering gait, no vicious memory staining his thoughts. She had often dreamed of what that encounter would be like, how she would stab him in the chest again and again with some blade miraculously come to hand. But when the time had actually come, she felt nothing at seeing him. Just a numbness as she watched him disappear down the steps to the St. Enoch Underground.

She looked down now at all these men below her in the congregation, standing up to face the Ark for the *Amidah* prayer. Her own father, frail and forgetful, clinging to his community. Dear Uncle Mendel beside him, no longer a gambler but still fond of his glass of *schnapps*, dreaming of the revolution that will never come, looking more and more towards religion than politics for his answers. In the row behind, Solly and his father Lucky Mo who preyed on the vices of men but were full of weaknesses of their own. And there was Avram making his way along the rows, causing quite a commotion. No-one was allowed to leave during the *Amidah* prayer, especially on *Kol Nidre* night, except if it were a matter of life or death. He glanced up at her, she caught his gaze. She closed her prayer book, touched her mother's gloved hand.

"I have to go," she whispered.

"Go? You cannot go. It is *Kol Nidre*. It is a sin to go. It is *verboten*. Come back, Celia. Come back. You can't do this to me."

They took a hansom to Trongate. 16 Saracen's Lane the address was, the alley running dark and narrow behind the back end of pubs, even the cab driver anxious about drawing up close. With only the occasional gas lamp, she found it hard to grope her way in the dark. No air from above, the stone walls dank and dripping, rats scurrying in the shadows, the cobbles slippery from slops carelessly thrown. This was the hell women had to visit to rid themselves of the indulgences of men. She took out her handkerchief, held it to her mouth. If this was where Megan had ended up, she was fearful for the fate of the girl.

"How can people live here?" Avram asked.

She didn't answer, instead slipping by him, lighting up a match, holding it to a doorway, the number 16 chalked on the stone. Avram beside her, knocking on the damp wood.

"Whit?" a voice said sharply from behind the door. "Whit, whit, whit?"

"Is Megan Kennedy there?" Avram shouted.

No response.

Avram asked again.

"Who?" came the voice.

Celia indicated for him to be quiet. "Megan Kennedy," she said. "We're looking for Megan Kennedy."

The clunking of a key in the lock. The door opened slightly, the light of a candle washed out into the lane along with the stink of ether. The woman was tiny, the candle glow showing a square face, the top of a head sparsely covered with clumps of reddish hair.

"Is that her?" the woman asked.

"Who?" Avram asked.

"The Oban lass."

"No, no. That's who we're looking for."

The woman peered at them both. "She's no been," she croaked, quickly withdrawing the candle. "She was due a half-hour ago. But she's no been." The door closed in their faces.

She ran with Avram back to the hotel, only a few streets away. Megan wasn't in her room. He tried the communal bathroom but it was locked. He banged away at the door, not rousing anyone until Celia managed to find the concierge, handy enough to open it up quickly with a skeleton key. Megan lay unconscious in the bath, still in her slip, skin blue-wrinkled, a bottle of gin empty on the floor. She laid her head against the poor girl's cold breast, could just make out a faint heartbeat. Avram picked the body out of the water, the cotton fabric clinging, nipples visible through the material, water dripping all over the place. She covered her with a towel, the concierge leering, trying to get a better look, Avram giving him a ten-shilling note, telling him to go back down to his desk.

Back in the bedroom, she rubbed Megan's cold body hard with the towel. The girl's fair hair was fanned out wet against the pillow, and she could see why Avram could be taken with such a lass. "Old wives tales," she said. "Soak in a boiling hot tub. Flush it out with gin. Women can be so stupid. So desperate."

"Will she be all right?"

"I don't know. How am I supposed to know? Why should I know such things?" Avram stepped back from her, a helpless look on his face. "I'm sorry," she said. "We just need to get her warm first. Go see if there are any more blankets in the wardrobe."

"What about the baby?"

"We'll have to wait until the morning to find out. You stay with her. I'll ask the concierge for a hot-water bottle."

She stayed up all night in the hotel, wrapped in a blanket in a chair in the vestibule, Avram upstairs in a vigil by Megan's bedside. She had tried to call home to lie to her parents about where they were, but the operator was unable to put her through. By the morning, Megan had woken, temperature normal, no signs of any discomfort beyond a terrible headache. The baby would probably survive. She walked home through the park, still in her synagogue finery, the avenues dressed in their yellow and golden leaves. She picked up a chestnut fallen on the pathway, its prickly shell burst open to reveal the shiny nut within. There was such a beauty at this time of year, she thought. And such a sadness too.

Nathan brought in the card-table, set it up close to the fire, patted the green baize top, indicated that she and Avram should take their places. It was a good thing to do, play cards while the rest of the house sulked in such a terrible silence, Nathan was sensitive to situations like that.

Avram had done what he was supposed to do on *Yom Kippur*. Asked for forgiveness. He told Papa and Madame Kahn about Megan, about her attempted abortion, about how he would now take care of both mother and child back in Oban. Her own mother had then proceeded to bang out some patriotic British tunes on the piano while her father went off to take another nap.

"The shame of it," her mother said before following her father into the bedroom. "The shame of it." It was that shame that was shrouding the flat in such a tension.

"It's so damn hot in here," Avram said as he drew open a window. "It feels like thunder in the air."

Nathan dealt out the cards. "Come on, sit," he said.

In her first hand, the only hearts she held were the two and three. "Never be low in hearts," Uncle Mendel used to tell her. "Never be low in hearts."

"I shall leave tomorrow," Avram announced, as he laid out a flush of diamonds, ten to ace, on the table. "I've caused enough trouble."

"A flying visit," she said.

"Yes, a flying visit."

"Flies in, stirs up the dust, flies out again," Nathan added before laying out four kings on the beige. "I'll have to pick up the pieces as usual."

She leaned over, ruffled his white hair. "You're so good at that, little brother. A right little fixer."

Nathan shook her off, turned to Avram. "Do you know why this pretty young lady never went off to Palestine with Jonny Levy?"

"Do tell me." Avram placed another set of cards on the table. "I've got three left."

"Three left," she said, trying to find some kind of redeeming feature in the cards she held. "Three bloody cards. I've got nothing."

"I think you're bluffing." Nathan grabbed her free hand by the wrist, held it up to Avram. "You see, this urban miss was terrified she'd break these red-painted nails digging up the soil."

She flicked her fingers at Avram. "What do you think? Red. It's the modern style."

"I'd just like to know why you didn't go."

"It was so long ago, I cannot remember."

"Come on, Celia. I'm sure that's not true."

"All right then. I was asked for all the wrong reasons."

"You see, Avram. That's my sister. As enigmatic as ever. As I said, she didn't want to break these nails."

"Enough with the nails, Nathan. Jonny Levy just didn't know how to deal with a woman like me."

"I don't think any *kibbutz* would know how to deal with a woman like you."

"Going to a *kibbutz* would not be such a bad idea," she said as she discarded one card, picked up another. A joker. That changed everything. "At least, they treat men and women equally."

"You mean the men wear red nail varnish as well," Avram said.

She laughed at that. They all did. And she remembered how they used to sit together like this, just the three of them, in a far more innocent time.

Twenty-two

CHARLOTTE SAT ON THE ARMCHAIR facing her, slouched down so far her bottom was nearly off the seat, her long-trousered legs stretched out in front of her. As usual, she smoked a cigarette, drawing nervously from it in short inhalations, then breathing out the smoke through her nostrils. Like a dragon. Charlotte the Dragon. Celia thought the appellation appropriate. Suck, suck, suck. It was the only sound in the room. They both stared at the pile of boxes in the centre.

On the day before *Yom Kippur*, they had driven down in a hansom to the Clydeside docks to collect them, steeled themselves with brandy from Charlotte's flask on the way. But they needn't have bothered preparing any explanations for the customs officer. The cheery young clerk had just handed over the cartons no questions asked, tried to be friendly to the two tipsy young women in front of him. The delivery note read "French caps – six gross." "You'll never sell berets to Glasgow folk," he had told them. "It's bowlers or flat caps for the men around here." They had just giggled at that, Charlotte blowing him a scarlet lipstick kiss, just to make sure he remembered them for next time.

"Eight hundred and sixty four bloody caps," Charlotte said. "Is that right? Six gross? I was never very good at my times tables."

"Exactly right. Three sizes. Small, medium and large. Two hundred and eighty eight in each size. How many women can we equip?"

"Depends how active they are, doesn't it? Stopes suggests having a spare. But she's not someone who needs to worry about the price of things."

"Look after them right, wash them carefully, keep checking them, and they can last up to two years."

"But every woman has a different effect on the rubber. So let's recommend one per woman per year."

"Listen to us. It's like ration coupons all over again. Eight ounces of sugar, fifteen ounces of beef, four ounces of butter and one rubber cap from France, please."

Charlotte did her dragon nostril exhalation as she coughed out a laugh. "You can be quite funny sometimes, Celia. When you're not being so bloody serious. I thought you had just repented for your sins. That should lighten you up a bit."

"There's been a lot going on at home."

"You should tell me about it. I am your best friend after all."

"Just give me a cigarette, will you?"

Charlotte tossed the silver case at her. She took one of the ready-rolled, lit up. For some reason, she was feeling quite confident in herself. As if this was exactly what she was supposed to be doing, at precisely this time in her life, with the very person sitting in front of her. She exhaled through her nose like Charlotte. "What do you think? We'll hand out two hundred in each size. Keep the rest in reserve."

"Just for you and me?"

Celia threw back the cigarette case, harder than she needed to. "No. Not for you and me. For some poor wifie who might need a spare."

"That seems fair." Charlotte fished out a fob watch from her waistcoat, gave it a quick glance. She was looking more mannish than ever these days, now that she had her hair cut short in the latest style. Celia touched her own longish locks, wondered whether she had the courage to have these tresses shorn. It was something religious women did before they married, making themselves unattractive to other men.

"Do you think we can get away with this?" she asked.

Charlotte sniffed. "It's not against the law is it?"

"I don't know. It's against some people's religious law. You saw how angry Christine got with me. She thinks the Pope will excommunicate her for just thinking about birth control."

"It's also against some people's morality. This offer of pregnancy-free sex."

"They'll think we're promoting promiscuity."

"Turning Scotland's lasses into prostitutes."

"Jezebels from Jedburgh."

"Whores of the Highlands."

They both laughed at that, but Celia felt it was more nervous laughter than anything else. This offer of free contraceptives was a serious business.

"We need to have a strict policy about what we're doing here," she said. "We're not qualified to give out any medical advice. What we really need is a midwife to help us. Or even a sympathetic doctor."

"Well, I don't know anyone."

"Me neither. Which means we need to adopt a very practical approach. We need to tell people we have these devices available. Either through women's groups or just plain old word-of-mouth. Then we need to print up a copy of Stopes' instructions on how to fit them. And that's it. We don't give advice. We just provide availability and instruction. As with any retail product."

"*Caveat emptor.*"

"Yes, *caveat emptor.*"

"And I know someone who can do the printing for us."

"Settled then."

"Settled." Charlotte sat up in her chair, dipped her hand into one of the boxes. "Now I'm going to take two for myself if you don't mind. Size? Medium, I think. I trust Miss Social Purist won't be needing any?"

"Abstinence is the best form of contraception."

"I just don't understand you, Celia Kahn. A pretty lass like you. Is it a Jewish commandment? Thou shalt not have relations with a person of the opposite sex. Ever."

She laughed. "The Old Testament is full of immoral sexual activity. There's King David and Bathsheba. Lot and his two daughters and..."

A loud rap from the front door interrupted her.

"That'll be Brian now," Charlotte said. "Got to practise what I preach. You answer for me, will you darling? While I go and fit this thing."

Brian was a big, breezy, blond man. Some kind of ex-navy type, Celia guessed. What with his weather-roughed skin, peaked cap, coarse blue turtle-neck sweater tucked into the belt of his pants. All he needed was a kit-bag over his shoulder and he'd be off up some Clydebank gangplank, sailing off into the horizon. He wasn't at all what she expected. But then again what did she expect from Charlotte? Ivor Novello singing *Keep the Home Fires Burning*.

"She 'ere?" Brian asked in some kind of English accent. She would have put it down as Cockney if she had a mind to, just like these street urchins she had seen recently in a musical at The Alhambra. She immediately felt like imitating his dialect back at him. "Yeah, all roit, she's 'ere". Instead, her voice came out all prim, as if she were Charlotte's stuck-up maid. "She's just getting ready. Please come through."

Brian went into the living room, paced about restless, while she sat herself in an armchair, wished she had another one of Charlotte's cigarettes to keep her busy. He ignored the boxes in the centre of the room, instead picked up an ornament from the sideboard – a swirly glass ash-tray Agnes had used for guests – examined it, put it down again.

"Didn't expect someone else, see," he said.

She wasn't sure how to answer, didn't know what Charlotte had told him about this place. "I'll be off soon," she said noncommittally.

Brian grunted, went over to stand by the window, peered out as if the view out on to the back-green midden was of great interest to him.

"Brian," Charlotte called. "Are you there?"

Brian turned round, smiled sheepishly, then went into the bedroom. A few seconds later, Charlotte's head was at the door.

"You are going out, aren't you?"

"I'm on my way."

"I don't know why you don't just leave me a key."

"Agnes left this place to me. I feel responsible."

"I'm not going to set the building on fire."

"I said I feel responsible."

"You just like being in control."

"Let's not argue about this."

"Give me two hours then."

"I'll go for a walk in Kelvingrove. I like the autumn."

Charlotte gave her a quick smile, then disappeared back behind the door.

She went out into the hallway, made a noise and a fuss about opening and closing the front door, but then crept back into the living room, sat down in a chair close to the bedroom. She kept herself rigidly tight, her breath shallow and quiet. The wall clock ticked away. She noticed a layer of dust on the sideboard where the sunlight came in through a rear window. She remembered Brian standing there only a few minutes previously, his broad back to her, his neck red and scarred, smelling fresh and scrubbed-up, probably just been to the bath-house before coming here. She imagined Charlotte even making that a condition of his visit. She heard the springs of the mattress, Charlotte's murmur, then nothing. What was she doing here, head bowed, hands jammed between her knees, eavesdropping on her friend? She heard his voice this time, Brian's cocky Cockney, Charlotte giggling. She wanted it to be good between them, she wanted to know that his touch could be gentle and loving. The bed-springs again, she heard Charlotte gasp. A strange sound, caught between pleasure and pain, like too-cold ice cream on a hot summer's day. She remembered the vendor and his ice-cart that Sunday outside the Botanic Gardens on her own fateful day of sexual invasion. "Mr Luigi And His Famous Italian Ices" – that was the name. Penny-licks. She wanted to forget, to obliterate that memory. The bed-springs, Charlotte again. Short, sharp yelps like a trodden-on puppy. A loud groan from Brian. She rose quietly from her chair, tiptoed into the hallway, closed the front door gently behind her. When she returned later, she would strip down the bed, take the sheets to the steamie.

Twenty-three

THE TELEPHONE RANG IN THE COLD, EMPTY HALLWAY. That sound still made her jump. She knew in some homes, families used the device for ordinary, everyday conversation. But not in the Kahn household. That shining black daffodil set upon the hall table was only to be used for special occasions. Just like the sets of dishes stored away in the cupboards only to be brought out once a year at Passover. The phone continued to ring. She was kneeled down on the kitchen floor, her hands wet and soapy from the scrubbing brush. She thought to call out for her mother but remembered she had gone down to the bakery. Papa Kahn and Nathan were at the shop.

"All right, all right," she muttered to herself, as she stood, wiped her soapy hands on her apron. "Calm yourself down. I'm coming." She went into the hallway, sat down by the telephone table, wriggled herself up straight, picked up the earpiece.

"This is the Kahn residence."

The clipped tones of the operator. "Is that Glasgow South 390?"

"Yes, this is Glasgow South 390."

"I have a trunk call for you. Putting you through now, thank you." She listened to the clicks of connection, then from far away:

"Who is there?" the voice asked.

"It is Celia Kahn."

"Celia, Celia. It is your Uncle Mendel."

"I can hardly hear you. What is it?"

"For hours I try to book this call. It is not easy. But better than a telegram to tell you."

"Uncle. What has happened?"

"The news is very bad."

"Are you all right?"

"It is not about me. It is about Avram. I don't know how this to tell you. But Avram… he is dead."

"What did you say? The line is not very clear."

"Celia. Avram is dead."

"Dead? He can't be. He was here only two days ago."

"Yes, yes. I know, I know. A terrible tragedy. I need to speak to your father. Arrangements we need to make very quickly. I am sorry…"

She heard her uncle's voice disintegrate into a sobbing wail. She held the receiver away from her ear as if this distance might lessen the impact of what she had just heard. Perhaps if she just swept this black device off the table-top, she could somehow obliterate the dreadful information.

"Celia? Celia? Celia?" Her uncle's tinny voice. "Can you hear me?"

She leaned forward, spoke again into the trumpet. "Yes, I can hear you."

"Go bring your father. Tell him to telephone me at Avram's shop. Here I will wait."

"But what happened?"

"The details I have no time to give. Only one minute I have. The constable came to the shop to tell me. Avram was shot."

"He was murdered?"

"I don't know exactly. Accident? Murder? It is not clear. Please bring your father to telephone me."

"But what will happen to Megan and the baby?"

"A baby? About a baby, I don't know…"

Click. The line went dead.

When she told her father, he spontaneously bursts into tears. She herself hadn't properly absorbed what had happened, yet as soon as she had finishing pronouncing the word "dead", her father had fallen back on his chair, started to cry. Here she was being all stiff and practical while her father was a sniffling wreck. This ability to immediately access his emotions astonished her, made her think better of him, worse about herself. What was wrong with her? That her heart should turn so hard against such bitter news. Her mother, of course, had a different reaction.

"They hate us," she said, as she snapped open the piano lid. "They pretend to like us. But in their hearts they hate the Jews." Her fingers began to hammer out a tune.

"But mother," she protested. "We don't know what happened."

Madame Kahn stopped her hands mid-strike above the keyboard. "You will see. Mark my words. This will be the work of some anti-Semite." Her fingers hit the chords hard. "Anti-Semite!"

Her father shouted from the hallway. "*Shah!* I am speaking on the telephone. Quiet in there."

When he had finished his call, Papa Kahn came through to the kitchen. His face was a sickly yellowish-white. She jumped up from her chair, busied herself at the hearth preparing a pot of tea. Her father took a bottle of *schnapps* from the mantelpiece, poured himself a glass. Her mother stiffened, looked ready to scold him, but instead she closed the piano lid with the greatest care, went to sit beside him at the kitchen table.

"So?" she asked. "What did you find out?"

Her father searched in his trouser pocket for a handkerchief into which he loudly blew his nose. He then folded the linen neatly, returned it to his pocket. He picked up the shot-glass, tipped back the amber liquid in one gulp, replaced the receptacle on the table-top. All this, he did very slowly and deliberately as if the slightest unplanned movement might shatter his fragility and he would break down again in tears.

"Mendel is taking care of everything," he said hoarsely.

"What is everything?" her mother asked.

"The proper transportation."

"What did the rabbi say?"

"Of course, Lieberman says the burial should be within twenty-four hours of death. But in an extraordinary situation such as this, if there is to be an official examination of the body, then dispensation can be made. Meanwhile, Mendel will arrange with the railway company to bring Avram back to Glasgow. He will be buried at the cemetery in Riddrie. I have spoken to the Burial Society. A plot will be prepared."

Celia moved quietly beside her father, placed a glass of black tea and a bowl of sugar cubes by his arm. He reached out, grabbed her lightly by the wrist, looked up at her with his red, watery eyes. "Thank you," he said, with such a solemnity it was as if she had presented him with a gift of gold bars. "Thank you."

"So who will pay for all of this?" her mother asked. "All these special arrangements."

Her father placed a sugar cube between his teeth, then sipped on the black tea. "Of course, we will pay."

"You see, I knew he was trouble from the moment I set my eyes on him. When I opened the door to that orphan boy from Russia and saw him standing there, I knew it. It was as if a candle in my mind lit up. *Tzores*, it said. Trouble. Avram will be trouble. Is that not true, Celia? *Tzores*."

"Mother. I cannot believe you are talking like this. He was my brother."

"Your adopted brother."

"It doesn't matter which. He was a member of the family. And he has been killed. Somebody shot him."

"Nobody shoots someone for nothing. There has to be a reason. This Highland *shikse* he wanted to marry. What was her name? This Megan. I swear she is behind all of this too. Both of them. Nothing but trouble. And these anti-Semites too. Meanwhile, we have to pay for all of this mess. All this mess people make from their lives, we have to pay."

"Calm down, Martha," her father said. "Just calm down. Avram gave you very little trouble. You know that. He was sent here with almost nothing. A few coins sewn into a jacket pocket. Never understanding why a mother could say she loved him, yet send him away from her. For what? To stop him going into the Russian army. At the age of twelve these Cossacks wanted to take him. Such a terrible thing to do to a child. Quotas, quotas, quotas. Using the youngest Jews to fill their damn quotas of conscription. And yet you chose to dislike him. Why? Because you have a jealous heart."

"Celia," her mother hissed. "Go away from here. You should not have to listen to such things."

"Celia will stay," her father said firmly. "She is a young woman. A young woman can hear such things." The colour was back in his cheeks now. Whether from the brandy or his anger she did not know.

"What does Celia know about what is going on in this family. She is never here. Like a lodger she is."

"Mother…"

"Don't avoid the subject, Martha."

"What is the subject? My jealous heart? Well, it is true, isn't it? You and Avram's mother. You and this Rachel. You were… lovers."

"Martha, Martha, Martha. What does it matter? It was such a long time ago. I have forgotten all about my life in Russia. Why did you have to take it out on Avram?"

"He was trouble. See, he comes back here for three days and look at the trouble he causes. A man should walk out in the middle of the *Kol Nidre* service. On the holiest of days. Who should do such a thing? And you too, young lady. You think you can run about town all by yourself. Like a *zoyne*. A common prostitute."

Papa Kahn slammed his fist on the table. "For goodness sake, woman. Control yourself."

Her mother continued to whimper. "See, even in death, Avram causes us trouble."

"Bah," her father snorted. "If it is the money you are worried about, then I think you will find that Avram had plenty. Ask your brother. Mendel will tell you what a successful businessman Avram was. And you know who will inherit his estate? This Megan who was not his wife? This bastard child that was not his? We will, Martha. We will. His adopted parents. That's how much trouble he was."

Her mother didn't go to the funeral, took to her bed, claiming her nerves had gotten the better of her. It was a miserable day anyway, rain drizzling down, trees half-stripped of their foliage, damp yellowing leaves underfoot like sodden bunting after a parade. A few mourners had turned up despite the weather. Apart from Nathan and her father, Solly was there, as was Charlotte, the seamstresses from the shop, a few family friends. Uncle Mendel had come down from Oban with the coffin, the funeral-car picking up the wooden box from Buchanan Street station, bringing it straight to the cemetery, the label 'human remains' still attached until someone had the good sense to tear it off. On her way to the graveside, she asked her father:

"What happens when we die, papa?"

"We go to the *oylem habo* – the next world."

"What kind of world is that?"

"I don't know," he shrugged, his eyes staring off into the distance. "Once I asked Rabbi Lieberman the same question. But his answer was so vague. Either he didn't know, or it was a secret he wasn't revealing."

Rabbi Lieberman was officiating at the ceremony, standing by the open grave, such a frail man these days, his skin almost transparent, his own body not that far from collapsing into the *oylem habo* itself. One of the synagogue officiants held up an umbrella for him. The rabbi spoke feebly, recalling how he had tutored Avram in his *bar mitzvah*, how the boy's voice had soared so beautifully on that significant day, only to be cut off so cruelly now in its youth. Still no-one knew exactly who had cut off this life. Celia had assumed the killing must have somehow involved the father of Megan's child but Uncle Mendel doubted this was the case. The incident might have been nothing more than a tragic case of mistaken identity. There was to be an investigation. Persons would no doubt be charged. What did it matter? she thought. Avram was dead. Just when it seemed he might have found some real happiness, his life had been taken away from him. And how would she grieve for him? He hadn't been in her life for years. How did you mourn the loss of someone who had hardly been there?

One by one the male mourners stepped forward, grabbed a spade in turn, tipped the worm-ridden earth back into the open grave. What a horrible sound that was, the dull thud of the clods as they scattered across the wooden box. The not-hollow sound reminding her that inside lay the body of someone she had loved. She watched as her father stumbled over the recitation of the *Kaddish*, the memorial prayer for the dead. The rain came down heavier now, muddying up the fresh mound of earth, creating puddles at her feet. The whole world seemed to sag with a sadness at this mournful scene.

Charlotte, solemn-faced behind her dark veil, came to stand by her side, took her arm, gave her a squeeze of support. Her father finished his recitation, she responded along with the small congregation in a communal 'Amen'. That was it. She raised her handkerchief to dab at her dry eyes. Charlotte pulled her gently away from the graveside, arm-in-arm they took to the path that led back to the main building. Off to the side, standing under an umbrella, under a tree, a man she thought she recognised.

"My God. It's Jonny."

"Who's Jonny?" Charlotte asked.

"Someone I used to know."

"He's a good-looking fellow."

"Perhaps he is."

"I suppose you let him slip away."

"You know what I think of men."

"I know what you think about them. What you might feel about them is a different matter."

"Oh no. He's coming over."

"I'll walk on ahead."

"No, you won't."

"Oh yes, I think I will."

Their umbrellas met first. Then there were a few awkward moments until they had both adjusted their stances. Eventually, he turned to face her. She saw that his skin was tanned from a sun that never visited this city, so that his teeth shone white even on this dull day. His hair was unoiled, slightly longer than she remembered. If she didn't know better, she would have thought him a foreigner, some Italian painter perhaps – he had that bright-eyed, unkempt looked about him. He held out a leather-gloved hand.

"I wish you 'long life'," he said.

"Oh, I don't think you need to say that to me. I'm not a blood relation."

"It seems appropriate."

"Thank you." The rain dripped down between them. "What are you doing back in Glasgow?"

"My mother is quite ill. The family sent for me. Then I heard about…" He shrugged, nodded towards the grave where the diggers were already stacking their spades onto a small wheelbarrow. "We used to play football together."

"I remember you told me that."

He shuffled on his feet. She felt a raindrop fall beneath the collar of her coat, trickle down her neck. A smell of woodsmoke in the air. Who would be lighting a fire in the rain? she thought.

"Perhaps we can walk a little," he suggested. "Instead of standing here getting soaked."

"Yes, yes. I must join Nathan and my father. There is a motor car to take us home."

She could see Charlotte further ahead, then beyond her the huddle of mourners just outside the reception building.

"How is your mother?" she asked.

"She's very sick. It is good that I came. I don't think she has long to live."

"I'm sorry to hear that."

"Thank you. But it is not a tragedy. She is very old. What happened with Avram is a tragedy."

"Yes, I know. I don't think I've fully absorbed what has happened."

"Death can be like that."

She wondered how he would know. "Of course, you were a soldier."

"I see your father is waiting for you. Please pass on my condolences."

"Yes, yes. I will have to go. Thank you for coming. That was thoughtful of you."

He took her hand again. "I don't know how long I'll be staying here in Glasgow. But perhaps we could see each other."

"Yes, I would like that," she replied with the realisation that she genuinely meant it.

He seemed to immediately relax to the warmth in her words. "I can regale you with my tales of *kibbutz* life," he said with a laugh.

"And I can tell you all that you've missed in bonny Glasgow."

"Well, it won't be the weather. Can I telephone you?"

"Yes, we Kahns have one of these contraptions now. Glasgow South 390. The number is in the directory."

Twenty-four

"I heard Dr Levy is back from Palestine," Madame Kahn remarked as she polished the brass ornaments on the mantelpiece with spit and vinegar. A small dog, a tiny shoe, a tortoise, a fairy castle from Bavaria the size of a baby's fist.

"His mother's sick," Celia said, trying not to let the statement interrupt her own rhythm in the scrubbing of the sink.

"Yes, I heard that." Spit, rub, spit, rub. "What is wrong with her?"

"I don't know. I only spoke with him briefly."

"It is good he came to the funeral." Her mother looked over at her and smiled. Her mood had become more cheerful since Avram's death. As if some great weight had lifted from her shoulders. Unfortunately, that same weight appeared to have passed to her father who had taken to his bed almost immediately after the funeral. "It shows he cares."

"He is just visiting."

Spit, rub, rub. "Just visiting. That means nothing. Look what happened with your father."

She stopped with her brushing mid-scrub. "What happened with Papa?"

Madame Kahn ceased in her own task, held up the Bavarian castle, squinted it as if a miniature version of herself was imprisoned in one of the turrets.

"I never told you?"

"Told me what, mother."

"About how I met your father."

"This is the first time."

Her mother scraped out a chair, sat down at the kitchen table. "Well, your Uncle Mendel and I, we were already in Glasgow a few years before your father arrives from Russia. He comes first to Edinburgh, then travels here to take a ship to America. America, America. That was your father's big dream in those days. America with its golden pavements. Buildings as high as mountains. But he has to wait for his ship, one month, perhaps two months. And while he is waiting, he rents a room from Mrs Shulansky in Crown Street, he goes to the synagogue, he is invited here and there, after all he was an educated man, not the tailor he is now. He is introduced to the community, to my family, he meets Mendel, he meets me, and, and, and…"

"What do you mean? And, and, and?"

Her mother actually looked quite bashful. Her face, already hot from all the rubbing, glowed even more as she put her hands behind her head, untied and re-tied her headscarf. "A woman has ways to make a man change his mind. That is all I say. *Genug*. Finished." She slapped her palms, stood up quickly, returned to the brasses on the mantelpiece. "Anyway, this America. Better to be here, a big stone in a small pond. Than over there, a nothing. A nobody. Even with all the golden pavements. Now finish your work."

She resumed her scrubbing, quick glances to her mother who was smiling to herself, sluiced out the sink with water from the bucket Jonny had bought at the gypsy encampment. "I'm going upstairs to see Uncle Mendel."

"You will not say to him what I just told you."

"He invited me for supper."

"Is that him with the baking fish again? I can smell the stink from down here. Baked fish. A baked head is more like it."

Celia hung up her pinny on the kitchen door, went out to the hallway, ran her fingers across the base of the telephone as she passed, checked the earpiece was sitting proper on its cradle-hook. Such a strange contraption, she thought. With its ability to make the possibility of contact ever-present. So unlike the arrival of a letter just twice a day. Her father was talking about buying a radio next. If he could afford the licence.

Her uncle stood in his doorway, a black *yarmulke* perched on his head, his beard longer than it had ever been. He wore a grey woollen cardigan so stretched at the pockets that the hem came down past his knees. On his feet a pair of old slippers she knew would be stuffed with newspapers to replace the worn-out soles. If she opened up his wardrobe, there would be several new pairs stacked at the bottom, given as presents, still in their wrapping.

"Come in, come in," he said. She remembered a time when he would have taken her in his arms or at the very least given her a sloppy kiss on the forehead. Now he observed the religious rules that forbade him from touching her. Or any woman. "You are hungry?"

"A little."

"A little hungry is good. Speciality of the house I have. *Komm, komm.*"

She could smell the charred paper, the fish cooking inside their damp parcel on the coals. She sat down in a large battered armchair, close to the fire.

"This reminds me of Avram," she said. "Waiting for the food to bake."

"*Ya, ya.* I remember not so many years ago you two *kinder* squeezed together in that one chair. Like those twins who came to England with the circus. In all the papers, they were."

"Siamese twins."

"Yes, that's it. You and Avram sitting there. Siamese twins."

"It is so sad."

"It breaks my heart. He was a good boy."

"Do you have any more news?"

"Tomorrow I return to Oban. I will find out then from the constables."

"What will happen to the shop?"

"For the time being, the business I will try to manage. But everything will be complicated. There was no will, no direct family. In the end, I believe to your mother and father his estate will pass."

"I would like some money to go to this Megan. Avram wanted to take responsibility for her child."

"This you must speak to your parents about directly. Your mother,

189

I am sure, will not approve. Her heart was always set hard against the boy. Your father, as we say in the business, is a softer touch."

"I worry about Papa so much. He doesn't talk about Avram's death. He just takes himself to bed, hides in the darkness."

"As the Torah says."

"What does the Torah say?"

"The deeper the sorrow, the less tongue it has." He prodded the bundle of fish with a poker. "Dinner is ready."

He gave her a towel to spread on her lap, then laid down one of the parcels of wrapped-up fish. She wetted her fingers, gingerly pulled back the paper to reveal the steaming pink flesh.

"Salmon," Uncle Mendel said. "I bring back two pieces in my ice-box. For this special occasion. Sitting here together with my niece. A glass of sweet wine I can offer you. It makes the fish go down very well. And lifts the sad heart."

She agreed and he poured out a glass, placed it on the brass coal-box by her side. He pulled up a seat opposite, placed his own parcel of fish on his lap, bowed his head, muttered the blessing before meals.

"Aha!" he exclaimed, his eyes popping open. "Now you are ready to dine like a *mensch*."

She broke off a piece of flesh, still hot in her fingers. "Is it true that salmon leap upstream to spawn?"

"Absolutely true. I have seen with my own eyes. When the river is full and rushing, out of the water they jump. With a net you can catch them. If you are clever and quick, quick, quick." He made a flashing movement with his hand to imitate his fishing skills. "But, of course, your Uncle Mendel buys them fresh from the fishmonger like every-one else." He raised his glass. "To Avram. *L'chaim*."

She reached over for her own glass, matched his gesture. "To life," she said.

They ate in silence after that, except for her uncle's noisy munching and slurping which somehow had a comforting effect on her. It was good to see him eat, he had lost weight recently, perhaps the double impact of the *Yom Kippur* fast and Avram's death.

"So," he said, plucking the last of the fish bones from his mouth, flicking it into the fire. "What are the feminists up to these days?

When racecourses they are not burning down." He leaned towards her, his eyes always so full of interest.

"To be honest, uncle, I find it difficult to talk to you these days about such things."

"What? What do you say?" He drew back in mock offence. "Celia, this is me, your Uncle Mendel. That other Uncle Mendel, the drinker and the gambler, long gone away he is. *Avek, avek, avek.* Far away."

She laid aside her parcel with its own set of fleshless bones, sat herself straight. "It is not that other Uncle Mendel I am worried out. It is this Uncle Mendel, the one sitting here in front of me. You. Suddenly you have become so religious."

"As a man grows older, closer to God he wants to become."

"But what about all your talk of socialism and revolution?"

"Bah! We had our chance," he said sadly. "That one chance we had. After that riot in George Square. Before the army and the tanks they send in. That was the opportunity. Twenty-four hours to make a revolution. That was all the time we had. But no leaders we had to take control. Twenty-four hours. On the other hand, God is here all the time. For eternity. But what difference does it make? About issues close to our hearts we can still talk."

"I don't think so."

"Celia. You can tell your uncle."

"All right then. If you insist, I will tell you." She sucked in a breath, then on the exhale: "Birth control."

"What do you say?"

"Birth control. We are trying to promote female contraception."

"It does not embarrass you to talk about such matters?"

"No, I am fine with it."

"Aha! Of course, we can talk about such things. We are all human beings together. The stuff of life we can discuss. Why not?" He stood up quickly, the parcel of fishbones falling off his lap onto the floor. As he paced about the room, she had to stoop down, scrunch up the greasy paper, throw it into the fire. A few of the burnt embers floated back at her from the grate.

"My tobacco, where is it?" her uncle cried. "My pouch? Do you see? One minute I have it, the next gone. My tobacco."

191

"Here it is. On the mantelpiece."

"Yes, yes, of course."

But he didn't take it. Instead, he sank back down into his armchair, hands clasped around his bowed head, pressing down with his thick fingers onto his *yarmulke*.

"Are you all right?" she asked.

He looked up at her. "What can I do? What can I do? This kind of talk it tears me apart."

"I didn't mean to upset you."

"No, no, Celia. It is not your fault. It is this struggle going round and round inside my head. Round and round. A tempest in my brain. It splits me apart. Like an axe."

"I don't understand."

"You know what the Torah says about such matters? About making birth. It says the Jews must be fruitful and multiply on this earth. To have children is a duty. A commandment even. A blessing. To prevent it is forbidden. *Farboten*. But I know also too large families are the curse of the poorer classes. A curse. Poverty, overcrowding, disease it brings. With my own eyes I see it. *Mit meine eigenene oign*."

"It is all right, uncle. I won't say any more about it."

He leaned forward, took her hands, looked at her with his watery eyes. She felt his palms hot and damp. "What you do is a good thing, Celia. A good thing birth control is. Even if the Torah says otherwise. But trouble there will be. Many people will hate you for it. From all sides, they will hate you. Mark my words. Trouble there will be."

Twenty-five

JONNY'S VOICE SOUNDED QUITE DIFFERENT on the telephone. All tinny and shivery as if he were talking from some corrugated shed in the snow. Her own voice too must have sounded strange, given she was quite breathless in her rush to answer the contraption before anyone else in the household.

"That'll be Jonny Levy then," Nathan shouted from the kitchen where the rest of the family were having dinner.

She placed her hand over the mouthpiece, called back to the open door. "It's Charlotte."

"Why does that woman always ring at mealtimes?" her mother grumbled.

"Yes?" she whispered into the mouthpiece.

"Can you meet me tomorrow?"

She heard the hiss on the other end of the line, felt herself redden to the request, convinced the operator was listening in, could imagine the girl with nothing better to do than smooth her nails with an emery board, eavesdrop on conversations. She leaned in closer to the telephone. "I think I can."

"Do you know Miss Cranston's in Sauchiehall Street?"

"I've been there."

She arranged to meet him outside the tearooms at two o'clock. "Yes, of course, Charlotte," she said into the mouthpiece after Jonny had clicked off. "Tomorrow at two."

"You must invite this girl over for tea," her father suggested on her return to the kitchen. This was the first time he had attended table since Avram's funeral. He looked as pale as death itself, hand trembling so much that her mother had stuffed his napkin into his collar like a bib against the spillage from his shaking cup. "It would be nice to meet your friends." The cup rattled as it was replaced on the saucer. The sound made her want to cry.

The wind was doing what it was supposed to do at this time of year. Strip the leaves off the trees. Strip the skin off her face as well, an Arctic gust ripping through her in her walk up Sauchiehall Street, people shivering in their shoes in the queue for the matinee outside the Empire. Jonny was waiting for her, wrapped up in a bulky overcoat, cloth cap pulled down over his ears, his Glasgow University scarf whipping about madly.

"I'd forgotten how cold it was here." He picked up one of the loose ends of his long scarf, wrapped it round his neck thick like a horse's halter.

"This is just autumn," she said. "Wait until winter blows in."

"At least it will be warm inside."

He held open the door, and she recalled herself as a young girl crossing this very threshold, how fearful she had been of her entry into this elegant tea-room.

"I remember the first time I came here," she said, as she let Jonny help her off with her coat. She rubbed her hands together, noticed her ruddy complexion in the window's reflection as she sat down. "I was with my friend, Agnes Calder. We sat at this exact table."

"Red Aggie? Red Aggie was your friend?"

"The very one."

"I hope she wasn't intending to burn the place down."

"Oh Agnes wouldn't have struck a match against this tearoom."

"I still can't imagine this was her style."

"At the time I couldn't either. I was only a young girl but I had the cheek to ask how a great socialist like herself could frequent such a high-class place as this. And do you know what she said? Come the revolution… and we'll all be having tea at Miss Cranston's."

Jonny laughed at that. Then the waitress came over and still chuckling, he ordered a full afternoon tea for them both. None of your post-wartime austerity or *kibbutz* economy for Jonny Levy. Just a pot of India's finest along with a three-tier plate-stand for sandwiches, biscuits and the most expensive gateaux.

"You've changed," she said.

"Not surprising. I wasn't long out of a war the last time you saw me. I would have been a scrawny runt back then."

"It's not just that. You seem more comfortable in yourself."

He shrugged. "Perhaps you're right. What about you? What are you feminists up to since you won the vote?"

She leaned in to answer him in a way she would consider intimate. She could feel her skin glowing, and she had that wonderful sense of knowing she was being silly and charming at the same time. What was happening to her? All her senses seemed more acute. She could smell his pomade, even her own French scent, those few stolen drops from her mother's dresser. The cacophony of overheard words from a nearby table, a high-pitched voice "…should have seen the way he…", the sound of a teaspoon replaced on its saucer, the taste of lipstick on her tongue. She noticed the tanned skin of his hand as he held his head on a tilt to look at her, this sun-dark mark of the common labourer looking quite attractive against the whiteness of his cuff.

"I take much offence at such a remark," she said with a breathiness that sounded not unlike her friend Charlotte. "As you know, women can only vote at the age of thirty. Are you suggesting I am of such an age?"

He shook his head at her. "I do believe you are trying to wheedle a compliment out of me."

"Oh, I do no such thing. Compliments are not worth tuppence unless they are freely come by."

"So what *are* you doing these days?"

"The usual. Scrubbing floors and sewing buttons on shirts."

"I find that hard to believe."

"What else does a Jewish spinster do?"

She leaned back to allow the waitress to lay out their tea things, watching on as Jonny carefully monitored the young girl in her task, directing the teapot here, the cake tray there. She had to remind herself he would soon be back in Palestine with a pickaxe over his shoulder, some Russian Jewess on his arm, discussing Marxism and where to

195

plant the next olive grove. She selected a sandwich from the bottom tier, examined its contents. "What do you think this is? Meat paste?"

He had a closer look himself. "Yes, it probably is."

"Oh, I can't eat that. What about you? Do you keep *kosher*?"

"I was a soldier," he said as if this explained everything she needed to know about his dietary habits.

"You have the meat paste then if you want. And I'll have the cucumber ones."

She picked up another sandwich from the plate, marvelled at how the crusts had been cut off. Such a luxury. Such a waste. "I would rather hear about your exploits. I am sure stories of Palestine are far more interesting than life in the Gorbals."

He spoke to her of the desert, the coastal plains, the hill country of Galilee and Judea. Of the date palms as tall as cathedrals, of olives that flowed from their branches like milk from an udder, the Jordanian hills that changed colour spectacularly throughout the day – the glorious pinks of sunrise, the burning red of the morning, the yellow of mid-afternoon, the purples of dusk.

"Stand at the top of Mount Tabor," he said, replacing his cup from which he had yet to drink. "Look down on the Jordan Valley and I do not believe there is a more beautiful place on earth. They say it was where the Garden of Eden was situated and it is hard to think otherwise. The Sea of Galilee gleams back at you in the sunshine, dotted with its little fishing boats. It is a paradise." He clapped his hands together with all the enthusiasm of a Zionist recruitment officer. "And you should see the light. There is something quite magical about it. It makes everything look cleaner, clearer." He gazed out of the window on to the heads of the shoppers in Sauchiehall Street. How gloomy this city must appear to him, she thought. The wind whipping up again, pedestrians holding on to their hats. Here there were belching chimney stacks instead of date palms, the dark alleys of the Gallowgate rather than the white light of the Galilee.

"And what do you do all day in this paradise?" she asked, moving the attention of her appetite to the pastry tier. "I doubt you are lounging in a deckchair reading the *Palestine Post*."

"The life is hard, I will give you that. The heat in the summer is almost unbearable. But I love the fact the work is so physical. And that we live as a community. There are about thirty of us. We're not like those Jews from the *shtetl* poring over each letter of the Torah. We ride horses and drive wagons. We live in tents, just like in the army. A lot of the land is marshland and we're trying to drain that, reclaim it for agriculture, hopefully get rid of the mosquitoes and the risk of malaria with it. Then there are the weeds, the thistles and the field mice to clear. Where we can, we've planted vineyards, banana plantations, orchards of lemons and grapefruits. And of course, there are date palms and olive trees that have been there for centuries."

"But where does all this land come from?"

"From the little blue *pushke*."

"The *pushke*? The Jewish National Fund collection box?" There was one on the mantelpiece at home. Her father used to give her a farthing, a half-penny or even a threepenny bit to stuff into its slot until it was so full she could hardly lift it. Then there would be a knock on the door, some mysterious figure would empty the contents, a receipt would be given, the contributions would start all over again. "I always thought that was for Jewish charities."

"Well, you thought wrong. The Fund uses the money to acquire land in Palestine for Jewish settlement. They buy from the *effendi* – Arab landlords happy to sell for a good price."

She tried to imagine these huge swathes of paradise on earth just waiting to be bought up with her *pushke* farthings. A date tree here, an olive grove there. How about those mountains that change colour throughout the day? And that lake where Jesus walked. How many *pushke*s for that? "Is all this just empty land?"

"Some is, some isn't. What's empty are the marshlands and the non-irrigated areas. The fertile areas are worked by the *fellahin*, the local Arab farmers."

"So what happens to them?"

"They don't have any rights of tenure with the *effendi*. So they have to leave on purchase."

"But where do they go?"

Jonny shrugged, looked down at his coarsened hands that had chosen to wield mattocks rather than scalpels. "Arabia is a big place.

As far as the Fund is concerned, Jewish-bought land is for the Jews. It's hard enough trying to eke out a few crops from the soil for yourself without having to worry about the *fellahin*."

"I thought you were a socialist."

"I still am, Celia. That's why I don't want to see the Jews as big-shot landowners with the *fellahin* as their slaves. I want to see a community of Jews as equals. The *fellahin* can go and live their lives where they want and how they want."

She picked out an éclair from the cake plate. She remembered how at this very table those several years ago, Agnes had persuaded her to come out with her to Govan, to ring the fishmonger's bell at the sight of the sheriff officers, how the women were all riled up and excited about the justice of it all, about the power of sisterhood to prevent the eviction of tenants by greedy landlords. And now her very own farthings were contributing to another form of eviction. All in the name of socialism. And Zionism. She had never missed her dead friend so much as at this moment. She had a thought to replace the gateau in her fingers back on to its paper doily. Instead she bit into the chocolate and cream. It was delicious.

"Why do you make me feel guilty about this?" Jonny asked.

"I haven't said a word."

"That's exactly why I feel guilty. So what would you like me to do? Go off to Africa, start a commune there?"

"I don't know why you want to go off anywhere. We Jews are treated well enough here in Glasgow. What's the point of trying to build a socialist homeland elsewhere?"

"I'm sure the Jews in Russia used to think the same. Until the pogroms started."

"That won't happen here."

"So would you rather I stayed?" He sat back in his chair, folded his arms against her. She noticed the sleeve of his jacket worn at the elbow. What he needed was a good leather patch, she could stitch that for him if she had a mind to. "Well?" he said, the word sounding like a challenge. "What do you say?"

"There's plenty of work here for a good doctor."

Twenty-six

"No-one's coming," Charlotte declared from her vigil by the window.

"It's still early." Celia was stoking up the fire in the grate. She'd made some scones, there was a pot of tea warming on the stove. There were even some pink roses, the very last of the year's bloom, in a vase on the kitchen table. She wanted Agnes' place to look homely and friendly, just women sitting around the hearth for an intimate chat. The boxes of caps she'd put in the bedroom for fetching when required. Samples of each size were available for trying out. She'd manage to fit one for herself no problem. It only required a certain amount of dexterity and intelligence in following the instructions. If their client or customer or whatever they were supposed to call them encountered any problems of discomfort or difficulty in fitting, then the whole process was to be abandoned. However, if matters went smoothly, the woman would be supplied with two rubber caps in her size and an information pamphlet. No medical advice of any kind was to be given. A short questionnaire to be answered. Anonymously, of course.

She had been in correspondence with two fledgling birth control clinics down in London – the first founded by Stopes, the other the Malthusian's League Walworth Clinic. Both had medical advice on hand although finding doctors and nurses both willing and knowledgeable had been a hard task even for them. But she had agreed with Charlotte a very clear policy. Their task was provision only. Any risk lay with the recipient. These women also had to confirm they were over twenty-one years of age, married or about to be married, and that they would not allow the device or the information pamphlet to fall into the hands of any young or unmarried person. Charlotte had produced a short waiver-and-consent form to this effect for signature, her recently acquired legal acumen coming courtesy of her current lover, a solicitor in the city.

"There's someone now," Charlotte squealed.

"You should get away from the curtain. You'll put people off."

"Oh no, she's gone past. I don't think anyone will come."

"We have to be prepared for that. Or perhaps it will just take time for word to get around."

"I feel like an actor on first night. Hiding behind the curtains, waiting for the theatre to fill up."

Celia thought that an apt description of her friend. A strutting actress always performing on some stage of her imagination. "Maybe you should put on some greasepaint then," she said rather unkindly. But she was feeling anxious herself and Charlotte's impatience was irritating. She would rather lay herself down on a bed in the dark, swallow two teaspoons of nerve tonic, wait for the doorbell to ring.

"I only make-up for the men. The women can see me for who I am." Charlotte turned away from the window, combed her fingers through her short bob. "Anyway, I don't want to intimidate some wee wifie, do I?"

"Sometimes I wonder why you bother with all of this?"

"Because beneath this sophisticated exterior, a Marie Stopes is waiting to burst out." Charlotte dumped herself down in an armchair. "To be honest, sometimes I wonder myself what I'm doing here. I don't really fancy having children. So I suppose I'm quite happy to help others who feel the same. There's too many stinking urchins running about in bare feet, with rickets and lice and polio and TB, sucking on gobstoppers, cluttering up the streets with their stupid games. The horrible little monsters. In fact, I hate children. I'm probably a eugenicist at heart. We should just sterilise the whole human race, let ourselves die out, start all over again. Just you and me."

"We'd still need some man to impregnate us."

"I'd choose Ivor Novello. We'll keep him for ourselves. And when he's not impregnating us, he can entertain us with a quick song and dance."

"You came up with his name quick enough."

"I've just seen him in that new picture. *The Bohemian Girl*."

"You can be his Bohemian girl then."

Charlotte laughed, flicked away with her fingers like castanets. "All right. I'll have Ivor. And you can have your Jonny boy. Is he still wooing you?"

"He's trying his best." Jonny had already taken her to the pictures three times in the last week – once with her mother, then with Nathan and finally with an imaginary Charlotte as chaperone. That third time, he had held her hand through both features, only letting go to bring her an ice at the interval.

"But will his best be good enough, I wonder? To break down that hard exterior?"

"I'm warming to him. A few years ago, I hardly gave him the time of day."

"Well, even now you don't sound very enthusiastic. Maybe I should have a go at him. The more I think about it, the more I think he looks a bit like Novello. A slightly darker version though. If he just swept his hair back a little, got rid of that working-class tan."

She felt her stomach tighten. Charlotte probably could have Jonny if she wanted to, the way she behaved around men was almost sinful, always touching their hands, rubbing against them like a purring cat, hard for a man to resist. "You're not his type," she said sharply.

"So what is his type then? Straight-laced virgins?"

"I've never said I was a virgin."

"So who was the lucky one then?"

"Charlotte. Can we stop this?"

"I'm sorry, I'm sorry, I'm sorry. I'm just tense. My nerves are all on edge about this. Do you have anything to drink in this…"

The bell went. Charlotte jumped out of her chair. "Thank God," she said as she raced to the door. Then she stopped herself, took a couple of deep breaths, then went out into the hallway. Celia poured some boiling water from the kettle into the teapot, fiddled with the flowers, fussed with the pleats on her skirt. The door to the kitchen opened. A refined-looking lady entered dressed in a full-length wrapover coat and a broad-brimmed hat. Behind her, Charlotte making all kinds of strange faces to confirm what they both thought. That this was not the kind of client they were expecting.

"What am I supposed to do?" this woman asked, looking around the room rather disdainfully.

"Please, please sit down," Celia said, pulling out a chair by the kitchen table. "Would you like some tea?"

"That would be fine." The woman sat down, took off her hat, put her handbag on the table, folded her hands in her lap. She wore her hair long and upswept in the old style. "Well?"

Celia placed the questionnaire on the table while Charlotte finished preparing the tea. "First, let me introduce myself. I am Celia Kahn, and this is my colleague, Charlotte Maxwell. Secondly, I would like to ask you a few questions."

The woman nodded.

"Are you married?"

"I most certainly am."

"We don't need a full name. But would you mind providing an initial?"

"You can put me down as Mrs B."

"Good. Now, Mrs B. May I ask your reasons for coming here?"

Mrs B twisted her neck first to the left, then to the right, Celia hearing the muscles unwind and crack as she did so. Charlotte placed a cup and saucer in front of their guest, along with a bowl of sugar and a jug of milk. Mrs B added the milk but not the sugar. "I am a Roman Catholic. As is my husband, of course." She lifted the cup to her lips, deemed it to be too hot, returned it to its saucer. Celia noticed the slight tremor in her hand, then in her voice as Mrs B said. "I have had ten pregnancies. Four children living. Two girls, two boys. The oldest is now twelve, the youngest just eight months. I am thirty-one years of age."

Celia noted all this down, glad of the distraction. Charlotte had sat down in the armchair, plucked a cigarette from her silver case, but remained with it unlit between her fingers.

"Do I have to go on? All I want is to purchase some items. I didn't think I would be attending confession."

"I'm sorry, Mrs B," Celia said. "We don't want you to feel that way. It's just that a little detail would be helpful to ascertain people's needs. And anyway, the contraceptives are free."

"I must insist on paying. I am not someone in need of parish handouts."

"Perhaps we can discuss this later. In the meantime, if you feel comfortable, would you mind continuing with your reasons for coming here."

Celia thought Mrs B was going to get up and leave there and then. She had picked up her handbag from the table, laid it on her lap, her body stiffening as if she were about to raise herself from her chair, take her hat and scarper. Instead, she unclasped the fastener on her bag, brought out a lace handkerchief. "My husband will not permit contraception of any kind. I spoke to him once about it a few years ago but he flew into such a rage, accusing me of such sinfulness against God, the Holy Father and the Church that I dared not raise the subject again. But I have no wish for another pregnancy. My nerves are so distraught by the thought of another miscarriage or a baby dying young. It is like some kind of dreadful lottery. Either a dead or a living child. Four is enough to bring into this world, don't you think? Yet my husband continues to want to… to know me. And I can't bear it." Mrs B played with the clasp on her bag. "I am not a stupid woman. I am aware of these contraceptives. I also understand they can be employed without the husband even knowing they are in place. But Boots the Chemist won't provide them without a prescription. And I cannot possibly visit my family doctor about this. He's worse than the Pope in these matters. So when I heard about this…"

"How did you hear about us?"

"Through my sewing circle. You know how women talk about these things."

Celia put down the questionnaire. "Charlotte will take you through to the bedroom, Mrs B. There is a choice of three sizes. Please feel free to use our samples to ascertain the one most appropriate. We have prepared a page of instruction along with diagrams according to the practice of Dr Marie Stopes. It is important that the device feels comfortable for you. There is a hand-basin, soap and a towel for cleaning the samples after use. We will provide you with two items in your size. I am afraid we cannot offer any clinical advice as we are not qualified to do so. Once you have found what you want, there is a waiver we would like you to sign."

Mrs B stood up. "Thank you," she said and followed Charlotte through to the bedroom.

As soon as the door had closed, Celia blew out a breath. She could feel the little pool of sweat that had formed just above her collarbone, soaked into her blouse. The whole conversation could not have taken more than five minutes yet she felt exhausted. She leaned over to the untouched cup of tea, picked it up, took a couple of sips. She usually drank it with sugar, but she didn't care, her mouth was so dry. The door to the bedroom opened. Charlotte.

"Bloody hell," her friend hissed. "What have we let ourselves in for?"

Celia motioned for her to stop talking, move away from the door. Charlotte plonked herself down on the armchair again, lit up the cigarette she had been holding for the last few minutes.

"How was she in there?"

"Fine," Charlotte whispered. "The poor woman. Well, she isn't poor, of course. If we get any more like her and the word gets around, we'll have the whole of Catholic Glasgow's wealthy women waiting in the hallway."

"I wasn't expecting to be serving the middle classes."

"Me neither."

"But what can we do? I don't know about you. But I'm a feminist first, a socialist second."

The bedroom door opened again. Mrs B stood there, slightly flushed, her coat open. "Thank you. I have taken two items in my size." She strode across the kitchen floor, pausing by the table to place a ten-shilling note by the saucer the same way she might tip a wait-ress. Without waiting for a word of protest, the offer of a scone or the request of a waiver to sign, she proceeded on her journey out of the kitchen, out of the flat. Charlotte jumped up to the window, peered out from behind the curtain. "Look at her go," she said. "She's walking as fast as she can without running."

The bell rang again.

"Round two," Celia said, getting up to answer the door this time. "Can you check in the bedroom to see if everything's in order."

The poor woman stood in the doorway trembling, clasping this flat, round object wrapped in newspapers like it was the crown jewels themselves she was holding. Celia could see she had once been an extremely pretty girl but her cheeks all rouged up now couldn't hide the gaunt pallor and desperation that had come to reside on her face. Once Celia had brought her through to the kitchen, she decided against making an offer of tea, went straight to the drinks cupboard to bring her a shot of brandy which she quickly accepted. Charlotte offered her a cigarette, also gratefully received. Celia had just managed to get an initial out of her for her name when Mrs T started unwrapping the newspaper from her parcel, not pausing to undo the string properly, just scraping away at it frantically with her fingers.

"See," the woman said.

What Celia could see was a large plain dinner-plate with the name of a well-known city newspaper embossed in the centre. "What is it?" she asked.

"The paper give me this. For having ten bairns. You had to write in and tell them. They printed a list so readers could check you weren't lying or anything. See my name's on the back. Mother of ten, it says. Just so you got proof of what I have to tell you. So you dinnae think I'm trying to get something for nothing."

"We're not here to pass judgement on you, Mrs T," Celia said. "Nor to investigate. We would just like to know the reason for you coming here."

"That's bloody simple. I need help, that's what. I've had thirteen bairns, ten are still alive by some miracle. I've done my duty for King and country, that plate of mine proves it. My man lost his job at the pickle factory a few years back so he's no bloody use to anyone. After the last bairn, the hospital told me my womb was prolapsed or something. Is that the right word? And if I had any more weans, it'd probably kill me. Not that they told me how to stop having the bloody things. Even when I asked them. It was like I'd spat in their faces the way they turned their heads so quick. My drunkard of a husband disnae seem to care that banging me up again is like a hangman's noose around my neck. As long as he satisfies himself whenever the fancy takes him. So I come to you. I couldnae have another wee drop of brandy, I'm shaking something terrible."

Charlotte poured Mrs T another glass, one for herself while she was at it. Celia went on to explain the service on offer, then Charlotte directed her towards the bedroom.

"These caps are no going to make me epileptic or something," Mrs T. asked, as she rose unsteadily from her chair. "Or send me to the loony bin. I hear they can do that, make you go doolally. Promise me that's no true. I dinnae want to go to no loony bin for this."

"I promise you it's not true. Now Charlotte will show you what to do."

Celia poured herself a brandy this time, knocked it back quickly, thought about having another, her nerves so fraught. The plate was still on the table, she had a quick look at it, front and back. The name of the awardee was a Mrs Frances Dixon. So much for a Mrs T then. She pinched a cigarette from Charlotte's case, lit up, let the tobacco rake her lungs, relax her a bit. As she sat back, watched the smoke drift up towards the clothes pulley, she thought of Jonny. His mother was getting more ill by the day, he didn't think she had much longer to live, her lungs were giving out fast although it didn't stop the poor dear smoking. She examined her own cigarette at this thought, took another drag. Compared to these beasts of men these two women had for husbands, Jonny seemed like an angel. He didn't drink much for a start. And perhaps he did look a bit like Ivor Novello if he'd just lose the tan. But then again, he might come across just fine in the courting. Who knows what kind of monster he might turn out to be later. You just couldn't tell with men. And where was that Charlotte, she was taking her time with this woman?

She stood up, felt a bit more calm in herself, the brandy quickly doing its work. She walked over to the bedroom, opened the door up a crack, poked her head in. Mrs T was sat on the bed with her skirts up, bloomers down, cigarette in her mouth, Charlotte crouched between her legs, sleeves rolled up, hands fiddling about where they shouldn't be.

"Oh for God's sake, Charlotte. I thought we were only giving advice."

Charlotte turned her head to the door. "I'm only helping out, one woman to another. I've fitted these things enough times to know what to do."

Mrs T resumed smoking, cool as you like, as if she was observing a plumber come in to fix her pipes, flicking the ash into the palm of her hand.

"I'll be outside," Celia said, closing the door on them.

There had been only the two clients that first session. But come the second session on Thursday, they had five visitors, three coming through meetings and pamphlets, two recommended by Mrs B of all people. The following week, seven women turned up on the Tuesday, ten turning up on the Thursday. Within two weeks, they had seen twenty-four women, given away forty-eight caps. Celia could also see that the women's reasons for attending were beginning to divide into three clear categories – religion, health and poverty, sometimes all three reasons present in one case.

That final day of ten clients, they had to extend the session by an hour, making it too cold and too late for Celia to return home any other way than in a hansom. She decided to save the fare, stay at the flat, Charlotte too, who telephoned Mrs Kahn from a neighbour's to tell that Celia was staying with her. They were both exhausted anyway.

Celia prepared the hot water bottle, wrapped the metal container in a cloth cover, slipped it into the bed, then moved in beside it. Charlotte came into the bedroom, her winter coat worn over her nightdress, with a couple of bottles of stout she'd picked up from the public house earlier, a straw placed in the neck of each. Charlotte got in beside her still with her coat on while Celia plumped up the pillows. She could see the reflection of the two of them in the mirror on the wardrobe door swung open but neither of them willing to bear the cold again to close it. What a pretty pair they made, she thought, puffing on their cigarettes, drinking their ale through a straw.

"Sucking the monkey," Charlotte said.

"Pardon?"

"Drinking your beer like this. That's what the sailors call it. Sucking the monkey. I can't remember why exactly. That Brian I used to see told me. He was in the Navy."

"Yes, I remember him." She thought how she had eavesdropped on their coupling on this very bed. "He did have the smell of the sea about him."

Charlotte sniffed heavily as if she was still trying to smell him out from between the sheets. "I'm absolutely exhausted."

"Me too. I thought all this work was going to make me feel good. It's just making me anxious and depressed."

"Which bit of it is getting you down?"

"Listening to these women's stories. It makes me so angry and tearful at the same time. And there's so little we can do. I'm sure half of these women don't really know how to fit these caps properly. They just take them from us so as not to be embarrassed."

"To be honest, for some I doubt there's much there to fit the cap too. Their whole insides have been ripped up and stretched apart. Who was that woman? Mrs P? Dropped sixteen children in seventeen years, half of them dead on arrival. It makes me want to be like you, practise social purity."

"We need a proper clinic. With proper doctors and nurses."

"I wouldn't bet on doctors knowing much about women's matters either. Look how many of our clients told us they asked their doctor for advice and he hadn't a clue what to tell them. I'm better qualified than them to know about what goes on down there. Not some quack who can't tell a valise from a vagina."

Twenty-seven

The next morning, she woke up early, head woozy from the stout, still dark outside, but the moon sending in a crack of blue-white light through the curtain onto the blankets. Charlotte sleeping beside her, lightly snoring, such a beautiful face, she would have reached out and stroked her cheek but for fear of waking her up. She would also like to have turned over, gone back to whatever dream she had emerged from, but it was Friday, the eve of the Sabbath, plenty chores to be done at home. She rose from the bed, peed into the chamber pot, raked up a fire in the grate, put a kettle to simmer on the hot-plate, left Charlotte to sleep, let herself out. She took a subway into St. Enoch station, walked the rest of the way, feeling much better in herself than she had done the day before. Dim sunlight was sneaking its way into the morning, those of the population with jobs were on the march to their offices, the factories, the shipyards, the steelworks and the mines. And here she was travelling in the opposite direction pleased with her own efforts towards the liberation of women from their yoke of poverty, religion and poor health. She entered her home, Papa Kahn and Nathan already gone to the shop, exchanged a few words with her mother who was giving a good polish to the silver candle-sticks that had been in her family since Napoleonic times. The one good thing about her mother was she didn't say too much first thing in the morning, taking a few hours to wind herself up like a bagpipe before moaning out her customary complaints. She picked up the shopping bag, her mother's list of messages with the usual bread and herrings to be collected for the *Shabbos* meal, went back out again. She was humming quietly to herself. That old tune by Ivor Novello. *Keep the Home Fires Burning.*

When she got back, she'd hardly had time to bring the shopping through the front door when her mother accosted her in the hallway.

"There's a gentleman here to see you. Just arrived."

Celia glanced at herself in the hall mirror. Her hair was all mussed up, she'd hardly given herself a wash that morning, her hands stinking of vinegar from scooping pickled herrings and cucumbers from the barrels outside Fogell's bakery.

"What will he think of me?"

"I wouldn't worry trying to tidy yourself. Just go on in. Hurry."

It wasn't Jonny as she had expected. Instead there was the long figure of a man sat with his back to her, legs stretched out to the fire, didn't even get up when she entered, just turned his head round towards her.

"I believe you two know each other," Madame Kahn said.

"Good morning, Miss Kahn. It's been a long time." It was Jimmy Docherty. Reporter for the *Evening Citizen.*

"Yes, it has, Mr Docherty. Four years perhaps."

"*Tempus fugit* and all that. Why don't you sit yourself down."

"This is my own home, Mr Docherty. I think I can do as I wish."

"Celia," her mother scolded before wriggling herself into a more polite demeanour. "Now, Mr Docherty, please tell me how you know my daughter?"

Docherty straightened himself up from his slouch, gave the knot of his tie a pinch as if this somehow proved himself a gentleman. "I can promise you my dealings with Miss Kahn have all been above board."

"I'm glad to hear that. But I cannot imagine what reason she has to be in the company of men of the press in the first place. I don't think I know my own daughter any more."

"Mother. Will you please stop being so dramatic."

"Dramatic? I never know where you are. You are like a lodger in this house. A mother cannot worry about her daughter?"

"There is nothing to worry about." She could see Jimmy Docherty smiling as he slowly turned in his seat, untangled his long limbs to take up a proper position at the table. He reached into his pocket, took out a notebook and pencil.

"Please sit down, Miss Kahn."

This time she did as she was told. She placed her hands defiantly in a clasp in front of her, then withdrew them when she caught a whiff of the pickled herring off her skin. "What can I do for you?"

"It's about your brother."

"Nathan?"

"No, the other one. Avram. The one that was murdered."

"I thought it was an accident."

"There might have been a misunderstanding. But they intended to kill whom they killed."

"I don't know what you are talking about, Mr Docherty. But my Uncle Mendel will know all the details. He will be back from the Highlands this evening for the Sabbath. He can tell you what you need to know."

"I don't need to know anything. I've already spoken to the constables. Two men have been arrested. One is a local pharmacist who mistakenly believed your brother to be having an affair with his wife. That was the unfortunate mix-up. Another man – the accomplice or the actual murderer, that is yet to be established – was a quarry guard whom I believe held a grudge against your brother."

"He was my adopted brother."

"I'm sorry. Your adopted brother then."

"He was always going to be trouble, that boy," her mother said. "From the moment I first saw him. *Tzores*, I thought. This can only be trouble. And was I wrong? Was I wrong? Now we have a murder in the house."

Docherty scratched his nose, then held up his hand in a languid, gentle gesture for her mother to stop. "Mrs Kahn. Please let me explain my purpose for being here."

Madame Kahn bit her lower lip, folded her arms. Docherty continued. "Like you, we understood this incident to be an unfortunate accident. Now that it is being treated as the murder of a young

211

Glasgow man, then, of course, it is of local interest. We have reason to believe the involvement of the quarry guard may have been due to some anti-Jewish feeling. I believe the phrase is 'anti-Semitic.'"

"Anti-Semitic," her mother shrilled. She pulled up the sleeves of her blouse, held out her bare arms to Docherty. "See these hands. I worked them to the bones for making Army uniforms for our soldiers. To the bones. And balaclavas I knitted too. Every day, balaclavas I send to the Front."

"Mother, will you please calm down."

"I am perfectly calm."

"I am going to telephone Papa to come."

"You will not do such a thing." Her mother raised the back of her hand to her head in another dramatic gesture. "I have such a headache now. I am going to lie down. If you will excuse me, Mr Docherty, I will leave you to speak to my daughter. When this headache comes, the pain is unbearable. I have to close my eyes."

"I can bring you a hot towel, Mama."

"No, no. Just speak to this man."

With Madame Kahn gone, Docherty stretched himself out again, plucked a cigarette from his top pocket, lit up without even asking a by-your-leave, causing her to get up, bring over an ashtray from the mantelpiece. She decided against offering him a cup of tea.

"Please excuse my mother, Mr Docherty. But she is of German descent. During the war she was interned in a camp as an enemy alien. It's an experience she's neither forgiven nor forgotten. Just the slightest criticism for being a German or a Jew sends her into a panic."

He tapped the end of his cigarette on the table, then lit up. "It's understandable," he said unconvincingly. "Now, about this other matter. The reason I came here is simple. We're interested in the Jewish angle. This anti-Semitic attack. Our readers probably don't know too much about the Jew community in Glasgow. How many are you? Eight thousand? Ten thousand?"

"I don't know. You would have to ask my father about these things."

"You see, we don't often get stuff involving Jews. I mean you pretty much keep yourselves to yourselves. Like some secret society. There was that famous Oscar Slater murder case, he was a Jew wasn't he? But that must have been before the war. There's been a few run-ins over gambling, accusations of sweated labour, that Manny Shinwell was a Jew, of course, but for the most part you keep your copy-books clean. So what I was looking for was a bit of background. And remembering you being of that faith, I thought you could help."

"This isn't really the best time to be coming here talking about this. My mother never liked Avram but the rest of us are in shock about his death. My father has only just got over his grief and returned to work. I don't find all this talk of anti-Jewish sentiment to be appropriate."

"I'm only doing my job, Miss Kahn. I'm not asking much. Just a few personal accounts of what it feels like being a Jew living in this city. Perhaps you could introduce me to some local dignitaries or tell me a bit about Avram. He was a credit draper, wasn't he? And this uncle of yours too. Selling goods on credit to poor Highland crofters and village folk. Was he lending money to them too? That's what this quarry guard is saying. Lending his sister money to buy things she didn't want on the never-never so she was always in his debt."

"I don't want to talk about this."

"I did you a favour those years back, digging deep to find out about Agnes' death. It's time to collect, Miss Kahn."

"I appreciate what you did for me. But I think you should leave."

"Oh, come on. I'm on a deadline with this. All the other papers will be running the same story. But you can give an old hack like me an edge. I could do with a hand here."

"Mr Docherty. Will you please go."

Docherty rubbed out his cigarette harsh in the ashtray, stood up, picked up his hat. "There's something I should tell you, Miss Kahn." There was an angry colour to his face, his eyes blazed down at her. "I lied to you about Agnes. I didn't want to upset you with the truth. Natural causes I told you. But the guards did get to her. They were force-feeding her till she got sick and died. It's a pity you left her to languish in the jail. Maybe if you'd gone to the press like she sugges-ted, she might have lived. I'll leave you with that thought, Miss Kahn."

No sooner had Docherty closed the front door than the telephone rang. She wanted to let it be but she had a sudden sympathy for her mother lying down with her splitting headache. Shaking, she picked up the earpiece, let the operator hand over the call. It was Jonny. His mother had passed away.

She didn't tell Papa Kahn about Docherty's visit. Her mother appeared happy to co-operate in the conspiracy for she didn't mention the matter either. Other events had taken over anyway. Jonny had sounded quite calm on the telephone, he didn't talk long, there were other people to notify. She wished him 'long life', as was the custom. Just prior to the commencement of the Sabbath dinner she told her mother, who surprisingly let out a wail on hearing the news before immediately beginning her calculations, her headache quickly forgotten.

"Now if this Mrs Levy, may she rest in peace, died this morning, then it was too late to bury her today. The funeral cannot take place during *Shabbos* so the service will be on Sunday. There will be time to think of the right approach."

"What right approach?" Papa Kahn said, looking up from his peeling of an apple. There was a time when he could pare the skin off in one complete piece, this skill with a knife having impressed Celia ever since she was a child. It was, he told her, the basis on which he decided he could be a tailor. Now the knife shook in his hand, she feared he might cut himself or that the apple spin out of his grasp.

"I think we should go to the funeral," Madame Kahn replied. "It is the right thing to do."

"What are you talking about?" her father said. "We don't even know the family."

"It is this Jonny's mother. We should put in an appearance."

"At the funeral? I'm not *schlepping* all the way out to the Necropolis. Anyway, there is no reason to start behaving like *machetonim*."

Celia paused in her vague reading about the progress of the British Mandate in Palestine as reported by the *Glasgow Jewish Evening Times*. She hadn't really been listening closely to her parents. She was still upset from the conversation with Docherty. It wasn't even what he had told her about Agnes. That event was so much in the past she could hardly feel guilty about it anymore. And how did she know that he hadn't lied just to hurt her? She was more disturbed about Avram

214

being killed in an anti-Semitic attack. Why should anyone kill him for being a Jew? She had always felt safe in this city, in this country. Perhaps this sense of security had only been an illusion. But then she heard her father talking about '*machetonim*', about two sets of parents brought together by the marriage of their children.

"What are you saying?" she asked.

Even her mother looked a bit embarrassed. "I am just saying that perhaps we should show some kind of consideration, that's all. Given our situation."

"What situation?"

"Between you and this Dr Levy. After all, you have seen a lot of him lately."

"Well, I won't be any longer. Now that his mother has died, he will return to Palestine."

"That's settled then," her father said, cutting his apple into not so neat segments. "No need to attend the funeral."

"What about the *shiva* house?" Madame Kahn asked.

"It is not necessary, Martha. We don't know the family. There is no need to pay our respects. Celia can go if she wants. After all, she is friends with the boy. What do you say, Celia?"

"I'm not sure, Papa. There is time to think about it."

"Why not have a piece of apple?" he offered, smiling at her. "Then please call Nathan and Uncle Mendel to the table. It is time to welcome in the Sabbath."

Twenty-eight

MRS LEVY'S FUNERAL AS PREDICTED took place on the Sunday. After that, there was to be a full week of mourning. With both the Levy's house and Agnes' flat being in the West End, Celia decided to go to the *shiva* on the Monday night, then stay over in the flat to prepare for the Tuesday evening birth control session. She would have preferred not to attend the *shiva* house alone but she didn't want to subject Charlotte to a room full of gossiping, tea-drinking Jewish women while the male mourners conducted their service elsewhere in the house. She would go by herself, remain as inconspicuous as possible, pay her respects to Jonny at the end of the service, retire to a night by herself at Agnes' flat while telling her parents she would be staying with Charlotte.

The Levy's home was quite magnificent. The upper apartments of a grand merchant house on Great Western Road. There was a pillared entrance, then a wide red-carpeted stairway leading to a long hallway with various rooms leading off. She knew Jonny's father owned a garment factory in the city but she didn't appreciate that his wealth could stretch to such a wonderful home. The whole of her parent's flat in Thistle Street could probably fit into the one front room here. She could almost forgive her mother's excitement at her notion of being *machetonim* with these people. The Gorbal Jews often talked about the *ganze machers* – the big shots – of the West End but she had never taken these comments seriously. She didn't appreciate that Jews could actually live in this high style in Glasgow. Like millionaires. But even with such spacious accommodation, the place was thankfully quite crowded. She was able to slip into the room reserved for women, take her place on a chair at the back by a tall, close-curtained window, gaze down at her handbag.

She found it quite pleasant, sitting like this, anonymous, the murmur of subdued conversation, the drone of the male prayers somewhere off in another room, the smell of expensive perfume, the rustle of dresses, the vague whiff of camphor, the clink of teacups, the covered mirrors, the heat making her drowsy. Wrapped up as she was within this cocoon of her race. This was no doubt how it would feel to be ensconced within that Jewish State the Zionists craved so much. Protected. For she still struggled with the thought that here in Scotland, a man could hate a Jew enough to murder him. This was not Russia, after all. Poor Avram. And poor Jonny. To lose a mother. What would it feel like to lose her own mother? She was so often at odds with her, so appalled at some of her behaviour. Yet she could never forget that this was the woman who had borne her, given her this life. Yes, poor Jonny. No doubt, once this *shiva* week was over, he would be booking his passage back to Palestine where the Garden of Eden and the *kibbutz* awaited, where he could ride his horses, drive his wagons, hack away at the soil with his mattock, plant his oranges and lemons on land purchased with her farthings.

She must have dozed off. For when she raised her head, many of the seats around her were empty. In their black dresses, black hats and veils, the women were quietly moving out like weary coal miners at the end of a shift. She could see the principal mourners taking their place on low stools in the hallway. There was Jonny, unshaven, his eyes hollow with tiredness, the lapel of his jacket cut by the rabbi's knife as a symbol of his grieving. Seated beside him, the man who must be his father, a drained face set off with wild eyebrows like hanks of cotton wool, a frail body lost within a too large suit, looking as if he hadn't much longer for this life either. Then came what must have been a couple of the deceased's siblings, tiny women for whom these low chairs appeared quite comfortable, followed by Jonny's own siblings – two older sisters and two older brothers. She wished them all 'long life', each of them clasping her hands in earnest thanks, not enquiring who she might be, for which she was grateful. Eventually, she reached Jonny at the end of the line.

"You came," he said.

"Of course, I came. Why wouldn't I?" Then she hurriedly put out her hand. "I wish you 'long life.'"

He took her hand in both of his. "Thank you." He held her there. His eyes were bloodshot. She wondered whether from tiredness or tears. She couldn't imagine him crying. "You are here alone?" he asked.

"Yes."

He let go his grasp. "Let me walk with you to the station."

"You should stay here with your family."

"What I should do is get out of this place. It's like being stuck in the trenches all over again. I need fresh air. I need to see life. All this talk of death. It depresses me."

"It's called mourning."

He smiled, a strand of spittle forming between his lips. "Everyone will be gone in a few minutes. Once the service is over, they pour out of here faster than the Children of Israel escaping Egypt. Please wait for me. And I'll walk with you."

"I can't really."

"Please."

"All right. I'll wait for you outside. But please don't be long."

She didn't linger outside the entrance to the house. Instead, she walked up from the gateway to the next corner and back just to keep warm. She had her muffler and her coat was decent enough for the weather but the contrast after the stifling heat of the *shiva* house made her feel cold. Perhaps it was the chill of death itself. There was a full moon, her breath misting the air in its beam, she felt very aware of the sound of her heels on the pavement stones as she walked, her steps quicker than they might have been.

Jonny had looked genuinely shattered back there, seated in his low mourning stool, giving her a feeling to put her arms around him, stroke away his grief. And now she would have to lie to him, let him accompany her all the way to Kelvinbridge Station, just so she could pretend to be seen off home before taking another route back to Agnes' flat. She should have come here with Charlotte. That was her mistake. Now she was caught in her own deceit. What she needed was a cigarette to calm herself. Or a bottle of nerve tonic. Perhaps she should not turn back at this corner, but continue walking to the flat.

"Celia."

She turned round, Jonny running towards her, his coat flapping, one hand holding on to his hat.

"Thank you for waiting." He took a rolled-up cigarette out from its tuck in his hat-band, lit up.

"I thought you only smoked a pipe."

"Emergency rations. Ran out of pipe tobacco. Pinched this from my brother."

She wished he'd pinched one for her as well. Even though it would be unladylike for her to smoke in the street. Although Charlotte would have done it, no bother.

"How are you feeling?" she asked.

"I'm just about holding it all together. She'd been ill with her lungs for a while, but it's still a shock when it comes."

"How old was she?"

"Sixty-six."

"That's still a long life."

"I was her last child. The doctor told her she should have one more. Just to clean out her system. That was me. The system-cleaner. The bleach baby. My oldest sister just told me that as we reminisced about our darling mother." He sucked hard on his cigarette, tossed it into the gutter. "Charming."

"I'm sure she loved you."

"I don't think she loved any of us. She never forgave the world or God or whatever for forcing her to leave Russia. Her body might have been here but her heart and soul were always back in Odessa. In *der heim*, as she used to say. Thirty years in this country yet she hardly spoke a word of English. To be honest, she wasn't much of a mother. Or a wife either. So my father put all his energy into his business. Making us a loveless but wealthy family. I'm sorry, forgive me for talking like this. I know you and your family have been burdened with your own grief."

They had reached Byres Road. Straight ahead, Great Western Road continued on to the station. Across the wide avenue to her left, the locked-up entrance to the Botanic Gardens. Since the day of her rape, she had never stepped through those wrought-iron gates. To her right, the street that led to Agnes' flat. Beside her, Jonny. It was if some divine force had brought her to this one spot. The Jews had a Yiddish word for it. *Bashert*. Fate.

"Celia? Are you all right?"

"I'm sorry?"

"You were dreaming."

"Come," she said, walking quickly away from him.

"Where are we going?" he asked.

But she didn't answer, frightened to break the force of her will with the sound of her own voice.

"Where are we going?"

She was almost at Agnes' street. She could turn back, of course. The road ahead didn't look too beckoning anyway. The trees were bare, the branches strangely eerie in the moonlight, the dead leaves swept into little mounds along the pavement to be collected in the morning if the wind allowed. A horse and cart approached from the far end, the driver shrivelled up inside his greatcoat, hat pulled down over his face. Such soothing sounds, that slow trot, the roll of the wheels, the lazy jangle of the harness.

"Evenin'" the driver called as he passed.

She didn't respond, but Jonny lifted his hat, called "Good evening" in reply. The cart trundled past. She didn't know why but this gentlemanly exchange calmed her as if everything was now all right with the world. She walked further up the street, searching in her pockets for her keys as she did so. She unlocked the main door, hurried up the steps to the first floor, again fumbling with the keys, Jonny standing at her shoulder, she knew he was desperate to ask what was going on but she was grateful he didn't for she didn't really know herself. She pushed in the storm doors, then finally only the flat entrance to deal with, so many obstacles in her path. With that door unlocked, she entered the flat. She didn't bother with trying to find the switch for the electric light, the moonlight was enough. Jonny came in behind her, she turned, closed the door with her rump, leaned up against its panels, grasped the lapels of his coat as if to keep herself from falling.

"Hold me," she said.

He swept off his hat, did as he was told. She leant against the front of his coat, felt the roughness of his unshaven chin against her forehead, smelled the staleness of his body and breath, these unwashed symbols of the mourning son, feeling all the closer to him because of it. She rocked back and forth in his embrace, listened to his heartbeat, her own heartbeat, the touch of his hands on her hair, his lips close to her ear, making her tremble. She pushed him gently from her, let her hand find the cold nipple of the electric light switch, pulled it down with a harsh click. The spell broken.

She rushed to close the curtains while he wandered around the room. Then she was busy kneeling at the fire, until he touched her shoulder.

"Let me do that," he said.

"What am I supposed to do then?" she said with a laugh that was a bit too shrill for her liking.

"Why don't you sit down over there and tell me what's going on."

She went over to the mantelpiece first, thank God for Charlotte's cigarettes, offered him one which he refused, took one for herself, sat down in an armchair. Jonny with his back to her, still in his overcoat, scuttling the coal on to the grate.

"I could lie to you," she said, suddenly feeling quite in control of herself and the situation. "I could tell you this flat belongs to a friend of mine. Which is true up to a point. But that friend was Agnes Calder and you know she is dead. But she left me with a liferent to her property. Do you know what that is? A liferent?"

"I know what it is."

"So I have had access to this place, to my own little nest, for the last four years. Nobody knows about it."

"Nobody?" he said, rising from his kneel before the fire as it started to take. He looked at his hands for stains of coal dust. Such slender fingers he had. She was surprised she hadn't really noticed that before. She waved her own hand about with the lit cigarette. It was something Charlotte would do. "Well, the lawyer knows, of course." She felt almost drunk now with a kind of silly giddiness. "And a few of my female comrades. But no-one from my family. Or the wider Jewish community in the Gorbals. I am a mystery woman of property. The Jewish Mata Hari of … of Maryhill. And I would like to keep it that way."

"So why tell me?"

"You are leaving for your Garden of Eden," she said. "My secret is safe with you."

He took off his coat, laid it down on a chair, stuffed his hands in his trouser pockets, played with some coins, while he had a good gaze around the place. "Cosy," he said. "What do you use it for?"

"That would be telling, Jonny Levy. But since you seem to be so good with your chores, why not put on some water to boil while I clean up."

She rose from the armchair, strode into the bedroom, locked the door behind herself. She gasped in a cold breath. The room was freezing. She flicked on the light, drew the curtains closed. "What am I doing?" she asked herself. "What am I doing?" Meanwhile, she realised her body was doing other things. Taking off her coat. Going over to the small sink, splashing water on to her face, washing her hands. She sat down in front of the dressing table, dabbed some powder on her cheeks, freshened up her lipstick. In the reflection in the glass, she saw the boxes of rubber caps stacked in the corner. 12 x *douzaines*, it said on the labels. *Importe de France.* She kept on watching them as she brushed her hair before eventually getting up, going over to the pile, taking out one in her size, then covering up the boxes with a blanket. She went over to the sink, washed the cap in soapy water, sat down on the edge of the bed, took down her drawers, eased her buttocks off the bed towards the floor until she sat in an appropriate squat, then carefully fitted the appliance. For extra precaution, she inserted a quinine suppository, wiped the grease off her hands with a face cloth. A shiver passed through her, a sign her body and mind had reunited again. "What a woman has to go through," she thought. She adjusted her clothing, stood up, opened the bedroom door.

"Come here," she said.

He was in the process of pouring boiling water into a teapot. Poor man, she thought, he doesn't know what to do. One minute he's being asked to behave like a domestic servant, the next like Rudolph

Valentino. And all this on the day after his mother's funeral. He put down the kettle, followed her into the bedroom. She switched off the light, sat down on the far side of the bed with her back to him, began to undress. She was hoping he would stay on the nearside of the bed, take off his clothes as well. She didn't want to have to talk, try to explain anything, for if conversation were to get in the way, she was sure her courage would fail her. She stripped down to her shift, swung her body round and under the blankets in one swift movement. She almost screamed as her skin touched the freezing sheets. He moved in quickly beside her, she clung to him for warmth more than anything else, felt the rough cotton of his long underwear against her thighs where her own garment had ridden high. She lay with him in silence, their bodies warming against each other. It was quiet outside but there was a gentle "thump, thump, thump," on the ceiling above the bed, a neighbour's child perhaps playing with a ball. He lay on his back, she could just make out the outline of his features in the darkness, the light through the too-thin curtains. She had expected him to be relaxed and in control like some silent movie sheikh. Or like those soldiers who went to the Front, returning home with their sexual craft honed in the arms of French prostitutes with their French kissing and their French letters and whatever else the French did that was supposed to be so sophisticated between the sheets. But he looked as terrified as she did.

"I'm not a virgin," she said. Then added quickly. "I was raped when I was eighteen. There's been nobody else since. I thought you should know."

He turned on his side towards her, raised his head onto the crook of his arm, stroked her cheek.

"You're shivering," he said.

He moved his body closer into hers, continued to stoke her.

"I'm ready," she said softly.

Their lovemaking was considerate but tense. Her head was so full of concerns she could hardly allow her body to take over. Was the cap properly in place? What was she supposed to do afterwards? Leave it in, take it out? Should she douche or not? She couldn't even feel it inside her. But that's what that Mrs B had told her – that the man couldn't feel if it was in place either. Strange she should pick up on this piece of advice from a client. Jonny rolled over on top of her and she had a moment of anxiety, a flash of memory of her young assailant with the dishwater blond hair. But as soon as she felt Jonny move himself inside her, that tainted thought disappeared. She arched her back to receive him, the action bringing just a stretch of pain that quickly turned to pleasure. He raised his weight on to his arms, pushed himself in and out of her, she could see his face now in the half-light, unshaven in grief, eyes pressed closed, his lips stretched over his teeth, those slender fingers digging into her shoulders, his pace gathering until it was all over. He eased himself off, let out a groan as he fell back on to the sheets, grappled for her hand, held it tight when he found it. She listened to his breathing as it began to subside, sucked in the warmth and smell of this masculine presence.

"I will go back to Palestine," he said. "You know that."

She stared at the ceiling rose, felt the grip of his hand strengthen in expectation. She knew what he wanted her to say. Instead she whispered: "You should go back to the *shiva* house. They will be wondering where you are."

He breathed out a long sigh, turned on to his side to face her, traced a finger lightly along her arm from her elbow to her wrist. She shivered. "I'm the youngest child," he said. "It's unlikely anyone's noticed I've gone."

"Still, it's best you go."

"Whatever you say. What will you do?"

"I'm going to stay here tonight."

He rose out of the bed, she watched him as he dressed. She'd never seen a man putting on his underclothes before, tucking in his shirt, buttoning his trousers, looping his braces up and over, fiddling with his cuff links, such an intimate scene, almost more intimate than their lovemaking. He leaned over, kissed her lightly on the lips.

"Stay in bed," he said. "I'll let myself out."

Twenty-nine

THE SOUND OF THE FISHMONGER'S BELL WOKE HER. Then his shout of prices for his herrings, smoked haddock and salted cod. His cart must have been just below her window for she could even hear the snort of his horse. There was bright daylight behind the curtains, she knew it had to be late in the morning, later than she had slept for a long time. But this was a remarkable day. Her own personal holiday. St. Celia's Day she would call it. A day devoid of chores. She could do absolutely anything she wanted. She stretched her arms out wide, felt the slight soreness between her thighs. She remembered Stopes' instructions. She could either take out the cap and douche if she felt anxious in any way about its effectiveness. Or just leave it in for a couple of days until 'the usual processes of Nature disposed of the now impotent sperms.' She would leave it in. At least for today, St. Celia's Day.

She thought about getting up but the lure of the warm bedclothes was still too much. She wanted to just lie for a while, recall the events of the night before. She couldn't believe she had acted in such a forthright way. "Come here," she recalled herself saying as she had beckoned Jonny into the bedroom. Charlotte would have been proud of her. She just hoped he didn't think of her as one of those flapper girls, so easy to pet, so easy to get. The act itself hadn't been anything special. If she were to be honest, she was just glad it was over. And that all these contraceptive issues had been properly attended to. The sexual life of the responsible modern woman was such a fussy one. But now she could relax about it. She was sure the next time would be better. And there was that fishmonger with his bell and his banter again. Time to get up. His prices weren't even that attractive. But then, this was the West End, not the Gorbals.

Even on this, her special day, she spent a few hours cleaning and dusting the flat in preparation for another cap distribution session that evening. She wondered how many poor souls would turn up this time. At least, she could counsel them from the standpoint of one who knew what it was like to have used the device. She thought about calling on Charlotte, telling her what had happened, her friend no doubt getting all crude and smutty, desperate for details, full of questions. Especially the one she didn't want to ask herself. "Isn't he supposed to be returning to Palestine?" But she decided she wanted to keep this day to herself, wrap herself up in these warm feelings before they melted away. She went outside, bought herself a newspaper, sat down at a window-seat in Urquhart's Coffee House, watched the world go by. She wondered what those passers-by on the other side of the glass would think if they knew this was a woman who had lain with a man, a woman who now carried a cap full of sperm between her thighs. She wondered also what her lover was thinking as he sat on his low seat of mourning in a room full of covered mirrors.

The weather remained dry for her St. Celia's Day. A glorious autumn of azure skies with air as cold and sharp as a knife. She bought an iced bun, a bag of apples and did something she never thought she would ever do again. She decided to go for a walk in the Botanic Gardens. At first, she lingered at the gates by the red-brick station, its clock towers topped with its ornamental domes that always used to remind her father of Russia. Then with a sharp intake of breath, she strode through the gates. Just like that. An invisible line so easy to cross. She passed the glasshouses with their towering ferns, a battery of seated nannies rocking their perambulators, old men buried inside their overcoats watching the falling leaves, then down the winding stepped-pathway towards the river. She easily located the place where the socialist Sunday school had held its picnic, she remembered the tables laden with food, Agnes introducing her to this and that person. From this clearing, she moved on down to where that youth had taken her, the narrow walkway alongside the bank of the River

Kelvin, followed the path for some distance, it didn't seem as threatening as she remembered it. Back then in wartime, attending to its parks and gardens was probably not a priority in the minds of the Glasgow City Corporation. But now the rhododendron bushes and the branches of trees had been pruned back, the wooden fence fixed here and there with new railings.

She realised she had come too far, for up ahead was an unfamiliar stone bridge spanning the river. She turned back, her eyes scouring the bushes for the spot. What did she expect to find? The branches and weeds still flattened? A plaque? Her shoes? Yes, her shoes. Now she remembered. She had walked barefoot back to the picnic. Could her shoes still be here? How long did it take leather to rot away into the soil? Or would a dog or fox or other creature have come by and stolen them away? Or would a park-keeper have picked one up with his stick and said, "I wonder what happened here then?", scratching his head as some lascivious thought passed through his brain before tossing the shoe back into the bushes. But trying to locate the scene became futile, she would just have to choose a spot at random. A symbolic area. A white cross for the unknown soldier that was her innocence. She found somewhere suitable. A bush not so thick as to prevent a couple disappearing into its bowels to consummate some sinful act. She stood looking at the earth with its mulch of decaying leaves, twigs broken from bodies that could have lain there many years ago. It was like visiting a grave. But she felt stronger now. Not sad or bitter or angry as she might have expected. Last night had changed everything. It hadn't eradicated what had happened in this place but diminished its importance so that perhaps the memory would eventually shrivel up into a nothingness. She took out an apple from her pocket, polished its skin against her sleeve, took a bite, then threw it into the bushes.

She left the Botanic Gardens, strolled past Jonny's house on Great Western Road, not even with a sideways glance, just for the excitement at the chance he might be standing at a window, gazing across to the Gardens, thinking about her. She then continued on into the city, window-shopping the shoe shops, the furriers, the department stores, even with a mind to browse the jewellery emporia in the

Argyll Arcade, until the rain started spitting. Green's Playhouse was presenting a matinee of *The Bohemian Girl* so she was happy to go off and sit in the darkness in the company of a few old biddies as well as Ellen Terry, Gladys Cooper and of course, Ivor Novello, as they played out their parts in this gypsy tragedy. Reminding her of that day berry-picking with Jonny in Blairgowrie, the tinkers' encampment, the dancing bear, that fearsome woman telling her that she too was a traveller in this world. She kicked off her shoes, sank back into the plush velour, nibbled at her bun, happy in herself on this St. Celia's Day.

It was dark by the time she emerged from the flickering silence of the black-and-white picture world, the rain stopped now, she took the subway back to the West End. A hot-chestnut seller stood on the corner of Agnes' street, she caught sight of the lamplighter still on his rounds, and those little mounds of swept leaves still uncollected from the night before. She passed the lights in the tenement windows warm-bright and welcoming in these dark early nights of the approaching winter before the weather became too fierce.

At the entrance to Agnes' tenement, she found a toppled plant pot, its earth scattered across the steps, forcing her to scrape the terracotta shards and soil to one side with her shoe, something she would sort out later with a pan and brush. She glanced up to the first floor window, searching for a light that would show if Charlotte had arrived before her, the darkness meaning it took her a few seconds to realise the pane was broken, a large jagged hole where the glass had been. She pushed open the main door, rushed upstairs. The landing walls were daubed with white-paint slogans as were the double storm-doors. She had to climb halfway up the next flight to see what had been scrawled. "Hores". "Bitches". Those were just two of the words, she couldn't make out the rest especially where the paint had run. She raced back down to the first floor landing, pulled out the pamphlet stuck in the letter-box, fumbled for her keys, pushed open the door, careful to avoid touching any of the wet paint. When she entered the flat, the door into the kitchen slammed, locked against her. My God, the perpetrators were still here. But how could that be? The storm doors had been locked, the first floor window too high to scale. She knocked gently on the kitchen door.

"Charlotte. It's all right. It's only me. Celia." She put her ear to the door, could hear the footsteps of approach on the lino. She rapped again. "It's Celia."

The key turned in the lock, the door quickly pulled open. An ashen-faced Charlotte, a kitchen knife in her hand, fist knuckle-white around the handle. "Thank God. Thank God, it's you."

Charlotte fell into her arms, her head against her shoulder, they stood like that a good few moments, the mounds of Charlotte's small breasts pressed against her own, the silk of her blouse cool against her finger-tips. With a sigh, Charlotte pulled away, looked at her straight, eyes veined red from the sobbing. "It was terrible," she said.

"What happened?"

"What do you think?" She switched on the light, held out her hand with the knife to indicate the broken glass, a half-brick on the floor, a piece of paper tied around it in a neat bow. "All this."

Celia stooped to pick up the brick, rough and heavy it was in her hands, placed it on the kitchen table, pulled away the paper. A pamphlet the same as the one she'd plucked from the letter box. "Who did this?"

"A group of women. I don't know how many. Five. Six. Hard to say in the dark. They started banging on the storm-doors. I nearly went to open them, thought it might have been the constables or something, until that brick came through the window. Two or three of them outside shouting obscenities at me. Then it was over. They were gone in a flash. Like rats down a drain. Then it was you at the door. You must have missed them by a couple of minutes. Now where are my bloody cigarettes? I'm sure I left a packet on the mantelpiece."

"Have you seen what they've done to the close?"

"I've been holed up here in the kitchen."

"You'd better have a look. I just hope it's water-based paint. Otherwise we've got a job to do."

She let Charlotte go out to see for herself, went to fetch a broom and shovel to lift up the glass. She would have to get some newspaper or cardboard to tape over the hole in the window. Then there would be a tin bucket to fill with soapy water, add in a bit of bleach, hoped it would be easy enough to wash down the walls with a mop before their clients came. She was down on a crouch on the floor, picking up the larger pieces of glass when a huge tiredness came over her. Not some lack of physical energy but a kind of emotional lethargy. She couldn't believe how happy she had felt this morning on her St. Celia's Day. And now this. She stopped in her task, pushed herself up onto her feet, sank down in an armchair. Tiny specks of glass had dusted her fingertips. She rubbed her fingers together, the sensation quite pleasant. Then Charlotte came back in from admiring the handiwork in the close, she must have cadged a cigarette off a neighbour for she was trying to light one up as she entered, the draught from the broken window making it difficult.

"Can't even spell 'whores'," Charlotte said, back to her usual self. "Fucking ignorant women. It's a mess out there. I told our neighbour not to worry. We'd clean it up." Charlotte moved across the room, sat herself down in the armchair opposite in her usual slouch. "We should install a telephone. I could have called the police station."

She let Charlotte ramble on, the cigarette forgotten between her fingers, couldn't blame her, she must have had quite a shock, wanting to talk out all her anxiety. She could hear some noises from out on the street, children playing hopscotch, there had been a grid chalked on to the pavement outside the flat. She remembered herself doing the same as a child, hopping through the numbered squares, avoiding the beanbag, a single-hop there, a double straddle, then base. Life was simpler then. She wished she could do that now. Just a few steps and she was 'home'.

"Perhaps they're right," she said, stopping Charlotte in her tracks.

"Who?"

"These women. Saying we're whores. Look at what their pamphlet says." She read from the paper she'd untied from the brick. "'The distribution of birth control devices encourages sexual intercourse out of wedlock, a sin against the will of God'. Isn't that what we do?"

Charlotte laughed. "It might be what I do. But you're a bloody paragon of virtue."

The flush to Celia's neck and cheeks made it useless to disguise the truth even though she didn't feel too much like confessing. "Not any more," she said softly.

"I don't believe it." Charlotte, wide-eyed now, her red lips broadening into a sloppy grin. "You slept with your Jonny boy? Please tell."

Celia shrugged, as if sex to her was the most natural thing in the world. "Last night. Here in this flat. And I could do it because I was sitting in a room full of contraceptives."

"Oh, Celia. At least tell me you enjoyed yourself."

"It was fine."

"Fine? Just fine?"

"I don't want to talk about it. I just want to say that here we are getting all these women to sign declarations they are married before we can help them. And here I am dipping into our supplies whenever the fancy takes me."

"You're just upset about the broken window and the…" Charlotte waved a lazy arm in the direction of the front door. "Paint."

"Upset? I'm terrified. You could have been hurt. We both could have. I really feel threatened right now. And I don't have the energy to fight back. It's all too much. Jonny was right."

"Right about what?"

"Glasgow's problems run too deep. We keep trying and trying to make change, and look what happens? Threats against us. By other women. I don't think we can make any difference at all. Not here."

"Well, I want to carry on."

"I don't think I can."

A knock at the front door. Charlotte fished out a fob-watch from her trouser pocket. "Well, that's probably our first client now. What do you want to do?"

"I'm not staying."

"What about the paint in the close?"

"I'll worry about it tomorrow."

"Where will you go?"

She didn't say. But she knew exactly what her next destination was going to be. On this, her St. Celia's Day.

She managed to get there just as the service finished, visitors quietly pouring out the front door, murmured farewells and quick handshakes, the mourners still there on their low stools in the hallway. She stood in line with the rest of them, trying to compose herself, feeling hot and sweaty beneath her garments both from the hurried walking and the stale air in which she stood. She wondered if there was a religious law about keeping a window closed in a house of mourning so as to seal in the grief. A woman behind her in tall dark hat and veil asked:

"Are you family?"

Celia just shook her head solemnly in a gesture that thankfully didn't inspire further enquiry. She moved along the line, Jonny's father no longer present, but she wished the two aunts a 'long life', then Jonny's two older brothers and sisters, all of them looking more relaxed and professional in their acceptance of these condolences. Jonny looked pale but smiled generously on seeing her. She held out her hand and he took it in a way that somehow felt more intimate. Or perhaps it was just her imagination. Or her over-sensitive state. For she was trembling as she tried to find her voice. She didn't wish him 'long life'. Instead, she spoke those other words she hoped would console him.

Thirty

CELIA CAME OUT ON DECK, the first time she'd breathed fresh air in four days, not that the air had been so fresh back in the Liverpool docks when last she'd surfaced. There was close to a full moon in a star-filled sky, the temperature still warm, she'd never experienced that before, being able to wear just a blouse in the evening time. She felt better now that the ship had turned eastwards from the Atlantic into the Mediterranean, gone was that rolling sensation that made her stomach turn, not being able to hold down her food, vomiting into a bunk-side bucket as if it were her whole past life she was getting rid of. Which wasn't far from the truth. One of the other girls in the cabin was the same, sometimes the two of them throwing up together in some kind of vile symphony that would have made her laugh if her stomach muscles hadn't hurt so much already. She didn't know what had happened to the other two girls she shared third class with, not occupying their bunks since the steamship had set off, probably had some sailors for company somewhere, all the better for her and her other sick-mate with more room to throw up in. The smells of the lower deck didn't help her queasiness either, too near the engine rooms with their stifling ooze of diesel, and the kitchens with their reek of whatever was lard-frying in the pans. 'Getting there is half the fun,' was the steamship line slogan. Not if you're travelling third class.

She ran her tongue over her teeth, still a taste of staleness there even though she'd rubbed them with bicarbonate of soda. But the sea air felt good against her skin, pulled hard into her lungs, she was getting her strength back, that was for sure. She was even feeling hungry. She gripped the thick wire of the railings, let her body sway and swing in the breeze as free as a child, an elderly man with a huge walrus moustache giving her a strange look under his hat as he tapped by with his cane. She wondered about Jonny, how she would be able to find him again in this warren of corridors and stairs, like a game of snakes and ladders. But she wasn't prepared to move from her spot just yet, didn't want to get too cocky about the reliability of her sea-legs to sway down these steel tunnels.

Jonny would come down to see her soon anyway. He came at least twice a day, showed his concern, practised his bedside manner, but happily he didn't stay too long, realising that having him witness her constant retching was as embarrassing to her as it was uncomfortable for him. He was probably off somewhere playing cards, happy again to be in the company of soldiers, drinking their heads off, talking their strange Tommy talk with words like "whiz bangs" and "Blighty", smoking their coffin-sticks and telling tall tales of Kitchener's Army. The ship was full of these eager young men in uniform, no doubt a stint in Palestine offering an easier tour of duty than in the old days being dug down in trenches in northern France. She'd also spied a group of nuns crowding the passageways like flocks of trapped birds, their faces virgin plain and earnest, off to the Holy Land to see where Jesus had walked, stumbled and died. There were tourists too, mostly American and Canadian, they had started out in New York, she hadn't seen much of them, just on embarkation at Liverpool on their way back up to the upper decks. Well-dressed they were, the men in their fancy suits, one even with a top hat, the women with their mink coats over summer dresses, all these strange accents exciting her. The furthest she'd been from home on a boat was down the water on a Clyde steamer to Dunoon and Rothesay. And even then she had been seasick.

The ship rolled slightly and she had to steady herself. It was such a monster of a vessel, this Empress of Scotland with its two giant funnels and six decks above the water line, yet the merest wash in the water seemed to rock it in its tracks. If she had been honest with herself, she hadn't expected to be travelling third class. What with the size of the Levy family home, she'd imagined a more romantic voyage. As Agnes would have said – come the revolution and we'll all be travelling first class. It was a sentiment Jonny's father hadn't approved of, the senior Mr Levy so dismayed by his son's abandonment of his medical career that he left it up to his son to finance the price of his socialist ambitions. And certainly her own parents hadn't been too keen about her plans. She had waited until the Friday night dinner to tell them.

"Pa-le-stine," her mother had shrieked as her father ignored the proceedings behind the *Jewish Evening Times*. "Tell me I didn't hear correctly. You are going to Palestine?"

"That is my plan."

"Your plan? Who has a plan? To live from day to day, that is all we can hope for. But a plan? Please God tell me you have a plan to marry this Jonny Levy?"

"No, mother. I do not have a plan to marry Jonny. We are merely travelling together to Palestine."

"How can you do such a thing?"

"What thing?"

"To be like this. With a man?"

"It is the modern age, mother. I don't need a chaperone for everything I do. I thought you would be happy for me. Isn't that what good Jews are supposed to do? Return to the Holy Land. And then the Messiah will come."

"To marry this doctor would make me happy. Then the Messiah will come. But this? What does his father say?"

"To be honest, his father is not happy either."

"You see. Someone in that family is talking sense. Anyway, you cannot go. I forbid it."

"You cannot stop me."

"Papa. Tell her. She cannot go. If she goes, she will be dead in my eyes. I will have no daughter. I will say *Kaddish* for you like a mother in mourning."

Papa Kahn lowered his newspaper. He was not happy to be interrupted in his usual Friday evening ritual, the reading of the obituary columns in Yiddish. "Please calm down, Martha. Let us see if we can talk about this reasonably."

"There is no reasonable talk in this matter. And where is Mendel? He is the one to put such ideas into her head. All this talk of socialism and revolution. This Glasgow is a fine place for us Jews. What need is there to go digging holes in Palestine."

"Scotland was not such a fine place for Avram," Celia countered.

"Avram was an isolated incident," her father said. "There is no real anti-Semitism here. The Protestants and Catholics are too busy hating each other to bother with us Jews. Believe me, Celia. I know what real anti-Semitism tastes like." Her father waved his hand over the proceedings as if this somehow would calm everybody. "Now," he said firmly. "Please tell us about these plans of yours."

"I'm going to sail to Palestine with Jonny."

"And when did you become such a Zionist?"

"I am not a Zionist. I am a socialist. I want to see what this *kibbutz* is like. I want to go somewhere where I can make a difference, do something useful in the world."

"This Jonny's *kibbutz*?"

"Yes."

"And where is it?"

"It is south of the Sea of Galilee. Close to the River Jordan."

"And what of your relationship with this Jonny Levy? Is it an honourable one?"

She wished she knew what her father had meant by that question. Even now as she stood under these stars and this moon in these Mediterranean waters, she still desperately wanted to know. What was an honourable relationship? One where she had refrained from intercourse before marriage instead of behaving like some kind of common prostitute? Or one where there was true love and respect for each other? "Which one did you mean, Papa? Because it would have told me so much about you if I had asked, instead of me just answering: 'Yes, it was an honourable one.'"

Uncle Mendel had come in then, happy to be back home from the Highlands, his enthusiasm quickly deflating once he had gauged the family mood. He held back from saying anything during the Sabbath meal but later in the evening he eased her gently into an armchair by the fire. He squatted next to her on the lid of the brass coal-box, a glass of *Shabbos* wine in his hand, the ruby liquid glowing in the flames.

"This what you do is a brave thing," he said.

"I am not brave, uncle. In some ways, the opposite. I fear for what happened to Avram. I fear what happened to my friend Charlotte. I am escaping my fears."

"Sometimes to run away from danger is the braver thing to do." He picked up a poker, prodded away at the coals, until the fire sprang back to life. "Look, Celia. A Zionist I am not. If a homeland for themselves the Jews want, then it can be in Australia or Uganda for all I care. But this idea of *kibbutz* interests me. Socialism and Jews together. It is a potent mix. I am interested to find out if it can work. You must promise to write your poor old uncle."

She looked at the fire, how she used to stare at the flames for hours as a child, at all the different worlds and stories she created there. "I promise."

"Now tell me. With this Jonny Levy, what is your plan?"

"The plan is to wait and see."

"There you are."

Jonny sauntered up to her with his sweater tied over his shoulders like some Monte Carlo millionaire, he was an old hand now at these shipping voyages, knowing just the right clothes to wear. He gently laid his hand over hers, the railing wire digging slightly more into her skin, she didn't mind, she would have felt there was something wrong between them now if he didn't touch her. She looked down at their clasp of fingers, this touching of skin, the back of his hand tanned already from a sun she had yet to see. This union of flesh feeling quite natural, at least here on the ship, caught in limbo between the past and the future, wondering how she would feel when they were both together on dry land with their lives stretching before them.

"How's the patient?"

"Better thank you."

"I can fetch you some soup and bread."

Hot soup. She could probably manage that now. But she didn't want to break the spell. "It's all right. I don't feel like eating just yet."

His fingers relaxed over hers, she moved her head so that it rested lightly against his shoulder, she looked out over the moonlit water, the hiss of the hull steaming across the flat sea, the warm breeze of a Mediterranean night. She felt she could stay like this forever. Please don't pull into port, captain. Just keep sailing on. To Australia and back again, if you must. She heard the sound of an accordion. A violin. The melodies familiar. Jonny pulled away to see what was going on.

"Come, Celia. Come and see this."

She walked over to where he was standing, her legs still a bit wobbly, she grasped the railing again, looked down onto an open lower deck. A violinist. An accordionist. People dancing. They were Jews. Orthodox Jews. The men with their skullcaps and ringlets, their black medieval garb, the women in their modest dresses on a separate side of the deck, their heads covered with scarves. Clapping their hands, and laughing, and singing on this moonlight night. To some melody buried deep in her own soul that spoke of vast forests and icy winters, wild bears and wooden huts, silver candlesticks from Napoleonic times. She found herself patting her own palms together in time to the beat.

"How I envy them," she said.

"Why is that?"

"They seem so committed. So sure of themselves. That this land they are going to is their land. While this Palestine means nothing to me. I am of Eastern European stock. I am from the *shtetl*. What relationship do I have with Abraham of Ur of The Chaldees? With this Middle Eastern camel merchant?"

"Why don't you wait until you get there. Then see how you feel."

He had been right about the light. She had her face tilted to it now, letting the sun warm her skin, she could feel her Glasgow cheeks red-burning in its glare as she waited to disembark. The ship was anchored offshore, swaying slightly in its moorings, people crowding in on her as they waited for the doreys to come alongside, take the passengers ashore. She couldn't find Jonny but she decided she would get off anyway, meet up with him on land. A battalion of soldiers had swarmed around her, she could hear their saucy comments, unusual to find a young woman without a chaperone or without one of the stewardesses assigned to protect her from such behaviour. She wondered how they would survive in this heat with their thick serge uniforms until their quartermasters provided them with their khaki. For her part, she wore her only decent summer dress.

"Any more women back there?" one of the crew shouted. "Any more women? Room for one more."

"Come on, love," one of the soldiers ahead of her called, couldn't have been more than eighteen, his pale skin already peeling and scabby from the sun. "Female boat only up front."

He drew to the side to let her pass as did the rest of his group until she reached the top of the external stairway hanging off the side of the ship to the boat below.

"On you go," the crewman said. "There's more of your kind down there."

She shrugged, not sure what he meant, made her way down the stairway, holding on carefully to the railings against the sway of the ship, some of the soldiers more cocky now with their comments. There were six Arab men sat relaxed at the oars of the dorey, dressed in loose robes, some wearing fezzes, all of them smiling, looking genuinely happy in their task. Crowded at the rear of the craft by the fluttering Royal Navy Standard were some of the Orthodox Jewish women she had seen dancing on the deck. They looked terrified, whether by the prospects of the row into shore or the possibility they might, God forbid, inadvertently come into contact with a male oarsman. Three nuns sat in the middle of the craft looking equally uncomfortable. A crew member took her hand, led her into a space at the prow.

"It's so small," she said.

"The bigger boats are for mixed company," he said with a cock of his head towards the rear of the boat. "Them women wouldn't travel with the men. They weren't too happy with the rowers either. That's us," he shouted up the steps. "Cast off."

The crossing to shore was rough but remarkably, she didn't feel ill at all. The rowers stuck to their task, some of the women letting out little gasps in unison if the boat rose forward on a wave. She watched Haifa draw closer, the crowds on the pier, its dockyard sheds, the waiting train, the palm trees, the low, sun-bleached houses scattered along the shoreline, across the hillsides surrounding the bay. She tried to imagine someone making a similar arrival on Glasgow's Clydeside. It would be like one of these photograph negatives – where Haifa was white, Glasgow was grey. The boat pulled into the pier. The Jewish women started to shriek, rushing to step off onto the jetty as soon as the vessel tethered. When she eventually disembarked, she saw these women further ahead, beyond the wooden decking of the pier, kneeling down on the ground, kissing the dusty soil.

She found herself a rough seat on top of a pile of jute sacks, waited for Jonny, not sure how she would spot him amidst this chaos in the harbour area. The army was there trying to assemble its troops as they disembarked, passengers stood around not knowing what to do next, all kinds of boats pulling in quay-side either dumping more passengers or with cargo stacked high. Donkeys came and went with their loads. An Arab boy, he couldn't have been more than ten, manoeuvred a liquor wagon through the crowd, another came with a tea urn and flatbreads for sale. And there was a man leading a camel as easy as if it were his bearded grandfather he was escorting through the crowd. The train stood waiting, impatient, coughing out its smoke, everybody asking what time it would leave. And it was hot. Still mid-morning, yet she could feel the rays bearing down on her skin, the trickle of sweat down her spine. She tied a scarf around her head, would have loved to take the tea on offer but she didn't have any money. Here she was, a powerless, penniless woman in a strange land surrounded by strangers, with only one man she knew within a radius of three thousand miles.

That man eventually turned up, all quietly efficient, located their luggage, engaged a porter to put their cases on the train. He bought her some tea and a box of dates – she'd never tasted them before, so sticky-sweet they were on her lips and her fingers, a woman with a jug on her head gave her water in a cup for the rinsing.

"Don't drink it," he warned.

"What am I supposed to do? I'm thirsty."

"Take the tea for now. There will be plenty of fresh water where we're headed."

Thirty-one

THE TRAIN'S FINAL DESTINATION WAS DAMASCUS. Although Jonny told her they would only be taking it for about fifty miles, first to Beisan, then to the station of their destination – al-Dalhamiyya.

"al-Dalhamiyya," she said. What a beautiful word, sounding like a name to describe the arid wind coming through the open windows as the train clattered along. "al-Dalhamiyya."

It was uncomfortably hot now they had pulled away from the sea and its breezes. She tried to keep her eyes open, take an interest, but the landscape was so bright in the sunshine, it was hard for her to stare at it for too long. Not that there was much to see in this barren land, a few olive groves on the hillsides, the occasional village, not a soul in sight in the midday sun, except for a couple of Arab men on horseback following the path of the train, their headscarves flowing behind them. The rest of the passengers too had quietened after an initial excitement, the heat and the rhythm of the train lulling everyone into a half-sleep. Only Jonny seemed to have come alive, his face brightening as soon as the train had left Haifa. She had never seen him look so happy, his eyes scouring the countryside, he pointed out this and that feature, it all appeared the same to her. She had her mind more on Charlotte, hadn't really thought about her on the whole sea journey, yet since she had landed, her friend was much in her thoughts.

"You have to bring me back one of those handsome princes," she had commanded. "Like Valentino's Sheik Ahmed Ben Hassan. Or if he won't come to me, then send a telegram. I will sail immediately to the Holy Land."

She had arranged for Charlotte to stay on at Agnes's flat. But the distribution of the caps they now left to others. A Labour councillor in Govan was close to setting up a women's welfare clinic there with a proper doctor and nurse in attendance. Charlotte had joined the general committee responsible, handed over their completed questionnaires and case notes from the over one hundred women they had already seen by themselves. From her own ringing of the fishmonger's bell in Govan to a clinic in that same area of the city, she saw the symmetry in that, the path of her own revolution.

She awoke when the train reached Beisan. Her sleep had been so deep, it took her a long time to realise that she was now in Palestine. Her eyes so heavy, she could just let her lids fall again, return to her dreamless state. She could smell coffee. The aroma of a strange spice.

"Cardamom," Jonny told her when she had asked, her lips so dry she could hardly form the question. "The Arabs use it in their coffee." He had been out on the platform but it was not coffee he had brought her but a glass filled with the pulp and juice of squeezed oranges. She drank it gratefully, felt she was imbibing the flavour of this land itself, then asked for more.

"Not long to go now," he said. "The journey should be more interesting too. The land is more fertile here with the Jordan River. You'll see fig trees, almonds, apple orchards."

She nodded as if she cared. But what did she know of fig trees and almonds? She was a Glasgow girl from the Gorbals. She didn't even know that figs grew on trees. She looked up as an Arab woman came into their compartment, sat opposite. Her features dark and handsome, her head covered by a long scarf, her wrists and ankles adorned with silver, her leathery feet bare. "We must be the same age," Celia thought. "But so different. Do you live in poverty? You have no shoes on your feet yet you wear jewellery of silver? Are you rich or poor? If you are poor, you have none of the haunted, pinched features of my countrywomen. How many children do you have? What methods do you use for birth control? How am I to know you?"

Jonny came back with another glass of orange juice. This time she didn't gulp it down, but sipped slowly, all the time watching the Arab woman over the cloudy glass.

"You'll have to learn Hebrew," Jonny told her.

"What about Arabic?"

"Perhaps that too."

al-Dalhamiyya turned out not to be a station at all, just a signpost in the middle of nowhere with its name scrawled in English and Arabic under the words 'Palestine Railways'. There wasn't even a platform. She wondered why the train had even bothered to stop. A bundle of spades, pitchforks, crates of tinned food had come off with their luggage. A man with a horse and wagon was already waiting.

"*Shalom*, Amos," Jonny called out to the driver.

Amos nodded. He wore a dirty vest, loose cotton trousers, no shoes. Tilted back off his forehead a peaked worker's cap, the type of headgear Celia had seen Lenin wear in photographs. He tipped his chin in her direction.

"Celia," Jonny said. Then in Hebrew. "*Hi gam baa m'Scotland.*"

Amos nodded again as if it were a matter of course a young Glasgow woman should turn up on his doorstep. His horse snorted, tried to nuzzle against her arm. He pulled the reins back hard.

"He's Russian," Jonny said, as if this somehow explained his reluctance for conversation.

Amos sprung down from his perch, started loading the railroad shipment onto the back of the wagon. He left their luggage for her and Jonny to pick up.

She would have preferred to sit up front with Amos but the space beside him was not offered. So she just hung on the back of the wagon with Jonny as Amos took off. It was a wild ride along what was hardly a track, dust stinging her eyes, stones kicking up from the wheels, the occasional high lurch as the wagon bounced in and out of a rut, the luggage and the rest of the load flying all over the place. She almost wished she was back in her cabin, the ship's ocean rolling not half as bad as this. Amos didn't seem to care. His job was to drive the wagon, what was going on at the back wasn't his concern. After about five minutes, Jonny shouted for him to stop. The wagon pulled up.

"We'll walk the rest."

Amos just shrugged.

She had hardly put her feet back on the ground when Amos rattled off again "Friendly," she said.

"He's a good worker," Jonny replied.

She realised this would be the judge of a person in this desolate landscape, wondered whether she possessed both the energy and commitment to meet the grade. "Where is this *kibbutz*?"

"Not far. You can just see it straight ahead."

She shaded her eyes, could just make out some wooden sheds, lines of tents in the distance, the smoke from a fire.

"I know you're tired. And it's hot. But I'd like to show you something first."

"As long as it's not too far."

He led her across what had been marked off as a field with posts and twine although how it would be possible to grow anything in this dry dirt she found hard to imagine. They came to an untethered wagon loaded with large rocks. Then on past a row of olive trees with their ancient twisted branches and dusty leaves. Her feet hurt, her head ached, her eyes stung, all she craved was some cool water to soothe her parched throat, moisten her dried skin, but she stumbled on, held her tongue back from any complaint.

"Here we are," Jonny said, holding out his hand like come proud conjurer introducing his lovely assistant. They had come to the edge of a plateau. Far down below them a valley that stretched for miles to a purple ridge of hills. Through this sun-bleached desolate landscape wound a narrow river, throwing up swathes of green where crops or grasses grew along its banks. The horizon was so wide she could not take it all in.

"On the *kibbutz*, we call this ledge *Merkaz Ha'olam* – The Centre of the World," he told her. "Straight ahead to the east, that's the Yamuk River. Beyond that is Trans-Jordan, then on to Persia and Arabia. Follow those hills to the north and you have Syria and Lebanon, to the south Jerusalem then on to Egypt and Africa. Behind us the Mediterranean and Europe."

All she noticed was the silence, the air still. Not a bird in the sky. Not a cloud in the sky. She really was at the Centre of the World. In the middle of her world. The rest of her life poised to begin from this spot. How it would stretch before her with this man beside her, she could not guess. She could feel Jonny restless beside her, standing apart, not touching, as if he too had the same fear of the future. He turned his back on the scene, stretched his arms out wide to embrace the terrain they had just crossed.

"And this is the land your little *pushke* bought. We're going to clear these fields, then irrigate them. Over there, we'll grow bananas and dates and lemons and grapefruits and more olives. We'll raise families, we'll raise cattle. And all according to just principles. From each according to his ability, to each according to his needs."

She turned round too, trying hard to visualise this socialist Utopia from the barren landscape facing her. Where Jonny could see cultivated farmlands and cosy communes, all she could imagine was hard toil from an unyielding earth. Then across this terrain, she spied some movement. Tiny matchstick figures approaching in a kind of dusty halo. She watched as they came nearer. Four of them. What looked like two adults, two children. With the sun throwing up some kind of dreamy haze on the hot earth, they shimmered and hovered magically above the ground as they approached, the man with a staff in his hand, the children swirling and dancing in the air. She could make out the adults' clothes. The male in a grey full-length robe, dun-coloured jacket and a matching headscarf. The woman dressed from head to toe almost entirely in black except for a trim of gold and red, a long veil drawn across her mouth. In contrast, the children's garb shone white in the sunshine, their hair black, long and free. She opened her mouth, felt the air breathed dry into her lungs, then the croak of her voice as she asked:

"Who are these people?"

Acknowledgements

I am grateful to the writer and critic Lesley McDowell for the title; and to Audrey Canning at Glasgow Caledonian University for helping me with my research. I would also like to acknowledge the generous support I have received from the Scottish Arts Council (now Creative Scotland) towards the writing of this novel.

About the Author

J. David Simons was born in Glasgow in 1953. He studied law at Glasgow University and became a partner at an Edinburgh law firm before giving up his practice in 1978 to live on a *kibbutz* in Israel. Since then he has lived in Australia, Japan and England, working at various stages along the way as a charity administrator, cotton farmer, language teacher, university lecturer and journalist. He returned to live in Glasgow in 2006.

He is the author of the *Glasgow to Galilee* trilogy which includes his novels *The Credit Draper*, *The Liberation of Celia Kahn* and *The Land Agent*. He has also written about contemporary and 1950s Japan in his novel *An Exquisite Sense of What is Beautiful* (2013). His work has been shortlisted for The McKitterick Prize and he has been the recipient of two Writer's Bursaries from Creative Scotland and a Robert Louis Stevenson Fellowship.

The Glasgow to Galilee Trilogy

While *The Liberation of Celia Kahn* stands as a novel in its own right, it is also the second part of a loose trilogy incorporating two other novels, *The Credit Draper* and *The Land Agent*, also published by Saraband. The three books can be read separately and in any order.

An Exquisite Sense of What Is Beautiful

An eminent British writer returns to the resort hotel in Japan where he once spent a beautiful, snowed-in winter. It was there he fell in love and wrote a best-selling novel accusing America of being in denial about the horrific destruction during World War II. As we learn more, however, we realise that he too is in denial, and that his past is now rapidly catching up with him. A sweeping novel of East and West, love and war, truth and delusion.